59372084136160

WITHD

D0389307

NEWS FROM HEAVEN

NEWS FROM HEAVEN

The Bakerton Stories

Jennifer Haigh

HARPER

www.harpercollins.com

HarperCollins books may be purchased for educational, business, or sales promotional use. For information, please e-mail the Special Markets Department at SPsales@harpercollins.com.

These stories have appeared, in slightly different form, in the following publications: "Beast and Bird" in *The Atlantic Monthly* (Kindle edition); "Something Sweet" in *Harvard Review*; "Broken Star" in *Granta*; "A Place in the Sun" in *The Common*; "Thrift" and "What Remains" in *Five Points*; "The Bottom of Things" and "Favorite Son" in *Virginia Quarterly Review*; and "Desiderata" in *One Story*.

FIRST EDITION

Library of Congress Cataloging-in-Publication Data has been applied for.

ISBN: 978-0-06-088964-7

13 14 15 16 17   OV/RRD   10 9 8 7 6 5 4 3 2 1

For my mother

CONTENTS

NEWS FROM HEAVEN

BEAST AND BIRD

Every Sunday morning, at seven o'clock promptly, the two Polish girls crossed the park and walked fifty blocks downtown to church. Early morning: the avenue wide as a farmer's field, the sunlight tempered with frost. The girls were bare-legged, in ankle socks and long coats, their blond hair dark at the ends from their morning ablutions. The younger, Annie Lubicki, was also the prettier. She had just turned sixteen.

Knowing less, Annie listened more than she spoke. Frances Zroka was three years older, a city girl from Passaic, New Jersey. Occasionally she went on dates. Annie had seen her waiting at the curb—wearing dark lipstick, nylon stockings instead of socks, a pocketbook looped over her elbow. Annie had never been on a date. She spent her free day looking in shop windows, or sitting alone in the park.

The girls walked quickly, both excited. A date had taken place the night before. Frances offered each detail delicately, like the tinned butter cookies Mrs. Nudelman favored, each in its own dainty paper cup. The young man had taken her to a restaurant.

"He wore a fancy shirt, with cuff links. You know." She panto-
mimed buttoning at her wrists.

"Yes," Annie said, because an answer seemed to be required. She
might have guessed what cuff links were, but she wouldn't have
been sure. She was a girl to whom people gave instructions. Mrs.
Nudelman directed her in English and in Polish, which Annie
understood; and sometimes in Yiddish, which she did not. The
repetition didn't bother her. She liked knowing what was expected,
the exact requirements of serving and washing up, which in the
Nudelmans' kitchen were precise indeed.

Church bells rang in the distance. In a few hours taxicabs would
clog the avenue; the neighborhood women would crowd the bak-
eries, wealthy matrons, beautifully dressed. But for now the girls
owned the sidewalk. They could have danced there, if they wanted
to. They could have turned cartwheels in the street.

"This way," said Frances, pointing down a side street. "It's
quicker."

They turned a sharp corner, Annie glancing over her shoulder looking for landmarks, knowing it was hopeless. At home in
Pennsylvania she could find her way through a forest at night.
The woods were full of helpful markers, simple and unmistak-
able. Water flowed downhill. The sun rose in the east. City streets
had their own order—surely they did—but to Annie the patterns
were invisible. Her first weeks in New York, she'd gotten lost
daily. Kind strangers had returned her to the apartment. Now
she could locate the fish market and the butcher; by retracing her
steps, she could find her way back. Any further exploration of the
city terrified her.

"He paid for everything," Frances reported. "After dinner we had lemon cake."

The bells grew louder, and Annie recognized the church half-way down the block, the familiar towering steeple. As always, her friend had been right.

In the street they tied scarves over their hair.

THEY WERE SERVING girls, employed by families on the Upper West Side. The families, the Nudelmans and the Grossmans, lived one floor apart. The girls inhabited the back corners of the apartments, small square rooms identical except for their color. Her friend's room had pink walls. Annie's was painted white.

She had come to New York three days after Christmas. A slow train had delivered her to Penn Station, a ten-hour journey from Bakerton, Pennsylvania. Until that day she'd ridden only coal trains; the rickety local had standing space for passengers in the rear. Because the Nudelmans had paid her passage, Annie had a seat in a compartment. At the halfway point she ate an apple and a boiled egg, the lunch her mother had packed.

She was the eldest of nine children. In school she'd gone as far as the eighth grade. After that she'd kept house. Her father was a coal miner, and her mother preferred outdoor chores. The family garden covered an acre. There were chickens and a Jersey cow. Her mother milked, gathered, fed, and butchered; she hoed, watered, picked, and weeded. Certain plants she set aside for medicine, to soothe colic, rashes, dyspepsia, croup. Annie was the cook and the cleaner, the bather and the mender. Mondays and Thursdays she washed tubs of laundry—coal-black overalls, dozens of diapers. On Tuesdays she baked six loaves of bread.

A neighbor had told Annie's mother about the job in New York. Her own daughter kept house for Mrs. Nudelman's brother, who owned a glove factory in Newark. Mrs. Nudelman wanted a Polish girl like her brother's: quiet, a hard worker, a girl who did as she was told. The Nudelmans would feed and keep her. That they offered wages in addition, Annie's mother found incredible. It was late fall then, the outdoor chores finished. She could manage the house herself until springtime, when Annie's younger sister Helen would leave school.

Mr. Nudelman had met her train at the station, a square little man with a round beaming face. "Miss Lubicki!" he said, sounding elated, as though he had made a great discovery. He took her small suitcase and steered her by the elbow through the crowd. All the while he peppered her with questions. Was this her first visit to New York? As the train approached the city, had she seen the Empire State Building? Annie groped for answers, unused to such attention. He listened intently to her replies and nodded sagely, as though she'd said something profound. His quick dark eyes unnerved her, so she kept her eyes on the feather in his hat.

The taxi ride passed quickly. She clutched the door handle as they cruised the wide avenues. Cars were rare in Bakerton. When one climbed the hill where her parents lived, her younger brothers ran into the street to stare.

Mr. Nudelman led her into the elevator, a contraption she recognized from the movies. He pulled shut the metal grille and the little cage rose noisily, a low grinding of gears. At the apartment door Mrs. Nudelman greeted her in Polish. She was a stout woman with a high bosom, her hair hidden by a flowered scarf. She showed Annie down a long corridor, past a series of closed doors. "My son's room," she whispered, stepping quietly. "He isn't well." Behind her Annie rose on tiptoe, conscious of her heavy shoes.

The apartment was not large, but its luxury astonished her. Thick curtains draped the parlor windows. There was a sofa with a curving back, covered in burgundy velvet. Matching chairs flanked the fireplace. The dark wood floors were softened by carpets, intricately patterned: fruits and flowers and diamond shapes, outlined in green and gold.

Mrs. Nudelman led her into the kitchen and flicked on an overhead bulb. Annie blinked. For a moment it seemed the light had tricked her eyes. The kitchen had two of everything: two sinks of gleaming white porcelain; in opposite corners, two separate stoves. One stove was for noodle pudding and custards; the other for cholent and brisket, for roasting lamb and frying kreplach. "Simple," Mrs. Nudelman said in English. Meat was cooked on the big stove. The smaller one was for everything else.

Annie stared in silent wonder. Her English was as good as her Polish; she used them without preference, as she used her two legs. But Mrs. Nudelman spoke with a strange accent. Perhaps somehow she'd misunderstood.

She listened intently as Mrs. Nudelman repeated the instructions in Polish. There were two sets of pots, two dish towels, two drawers of spoons and forks. Two complete sets of dishes: fleishig plates with a red stripe around the border, milchig plates rimmed in blue. The dishes were to be washed in different sinks, dried with different towels. Meat was to be sliced on one counter, cheese on the other. If ever Annie made a mistake, she was to tell Mrs. Nudelman immediately. This was the most important thing.

Annie nodded, keeping her eyes on the floor. She thought of the Klezek boy at home, who heard voices; a neighbor lady who scrubbed her hands until the skin cracked and bled. If Mrs. Nudelman were poor, her madness would be simpler; wealth permitted this elaborate variant. Annie's family had chicken soup on Sundays, meat on Christmas and Easter. There was nothing to keep separate. Her last supper at home had been fried cabbage and noodles, served on mismatched plates.

As Mrs. Nudelman talked, a boy appeared in the doorway behind her. He wore black trousers and a white shirt, open at the throat. He was perhaps Annie's age, tall and slender. His dark hair was wild, as though he'd come in from a storm.

"This is my son, Daniel," Mrs. Nudelman said in Polish. She spoke to him briefly in Yiddish. The boy smiled at Annie and bowed his head. Pinned there was a small black cap, nearly hidden by his curly hair.

WEEKS PASSED. IN the apartment Annie lived softly. She had never imagined rooms so easeful: the hissing radiator in her bedroom, the reliable heat of the bathroom tap, the clean simplicity of the gas stoves, the high smooth bed all to herself.

Outdoors was another matter. There wasn't any outdoors.

Her first free afternoon, she followed Mr. Nudelman's directions to the park. A handsome stone wall screened it from traffic.

Its lawns were clipped, its paths neatly paved. Annie sat on a bench and stared up at the sky. She thought of her mother, who would have lived as happily out in the open, slept in the field like a horse or a dog.

In New York the outdoors had furniture. The outdoors was just like the indoors.

The next morning she mailed two envelopes off to Bakerton: a letter for Helen to read to their mother, and one for Helen alone. In the first envelope she placed the bills Mr. Nudelman had given her, enough to buy flour and sugar, a little coal for the stove.

During the day she didn't think of her loneliness. She thought fleishig and milchig, red stripes and blue. She lived in horror of making a mistake, though what the consequences would be, she couldn't begin to guess. Preparing supper was her greatest anguish, the most taxing hour of the day. Serving did not unnerve her. It pleased her to move neatly around the table, silent as a ghost. Her employers scarcely noticed her. Their attention was focused, always, on their son. From soup to dessert, Daniel was questioned: what he had learned at school or read in the newspaper; his opinions and observations; the quality of his sleep and digestion; his worries, his plans. Poor Daniel, Annie thought as she cleared the table. She looked forward to cleaning up, the cheerful business of washing and drying. The dirty dishes she piled on a small table in the kitchen, afraid to place them on the countertop.

She preferred simple tasks, where the potential for error was slight: washing floors, mashing potatoes, chopping a mountain of carrots for the sweet stew Mrs. Nudelman loved. Then she could settle in and enjoy the warmth of the kitchen, the wash of sunlight from the window above the sink. The radio played Mrs. Nudelman's favorite programs, serials and news reports and, each day at noon, a musical revue. The announcer spoke in a booming voice: *From atop the Loew's State Theatre Building, the B. Manisch-ewitz Company, world's largest matzoh bakers, happily present* Yiddish Melodies in Swing! Between songs came a torrent of words, some English, some foreign; in the announcer's sawing accent, they sounded nearly the same. The audience erupted periodically in raucous laughter. Annie listened intently, longing to share in their good time.

At night, the floors washed, she took tea and cake to Daniel, who studied late in his room. She knocked softly, opened the door, and set the plate and saucer at the corner of his desk. He wore round spectacles, a wool sweater over his white shirt. He didn't speak, just nodded courteously. In the morning, outside his door, she found the dishes on the floor.

SHE'D BEEN AT the Nudelmans' a few weeks when she met Frances in the lobby downstairs. Another serving girl: Annie knew it immediately, without knowing how she knew. "Well, of course," Frances said when Annie told her this later. The daughters of the building had dark hair. All the serving girls were blond.

For two years Frances had worked at the Grossmans', where her duties were the same as Annie's: milchig and fleishig, the twin sinks and stoves. Mrs. Grossman was as crazy as Mrs. Nudelman. They shared the same mania for keeping things separate.

"But why?" Annie demanded.

"They're Jews," Frances said.

In two years she'd learned a few things about her employers. Mr. Grossman worked for his wife's father, a fat man who came to Friday dinner and ate enough for two. The Grossmans' youngest daughter was a little beauty, spoiled by her father. The older sisters were plain as milk. All three had large wardrobes, which required much ironing. Frances didn't care for these daughters, nor for any of the Grossmans. She was tired of living among Jews.

"Just wait until springtime," she told Annie as they walked to the fish market. "They'll work you like a slave." Last year Frances had cleaned late into the night, scrubbing down every inch of the kitchen. Mrs. Grossman had inspected all the pantry cabinets, looking for crumbs of bread.

Annie nodded, slightly puzzled. Though she cleaned the kitchen each night after dinner, it was never truly dirty. There was no coal stove to contend with, no small children's dirty shoes.

On Thursdays both girls were free. Together they walked the avenues, looking in store windows. One evening they returned to their building and stepped into the open elevator. Too late, Annie saw Daniel Nudelman standing at the rear. She hesitated a moment, inexplicably embarrassed. If she had seen him first, she would have taken the stairs.

Daniel nodded silently. He reached past the girls and pulled shut the grille.

The elevator stopped at the second floor and Frances stepped out. "See you later," Annie said softly, aware of how the small space amplified her voice.

Daniel closed the grille and turned to Annie. "You speak English?" he said, his black eyebrows raised.

"Of course." Why would she not speak English? This is America, she thought.

They waited in silence until the elevator stopped. He fumbled in his pocket for a key. Inside, the apartment was dark and silent. Annie went to the kitchen and put on water for his tea.

In a moment Daniel followed her into the kitchen. "You must think I'm very rude," he said. "I thought you spoke only Polish. That's why I never talked to you."

Up close, in the bright light, he looked older than she'd thought him, his cheeks dark with stubble. He sat at the small table and pulled out a chair. "Please, let's start over. I'm Daniel. How do you do?"

Annie sat, undone by the question. Her heart raced pleasantly, as it had in the taxicab with his father.

"I know maybe two words of Polish. My mother says the Poles never did anything for us. But you're a Pole, and you bring my tea every night. So that is no longer true."

"But your parents speak Polish all the time," Annie protested.

Daniel laughed. "Only when they don't want me to know what they're saying. The same way they speak Yiddish around you." He folded his hands. "So ask me a question, and I'll answer. Then I'll ask a question about you."

For two months her head had felt swollen with questions. Small questions nested inside larger ones, like matryoshka dolls.

She chose the smallest question, a timid one. "Why do you study all night?"

"It's my job. I'll be studying for the rest of my life." His smile was broad, like his father's. "My turn. Where did you come from, and why did you leave there?"

Flushing, Annie talked about the house in Bakerton, her eight brothers and sisters, the forest and the coal trains. The money she sent home each Friday, two bills folded in an envelope.

"You send them everything we pay you?" Daniel stared at her intently.

Annie felt her cheeks flush. "Almost," she said.

There was a long silence.

"But that was three questions," she said. "So now I can ask two more." She felt suddenly bold. "Why are there two sets of dishes?"

"You shall not boil a kid in its mother's milk."

Annie frowned.

"Not very helpful, is it? Listen, there are rules for everything. Foods we do not mix. Other foods we don't eat at all." He recited very fast: *"This is the law about beast and bird and every living creature that moves through the waters and every creature that swarms on the ground, to make a distinction between the unclean and the clean and between the living creature that may be eaten and the living creature that may not be eaten."*

Like his father, he seemed to enjoy explaining. He spoke with his entire body: eyes, eyebrows, shoulders, hands.

"But that doesn't answer your question, does it? Your question was *why.* So, Miss Lubicki: we eat this way as a reminder of our covenant with God, who led us out of slavery in Egypt. That's the official answer. Not my answer. My answer is, I don't know." He shrugged. "Is it the same for you? Do Christians do things for no reason?"

Annie thought of her mother, who saved Lenten palm leaves, tucked them behind the Last Supper hanging on the kitchen wall.

Each year, on Palm Sunday, the old leaves would be replaced with new ones. To ward off lightning strikes, her mother said, an explanation Annie found dubious.

"Oh, yes," she said. "All the time." One last question hung in the air. "Why did you think I spoke no English?"

He had his father's eyes, dark and quick, always moving. "It's what my mother told me."

"Why would she say that?"

"I don't know," Daniel said.

IN THE BEGINNING the languages had melded together; she'd scarcely noticed which was spoken. Now she began to pay attention. One Friday, chopping vegetables for cholent, she heard the Nudelmans argue in Polish. A secret from Daniel, then: they didn't care if Annie heard.

The argument began in the hallway. Like every Friday, Mr. Nudelman had come home early, but he'd forgotten to stop at the bakery after work. Annie felt a flash of disappointment. Mrs. Nudelman always offered her the leftover challah, a treat she savored. The braided loaf was dense and eggy—in taste and texture, identical to the paska her mother baked at Easter. This had been a remarkable discovery, surprising and somehow joyous, like glimpsing her sister on the street.

The Nudelmans went into their bedroom and closed the door. Their voices rose steadily. Mrs. Nudelman's was clear and sharp, easier to hear. "And where does he sleep, this nephew? The apartment is crowded already."

"With Daniel," said her husband. "We could put another bed in his room."

"And what happens when Daniel is ill? Our son can't share a room."

"The situation is desperate," said Mr. Nudelman. "If we wait a year, it may be too late."

"You're not his only uncle!" Mrs. Nudelman was nearly shouting. "What about that brother of yours? He can't be bothered to help?"

Mr. Nudelman answered in a low voice. Annie stood very still, listening, but she couldn't make out the words.

"HIS NAME IS Mitro," said Frances. "But he likes to be called Jim."

Annie smiled, for the first time in her life aware of her lips, coated in borrowed lipstick. They stood on the sidewalk waiting for the boys to arrive. Frances's beau had arranged the evening. His friend Jim drove a taxi and would collect the girls in his car. Annie glanced up at the third-floor windows. A single light burned in Daniel's, the bright study lamp at his desk.

A yellow car stopped at the curb, and a burly man stepped out of the backseat. "Eddie!" Frances squealed, and kissed him full on the mouth.

"Well, what are you waiting for?" the driver called. Annie bent to see him through the open window. He wore a wool cap and a leather jacket and resembled her father, her brothers: the broad cheeks, the eyes watery blue.

Frances and Eddie tumbled into the backseat. Another car pulled up behind the taxi, its horn blaring. Timidly Annie opened the passenger door.

"We don't have all day," Jim shouted. "Let's go, let's go!"

The car was close and warm inside, smelling of cigarettes. Jim turned the wheel sharply, and they darted into the avenue. "You're Polish," he told Annie. "I could tell a mile away."

Murmurs from the backseat, a stifled laugh. Annie glanced over her shoulder. Eddie and Frances sat whispering, their hands intertwined.

"You want to live in city, you need to move faster." Jim shook a cigarette from the pack in his pocket. "I know many Poles. All Poles are slow." He himself was not a Pole but a Ukrainian. He announced this with a certain drama, as though Annie had won a spectacular prize.

They drove. As in the taxi with Mr. Nudelman, Annie felt her stomach lurch. Storefronts flew past at a dizzying speed: laundry, delicatessen, shoe repair while you wait. She closed her eyes, knowing the signs would keep coming. That they would come to her that night, in dreams.

Finally the car stopped. Annie stared up at the bright lights of a theater. A crowd had gathered in front. ISLAND OF LOST SOULS, announced the marquee.

"Get out," Jim said abruptly. "I go park this thing. I come and meet you inside."

She scrambled out of the car and followed Frances through the revolving door. The high lobby was bright and crowded, the carpet soft as swamp grass under her feet. A long line had formed at the ticket counter. She took her place behind Frances and Eddie, who stood hip to hip. They seemed to have forgotten she was there.

The line moved quickly. Annie watched the revolving door—

endlessly turning, a constant stream of people pouring in from the street. Young couples and old ones; several well-dressed women, a group of boys in black coats and small black caps. One boy, the tallest, caught her attention. Annie turned away, flustered. For an instant her heart raced.

At the window Eddie bought tickets for himself and Frances. Again Annie glanced at the door. The ticket cost her a quarter, exactly the amount she had in her purse.

THEY FOUND SEATS in the dark balcony. The newsreel had already begun. Annie stared at the screen, reading quickly:

Work Speeded on Huge Structures for World's Fair in Chicago.
Some 20,000 Beer Cases in Skyscraper Pile Ready for April 7.

Beside her, Frances and Eddie sank into an embrace.

A stack of cased brew as extensive and as high as a city apartment
house block is the amazing sight that meets the eye on the grounds
of a large brewery here. Almost five million bottles, a veritable
mountain of drinks, await the Zero Hour when the 3.2 howitzers
will begin to pop.

"Here you are."

Annie turned. Jim sat heavily in the seat beside her. "I had hell of time finding parking space."

"That's too bad," she said, wishing he'd be quiet. She had never been a fast reader. On the screen a man gestured wildly. He took a handkerchief from his pocket and swiped irritably at his brow.

German Chancellor delivers a rousing speech to crowd of thousands.

"Why is he so angry?" she whispered.

"It's news." Jim leaned in closer. "It's warm in here. Take off your coat."

Annie did, leaning forward in her chair, a clumsy business. Then, finding nowhere to put it, she laid the coat across her lap.

The picture started. As always, the lilting strains of music swept her up completely; she barely noticed Jim's arm slipping around her shoulders. The stars' names flashed across the screen, written in swirling script. Only one was familiar. Unlike Frances, who spent half her wages on movie magazines, Annie had seen few pictures; but everyone knew Bela Lugosi.

Jim's hand reached beneath the coat on her lap.

For two hours her eyes didn't leave the screen; yet later, when she tried to remember the story, the details would escape her. She recalled only the warm weight of Jim's hand, burrowing like a small animal, tunneling under her skirt.

WHEN THE LIGHTS came up, Annie blinked, a little dazed, as though she'd been asleep a long time. Flushing, she adjusted her skirt. Beside her were two empty seats. Frances and Eddie had stepped out halfway through the picture, crowding past strangers' knees: *Excuse me. Pardon me.* It hadn't occurred to her that they wouldn't return.

"Where did they go?" she asked Jim.

"They want to be alone." He rose abruptly. "Let's go." .

He charged into the aisle, shoving his way through the crowd. Annie hurried into her coat. The aisle was swarming with people. It was a sensation unlike anything she'd experienced, the room humming like a beehive, strangers pressing at her back. In a moment Jim was several paces ahead of her. She watched his broad shoulders disappear around the corner into the lobby.

"Wait!" she called, fumbling with the buttons of her coat.

Rounding the corner, her head down, she collided squarely with a tall boy holding a paper bag. There was a shower of white blossoms, popcorn scattering to the floor.

"Oh!" she cried, catching her breath.

He reached out a hand to steady her. He wore black trousers and a wrinkled white shirt, but he was not Daniel Nudelman. He was only a boy.

"I'm sorry," she said, stepping back. To her horror, she felt her eyes tearing. "It was my fault."

"It's nothing." He looked puzzled. "Miss, are you all right?"

"I'm sorry," she repeated, hurrying past him. She pushed through the crowd. A leather jacket had disappeared through the revolving door.

The sidewalk was crowded with people and umbrellas. A steady rain beat the pavement. Annie looked both ways, but the Ukrainian had disappeared.

She stepped back under the marquee, crowded with people seeking shelter. Her mind raced. She had no umbrella, no money, and crucially, no idea where she was. She could walk for a week and never find her way back to the Nudelmans'. She swiped her eyes with her sleeve.

"Miss?"

She turned to see the boy from inside the theater.

"Are you all right?" His eyes flickered across her face. "Did I hurt you?"

"Oh, no." She found a handkerchief in her purse. "I'm just—lost."

"Where do you want to go?"

When she gave him the Nudelmans' address, he smiled. "Easy." He pointed down the street. "Just go left at the corner and keep walking. It's not quick, but it's simple. Thirty blocks, and you're home."

She felt a hand at her back.

"Jew, leave her alone."

Annie turned. Jim's face was very red, his fair hair sodden. A cigarette dangled from his mouth.

The boy looked uncertainly at Annie.

"It's all right," she said. "I'm fine now. Thank you for helping."

"Beat it," Jim said.

HE DROVE WITH the windows down, crashing through puddles. "Why were you talking to this Jew?"

"He gave me directions," she said. "I couldn't find you. I didn't know the way home."

"What, you think I leave you there? I go to get car." He tossed his cigarette out the window. "It's bad idea, talking to strangers. You should be more careful."

Annie stared out the window.

"It's bad part of town," said Jim. "Low class. Too many Jews."

They drove for what seemed a long time. Finally, with a kind of exaltation, she recognized the kosher butcher, the fish market, the bakery Mrs. Nudelman favored. For the first time in months she knew exactly where she was.

"Stop here," she told him. "That's my building."

"It's early," he said, stepping on the gas. "We go drink a night-cap. I know a place."

The rain quickened, nicking the windshield. "No, thank you," said Annie.

"You'll like it," Jim said, racing down the block.

When the car idled at a red light, Annie didn't hesitate. She threw open the car door and stepped into the street.

"Hey!" Jim called.

Annie hurried to the sidewalk and broke into a run. I'm not slow, she thought.

She didn't look back.

THE APARTMENT WAS silent at that hour. Her key clicked loudly in the lock. Annie slipped out of her coat and tiptoed down the hallway. At that moment Daniel emerged from his bedroom. He removed his spectacles and rubbed wearily at his eyes.

He seemed startled to see her. They stood there a moment, not speaking. Then a voice came from the Nudelmans' bedroom:

"Daniel? You are still awake?"

"Go back to sleep, Mother," Daniel said.

His eyes met Annie's; he raised a hand in greeting. Annie waved back, thinking of her rumpled skirt, her smeared lipstick. Her cheeks burned with shame.

ASH WEDNESDAY CAME, the beginning of Lent. A day of false spring weather: the crusty snow melting, the storm grates loud with runoff. Annie crossed the park quickly, her head down, a black smudge on her forehead where the priest's thumb had traced a cross on her skin. Mrs. Nudelman had given her the morning off, and she took the long way back from church, the route she had memorized. Alone, she didn't dare attempt a shortcut. Earlier that week Frances had been sent back to Passaic, her belly swollen. Annie's only friend.

Back at the apartment Mrs. Nudelman called from the parlor. Three large suitcases sat open on the floor. Her nephew was getting married on Sunday, she explained in Polish. The family would travel to Newark for the weekend. Just this once, Annie would work on Thursday, help with the laundry and the packing. In return, she would have the weekend free. She could do as she pleased until Monday morning, when the family returned.

In English Mrs. Nudelman repeated this incredible fact: for an entire weekend, Annie would stay in the apartment alone.

That night she slept badly, plagued by nightmares. She was lost in the city streets. A yellow taxi seemed to be following her, its horn honking angrily. When Annie turned to see the driver, the yellow car was gone.

. . . .

FRIDAY MORNING, AS usual, Annie went to the market. The sky was low and heavy. The spring weather had vanished like last night's dream. When she returned, Mr. Nudelman was sitting in the kitchen.

"Daniel is ill," he said. "Only a cold, but it would be unwise for him to travel." The doctor had already come and gone.

Annie nodded, not surprised. The night before, when she'd taken his tea and cake, she'd found the room dark. In a whisper she'd apologized for waking him. Quietly she'd closed the door.

"My wife is upset. She doesn't like to leave him." Mr. Nudelman shrugged. "I told her you'd look after him."

Annie laid the table for lunch, but Mrs. Nudelman would not come out of her room. Her husband drank coffee and stared at his newspapers, English and Yiddish. Annie bought them each morning at the corner store.

"The world," he said, "is a dangerous place."

He sat smoking as Annie cleared the table. At the front door she helped Mrs. Nudelman into her coat.

"Take Daniel some soup later." Mrs. Nudelman spoke in a whisper, her face flushed, her eyes red.

Her husband gave Annie a slip of paper. "This is the telephone number in Newark. If you need anything, please call."

From the window she watched them get into a cab. A wet snow was falling. The taxi was yellow, as in her dreams: the car the Ukrainian had driven. If he were the driver, would he speak to the Nudelmans? *I know a girl who works in this building.* What would he say about her?

In the kitchen Annie switched on the radio. The announcer joked in Yiddish or English. The audience roared with laughter.

. . . .

AT DINNERTIME SHE heated the soup and carried it to Daniel on a tray. His room was dim inside, the curtains drawn.

"How are you feeling?" Annie asked.

He sat up partway in bed. His eyelids were heavy, his hair wild, his face coated with a sickly sheen. Annie put down the tray and sat at his bedside. Without thinking, she laid a hand on his forehead. She did this automatically, as with her younger brothers and sisters. He seemed startled by her touch.

"You have a fever."

He smiled weakly. "How do you know? You don't have a thermometer."

She had nursed a brother through pneumonia, the little twins through whooping cough. "I know," she said.

The doctor had given him aspirin; there was more in the medicine chest. In the bathroom she found the bottle behind the mirror. She filled a glass with water and wet a towel at the sink.

"Cold," Daniel said when she laid the towel across his forehead. "Feels good. My mother left me in good hands." He shifted in the bed. "She's not happy about it, I can tell you that. But every once in a while my father puts his foot down."

"She wants you to eat."

"Always." Daniel lay back and closed his eyes. "Later. I promise."

"I can call your parents. On the telephone."

"Don't." Daniel sat up abruptly. "Please. They'll come back, and that will only make me feel worse. I'll be better in the morning. You'll see."

"All right," Annie said.

Outside, the snow was flying. A stiff wind rattled the windowpanes.

ON SATURDAY MORNING the city was quiet, the streets snow-covered. Daniel was sleeping deeply, wearing his spectacles. A book lay open on his chest. In that moment Annie felt her freedom. She had nothing to clean and no one to feed.

She put on her coat and wound a scarf around her neck. The elevator was empty, the street quiet. Her breath steamed in the cold. In the avenue, the traffic lights were blinking. There were no cars in sight.

Why not? she thought, and walked down the middle of the street.

Blanketed in snow, the park seemed larger, a vast plain of whiteness. I could stay here forever, she thought. A few strangers crossed the lawn, hands in their pockets. On this still morning everyone was smiling, as though the storm had been staged for their amusement. Annie found herself smiling back. For the first time she felt included in the joke.

When she returned to the apartment, it was nearly noontime. The indoor air burned her cheeks. In Daniel's bedroom the radiator was steaming. He had tossed aside the blanket. His pajama shirt was dark with sweat.

She sat on the bed and laid a hand on his forehead. His eyes snapped open. His lips were parched. A fast pulse beat in his throat.

In the hallway she took the slip of paper from her pocket. As she had seen Mrs. Nudelman do, she took the receiver from its hook and listened for a voice.

"I tried to phone your mother," she told Daniel. "It didn't work. I think I did something wrong."

Daniel closed his eyes.

"I can call the doctor," she said.

"It's Saturday. No one will answer the phone."

He was thirsty but couldn't drink. Water tasted like metal and turned his stomach. Annie brought milk and held the glass as he drank. Heat rose off him like steam from the stove.

IN THE EVENING she fixed herself a cheese sandwich, ate it standing over the milchig sink. Even alone, she followed the rules. In this kitchen there seemed no other way to eat.

For several hours Daniel slept deeply, his skin cooler. Then, at midnight, the fever returned.

In the kitchen Annie put on the kettle. She opened the pantry cupboard and scanned the shelves. The Nudelmans had no garden, no dry, aromatic plants hanging in bunches in the cellar. There was only ground pepper and cinnamon and coarse salt; a bottle, labeled Onion Powder, whose use she couldn't fathom; and a familiar yellow can. At home her mother kept mustard leaves for this purpose. In the city, Colman's Dry Mustard would have to do.

The kettle whistled. Carefully she mixed the paste. She spread it into a clean dish towel and brought it to Daniel on a tray.

"What's that?"

"A plaster." Annie sat on the bed beside him. "Take off your shirt."

His skin was moist and pale, matted with dark hair. He winced as she laid the hot towel on his chest.

"Leave it there until it cools," she said. "I'll come back in a little while."

"No." He reached for her hand. "Please. Sit with me."

For a long time she stared out the window, listening to the night noises: Daniel breathing fast and shallow, snowflakes scratching the windowpanes. Outside, the sidewalks glowed beneath the streetlamps; even at this hour, the city was bright. Annie was a sound sleeper; she had never imagined the night was so long. The city was full of restless people, a thousand Daniels lying awake, the horizon burning with their collective heat.

IT WAS DAYLIGHT when Annie woke. She stirred, her back and legs aching, and found herself kneeling at Daniel's bedside. Her blouse was wrinkled, her face creased. Her arms and shoulders rested on the quilt as if she'd fallen asleep in prayer.

She raised her head. In the distance, bells were ringing. Sunday morning, the Mass starting without her. Daniel was fast asleep, his bare shoulders visible above the blanket. His chest rose and fell silently. His hand was tangled in her hair.

She disengaged his hand. He stirred but didn't wake. She saw then that the bedroom door was open. Somewhere in the apartment a radio was playing, water running. Somebody was drawing a bath.

The Nudelmans had come home.

Annie stood, her heart pounding, and went into the kitchen. A breakfast had been cooked and eaten. In the milchig sink were two greasy plates.

AT HOME IN Pennsylvania she thinks often of that night: her vigil at Daniel Nudelman's bedside, the bright silent city closed in around them. There are words for what she'd felt as she watched him sleep, many words in many languages, but the one she knows is *longing*. Her mind wanders as she punches down the bread dough. She covers it with a towel and leaves it to rise near the stove.

Her mother speaks to her only in Polish and asks no questions. For several months she's kept an eye on Annie's waistline. Spring ended, then summer. Still Annie is thin as a deer. Now the mornings are cooler; the garden offers up its last tomatoes. Her brothers and sisters go back to school. Helen Lubicki walks across town to Bakerton High, the first in the family to do so. She is an excellent student. Now that Annie has returned, there is no need for Helen to leave school.

"I'll be studying for the rest of my life," Daniel had told her. Was such a thing even possible? Like everything she heard and saw in the city, it now seems fantastic, as though she made it all up.

His hand in her hair.

In the days after the snowstorm, Mrs. Nudelman had ignored her completely. It was her husband who told Annie the news. "I'm sorry, Miss Lubicki, but we will no longer need your help in the kitchen." His Polish was awkward; she stared at him, mystified, not sure she'd understood.

Instantly she thought of the dishes. "Oh, no. Have I made a mistake?"

"Not at all. Your work has been very good." He hesitated a moment, then spoke carefully. "But my nephew is coming from Poland. God willing. So we will no longer have an extra room."

Years later she will understand the reason. Her brother Peter will die in the war. Her brother John will see the camps, and Annie—married then, with sons of her own—will remember the Nudelmans and the Grossmans, the nephew from Poland who was given her bedroom. She will think of Daniel. Is he married, too? A husband and father and still studying? Daniel in his separate world.

Now she sets out coffee, a heavy clay pitcher in the middle of the table, milk and sugar already mixed in. Each morning for breakfast she bakes a dozen apples. Then the young ones leave for school, Helen and John and Peter and the rest, and Annie piles the dishes in the sink.

SOMETHING SWEET

The farm children were waiting in the corridor each morning when Miss Peale arrived at school: Henry Eickmeier,
Chauncey Hoeffer, Peggy Schultheis, and Richard Dickey, who'd
ridden into town at dawn on his father's milk truck. In the cloak-
room they stowed coats and galoshes, hats and gloves. Miss Peale
settled in at her desk and looked over her lesson plans. The farm
children did not speak to one another; familiar as cousins, they
didn't see the point. They sat quietly at their desks, waiting for the
town children to arrive.

First came the hoodlums, in a noisy pack: Jerry Bernardi, Joseph
Poblocki, and John Quinn. At the back of the room they sprawled
heavily in their chairs, scraping the linoleum. At the end of the day
Miss Peale would have a pupil reorder the desks, or simply do it
herself.

Gradually the others filed in, the studious boys who spoke up
in class, the shy girls—Dorothy Novak, Helen Lubicki—who never
said a word. At the front of the room sat the pretty girls: Nellie Stiffler, Theresa Bellavia in her tight sweater, Angela Scalia,

the homecoming queen. Evelyn Lipnic seemed out of place in that crowd, a redhead with a lovely complexion, sweet and mannerly and, in Miss Peale's estimation, not as fast. At the center of the hive, as always, was Alan Spangler, smiling and dapper in a plaid sport coat. Their arrival caused a reaction among the hoodlums, a kind of heightened alertness. From her vantage point, Miss Peale saw it like a ripple in the water. The pretty girls seemed not to notice. According to Edna O'Shane, who taught art and music, they had fiancés overseas, young men in danger. Boys their own age could not compete.

They were the class of 1943, that year's models. In other years there had been other quiet Schultheis girls, other lovely Scalias; a long series of incorrigible Bernardis, Poblockis, and Quinns. Most were coal miners' children, the sons and daughters of pinners and cutters—raised in company houses built by Baker Brothers, their chores and meals dictated by Baker shifts. There were a few exceptions: the Bellavias owned a bakery in Little Italy, the Spanglers a hat shop on Main Street. Bernardi's Funeral Home catered to the new foreign families, Italians, Irish, and Slavish—a business that, given the general fecundity of Catholics, seemed destined to thrive. Viola Peale was, herself, a lifelong member of St. John's Episcopal, built by her father's cousins Chester and Elias Baker—the original Baker brothers for whom the mines, and the town, were named.

The homeroom period was for administrative purposes. Miss Peale took attendance and read announcements. On Saturday morning the Key Club would sponsor a collection drive, old tires and scrap metal for the war effort. Students' families were encouraged to donate. Report cards would be issued on Thursday, the last day before Christmas vacation. Thursday evening the glee club would perform its annual Christmas concert.

"Starring Alan Spangler!" Nellie shrieked, squeezing his shoulder.

Miss Peale gave her a reproving look.

At the bell the students rose. The pretty girls collected their pocketbooks. Alan Spangler lingered at Miss Peale's desk.

"You have to try these, Miss Peale." His voice was warm and resonant, Edna O'Shane's best tenor. He reached into his jacket and produced a tin of lemon drops. "My dad buys them in Pittsburgh. My mom can't get enough of them."

"That's kind of you, Alan," she said, flushing. "Though it's a bit early in the day for candy." She was uncomfortably aware of the boys at the back of the room, Poblocki's gruff laughter, Quinn cracking a joke in a low voice.

Alan Spangler seemed not to notice. He grinned, showing his dimple. "Take one for after lunch. It's nice to have something sweet."

A FEW SNOWFLAKES scattered as Viola drove across town. She had stayed late to grade papers, and already dusk was falling. She groped for, and eventually found, the switch that turned on the headlamps. She was not a confident driver. The car, her father's ancient Ford, never traveled beyond the town line.

At home Clara was chopping vegetables for soup. "The basket came," she said.

Viola glanced into the parlor. A giant package sat in the center of the table, wrapped in clear cellophane. Her sister had shown unusual restraint. Each year at Christmas, their cousin Chessie sent a massive fruit basket—not the usual apples and oranges but bright, sweet clementines, tiny champagne grapes, a whole pineapple with the leafy crown attached. (Where one found such produce in Bakerton, Viola couldn't imagine. In winter the selection was slim indeed.) The basket arrived with a generic note, on company letterhead:

COMPLIMENTS OF BAKER BROTHERS,
MINERS AND SHIPPERS OF COAL

Delivered, always, by one of the Baker maids, as if to remind the sisters that their cousin was an important man, busy running ten coal mines, the welfare of an entire town heavy on his shoulders. The slight was lost on Clara, who would, if Viola didn't stop her, attack the basket like a hungry orangutan and devour its contents in a single day.

Her sister was sweet-tempered and didn't mind the scolding. At school she'd been called slow. As labels went, it was not inaccurate. Clara moved through life at a deliberate pace, as though the smallest decisions—shoes or boots, rice or potatoes—called for long consideration. And yet she was an excellent cook, a careful housekeeper, skills Viola had never bothered to acquire. Since their parents' death, the sisters had looked after each other. Neither had ever lived alone.

After supper, Viola took a walk uptown. The stores were open late for holiday shopping, the sidewalks busy, the windows bright. Even the Jewish merchants had decorated; Friedman's Furniture glowed with twinkling red lights. A speaker piped carols into the chilly air, Bing Crosby singing "White Christmas." The atmosphere was festive, and yet there were sober reminders—two blue stars in Izzy Friedman's window, his sons Neil and Morris serving overseas—of the boys who might not return.

She wandered down Main Street, studying the shop windows. Each year she bought a few modest gifts—scented soap for Edna O'Shane, a scarf or sweater for Clara, who would have preferred some useless trinket. She had always been indifferent to clothing. Without Viola's prodding, she would go to church in her slip.

She paused in front of Spangler's Hat Shop, known all over Saxon County for its window displays. In defiance of the season, someone had created a kind of Caribbean fantasy: against a painted backdrop of sand and ocean, mannequins sat in lawn chairs, dressed in colorful swimsuits and drinking summer cocktails. Absurdly, each wore a beautiful hat. The hats were strawberry-pink and lemon-yellow, nothing a woman would buy this time of year. And yet the tableau was irresistible. It was impossible to walk past the window, impossible not to step inside.

As she stood gawking, a hand snaked through a seam in the backdrop and placed paper umbrellas in the mannequins' glasses. Then Alan Spangler appeared in the window. He knelt to clip a bracelet around a mannequin's wrist. When he spotted Viola, he smiled and waved her inside. "Miss Peale! It's nice to see you." He had removed his sport jacket; his shirtsleeves were rolled to his elbows. "How do you like my display?"

"It's enchanting," she said. "This is your creation?"

He grinned. "I accept full blame. My dad thinks I've lost my mind." He lowered his voice. "It's working, though. We've never had a busier Christmas."

"Well, congratulations." Her eyes darted around the shop, the dozens of hats on wire stands. For her sister, it would be a wasteful gift: the hall closet was full of unworn hats. Each Sunday Clara donned an old green cloche of their mother's, stylish twenty years ago.

"We just got a whole truckload of new merchandise. I haven't put them out yet. You can have first pick." He crossed to the front door and turned the sign from OPEN to CLOSED. "We close at eight, but you're a special customer."

"I don't want to be a bother," she protested.

He disappeared into a back room, calling over his shoulder: "Don't move. I'll be right back."

Viola waited. Somewhere a radio was playing. On the counter was a pile of fashion magazines, *Vogue* and *Harper's Bazaar*. She hadn't bought a new hat in years. She and Clara lived within their means, her weekly paycheck plus the small inheritance from their father.

Alan reappeared with a stack of hatboxes piled to his chin. "I picked these especially for you." He opened a box and took out a maroon beret. "Try this."

Viola took the hat and placed it carefully on her head. He pointed toward a mirror. "It's lovely," she said.

"Don't make up your mind yet. Not until you see this." From a larger box, he took a simple woolen sailor. "Don't look yet." He placed the hat on her head, frowned, adjusted it minutely. To her astonishment, his fingers brushed at her forehead, loosening a lock of hair. "You have beautiful hair. We don't want to cover it completely."

It was a remarkable thing for a boy to say to his teacher, but Alan said it simply, without self-consciousness. He was a natural salesman, born, if the Creator actually thought of such things, to sell ladies' hats. Growing up around the shop, he'd developed a way with the female customers, a warm and practiced ease. It explained his popularity with the girls at school. Bakerton men were not known for social graces. Next to other local males—the girls' gruff fathers and crude brothers—Alan Spangler was a prince.

He stood behind her and studied her reflection in the mirror. "I had a hunch it would suit your complexion. Bring out the blue in your eyes."

Viola blinked. He was right: her eyes, gray in most lights, looked distinctly blue. "It's marvelous," she said softly—forgetting for the moment that he was her pupil, forgetting everything but this new vision of herself, no longer a dowdy schoolmarm but a striking blue-eyed woman with beautiful hair. Such was the power of an elegant hat.

She turned to face him, hesitating. It seemed indelicate to ask. "What is the price, exactly?"

"Nineteen dollars."

"Oh, my." She had never spent so much on a hat in her life. "It's very tempting. But Christmas is just around the corner. I should be buying gifts for others, not myself." She took a final look at her reflection, the vivid blue eyes she'd never seen in a mirror. Reluctantly she removed the hat.

"I'll put it aside for you, in case you change your mind." Alan's eyes twinkled. "This hat is made for you. There isn't a woman in Bakerton who could wear it so well."

"Thank you, Alan," she said, flushing. "You're quite a salesman. Your father must be very proud."

She buttoned her coat and headed out into the cold. A stiff wind had kicked up. Walking home, she felt warmed from the inside, hot with pleasure and embarrassment. Bakerton was a small town. Mindful of appearances, she had always kept a certain distance from her pupils. Any passing pedestrian might have seen her through the glass door, alone in the shop with Alan Spangler, giggling like schoolgirls as he placed the hat on her head. And yet in the moment, she'd felt no discomfort. She hadn't felt such freedom, such warm and easy happiness in another's company, since she was a girl.

That night, naturally, she dreamed of Edgar. She often did, but that night it was certain to happen. There was no doubt.

THEY HAD CALLED themselves cousins, though in fact their fathers were. Viola's, an accountant, had been brought over from England by his cousins Chester and Elias Baker. When the first Baker mine prospered, Herman Peale had been hired to keep the books. Edgar was Chester Baker's son—born, like Viola, at an extraordinary moment, the dawn of the new century. They had in common a feeling of destiny, a fascination with the future: the modern wonders not yet invented, the unimaginable miracles to come.

From birth they'd been closer than siblings. Viola's sister, Clara, was too slow for their games; Edgar's brother, Chester Jr.—known as Chessie—too serious, too old. As children they'd chased each other through the Baker house, a rambling mansion on Indian Hill. At Jefferson Elementary they were inseparable. Another boy would have been teased for playing with a girl, but Edgar was a Baker. At eight or nine or ten, the miners' children were old enough to know the difference.

Looking back on those years, Viola could summon few memories of her parents or Clara and none whatsoever of her schoolmates. Her long happy childhood had been spent in Edgar's orbit.

Then, when they were both fourteen, Edgar was taken away—enrolled, like his brother, Chessie, at the Wollaston School in Connecticut, impossibly far away. At Bakerton High, Viola was sick with loneliness. From the miners' children she felt hopelessly separate, and yet she was no Baker. The schoolmates she'd always ignored returned the favor, leaving her friendless in the small class. In those days, few pupils finished high school; they left for the mines or the dress factory, the family farm. In 1917, Viola's year, Bakerton High would graduate a class of twelve.

She lived for the summers, when Edgar returned for three glorious months of riding and long walks and picnics and tennis, a game he'd become obsessed with at school. On rainy days they spent hours at the piano. Viola played competently, Edgar beautifully. Every summer they mastered several duets. Each May their reunion was awkward. Edgar seemed at first a different person, a handsome and beguiling stranger with a shockingly deep voice. In a day or two the effect would dissipate, and Viola would recognize her own Edgar, dearer to her than anybody; as familiar as her own self.

They had three such summers, sun-filled, precious. Then,

in the fourth summer—they didn't know it would be the last—everything, everything changed.

Edgar came home in time to attend her graduation. Viola, the class valedictorian, saw him sitting in the audience next to a boy she didn't recognize. Later she was introduced to Bronson Baker—Edgar's first cousin and her second. The boy's mother, finding Bakerton uninhabitable, had divorced Elias Baker when Bronson was a baby and taken him back to England to live. When England went to war, Bronson had been sent to military school in South Carolina. Now he'd come to spend a summer with the father he barely remembered.

Viola loved him on sight.

He was their own age, their own blood, but stirringly different. Since birth Viola and Edgar had resembled each other, fair and slender, with fine blond hair that turned almost white in the sun. Bronson was not tall, but his body was thick and powerful. She loved his square shoulders, his curly hair, his cultivated accent. He was the first boy she'd ever met who could drive an automobile. On summer evenings the three cousins raced along the back roads in his father's Maxwell touring car, the only automobile for miles.

Each morning Viola watched the boys play tennis. She'd never realized—Edgar was too kind to let her see—that she was a weak player; now, watching him with Bronson, she understood how patient he'd been. With Viola he'd never kept score, but now each point was fiercely contested. Edgar played with grace and precision, Bronson with fury: explosive speed, a blistering serve.

In a trance of longing, Viola sat on the grass, hugging her knees to her chest.

She wished desperately for Bronson to approach her, though how a boy did this—with words, a look, a touch?—she couldn't begin to say. She had never been alone with him. Playing cards or croquet or riding in the Maxwell to the new picture show uptown, it was always the three cousins together. All her life, Edgar had been Viola's dearest companion. Now she found herself wishing—shockingly, horribly—that he would disappear.

Instead the opposite happened. Viola herself became invisible. Once or twice, when the moon was full, the boys set off on horseback to camp on Garman Ridge in an old canvas tent. On hot afternoons they went swimming in Deer Pond, an activity unsuitable for females. Miserably she watched them set off in the Maxwell.

"I won't go if you don't want me to," Edgar said sweetly.

"Oh, I don't mind," Viola answered, hating him and Bronson both.

The summer marched on toward its inevitable conclusion. America had joined the war in Europe. It was known, though not discussed, that the boys would be called up to serve. One morning in early August, the three cousins set off on a long hike, Bronson's idea. All summer long, he'd been itching to climb Indian Hill.

"Why?" Viola asked, genuinely curious.

"Because it's there," Bronson said.

The strongest by far, he carried their supplies in a rucksack strapped to his back. They attacked the hill and found a path into the wood. Bronson led the way, armed with a compass, Edgar a few paces behind. Viola struggled to keep up, encumbered by her skirt.

At noon they reached the summit. The view was picturesque: an alternating pattern of forest and farmland, the fields laid out like a patchwork quilt. To the north and west were two mine tipples, Baker One and Baker Four.

On a flat rock they ate their sandwiches. Viola rose and dusted off her skirt. The air had grown muggy; the woods hummed with insects. She wished herself at home in a cold bath.

Bronson pointed in the distance, toward Deer Ridge. "We can get there in an hour, if we pick up the pace. The first half is all downhill."

Edgar frowned. The downslope was steep and rocky, he pointed out, with few trees to grab on to.

"We'll go one at a time," Bronson said. Military school had taught him to give instructions; to all three, his leadership seemed inevitable. "Otherwise, if the first man stumbles, we could have a pileup. You first," he told Edgar. "When you get to the bottom, give a whistle and stand clear."

"I should stay with Viola," Edgar said. "In case she needs help."

More and more, the boys spoke of her in the third person, as though she weren't actually there.

"I'll go with her," Bronson said curtly. And then: "If she fell, what would you do about it? You can't carry her. You aren't strong enough."

Edgar flinched.

Why, he's insulted, Viola thought. She hadn't, herself, considered the words harsh. She'd been distracted by the thought of Bronson carrying her, his thick arms beneath her, pressing her to his heart.

Edgar set off down the slope, agile as a cat. As his white shirt disappeared from view, Viola was aware of Bronson beside her, so close she could hear his breath. "I hope he's all right," she said to fill the silence.

Without warning, he grasped her shoulders and kissed her hard on the mouth.

It wasn't at all what she'd imagined. She was conscious of their teeth colliding, his wet tongue pushing into her mouth, his hands grasping through her skirt. Later, undressing for her bath, she would see where his fingers had clutched her, a constellation of small bruises on her backside.

He pulled her roughly to the ground.

His body seemed heavy enough to kill her. Her lungs were panicked, useless. Her rib cage, surely, would shatter under his weight. Edgar, she thought, where are you?

She felt rough hands beneath her skirt and then a breathtaking, searing pain, his fingers up inside her. This isn't happening, she thought.

Finally he let her go. He rolled off her, breathing heavily. Her blouse was dirty, her skirt torn.

"Wipe your eyes, for God's sake." He got to his feet. "That's what you wanted, isn't it? You've been after it all summer."

The truth of the words cut her open. That, of course, was the shame of it: everything he said was true.

"I fell," she told Edgar when they met him at the bottom of the hill.

"I can see that." He took her hand. "You're not hurt, are you?"

Viola shook her head, not trusting herself to speak.

"This hill is too rugged for you. For me, too. I say we stage a mutiny." Gently he brushed some debris from her hair. "Come on. Let's get you home."

At the end of August, Bronson left for Camp Lee, Virginia.

Viola and Edgar rode with him to the train station; they stood on the platform waving goodbye. In September Edgar was drafted. Viola stayed behind and waited. Nothing happened for a long time, and then everything did.

EDGAR RETURNED IN May, as usual. Or so Bakerton was told. In truth his body was never recovered. Chester Baker arranged for a closed casket, an empty box to be buried in the family crypt.

As Viola had once wished him to, Edgar had simply disappeared.

The morning of the funeral, she bathed and dressed; at least she must have. Her memory was blurred like a photograph ruined by water, the endless flood of her own tears. She attended the funeral with her parents and Clara. At St. John's Episcopal they sat in the second pew, behind a row of Bakers. The service had already begun when Bronson Baker crept in through a side door, an old woman— his mother?—clutching his arm.

For a moment it seemed that Viola was dreaming. She'd believed him still in France, still fighting; no one had said a word about his return. Later she would understand the reason, but in that moment she felt she'd lost her mind. She hadn't forgotten what he'd done to her in the forest, the secret mutilation that would not heal. And yet the sight of him affected her as it always had. For an entire summer she had studied him hungrily, stirred by his beauty. She couldn't, now, see him any other way.

At the graveside she watched him, the old woman at his side. Mourners crowded beneath a black tent. Bronson himself stood a few feet from the coffin. During the hymns, the blessing, he seemed overcome by emotion. He bawled loudly, unself-conscious as an animal, his eyes streaming tears.

The other mourners stared at the ground.

The service ended; the coffin was lowered. The old woman took Bronson's arm. He was led away weeping, docile as a child. Viola hurried after them. Suddenly her wild grief had a focus: Edgar was gone forever. But Bronson, by some miracle, had returned.

She called his name. Later she'd wonder what exactly she'd hoped for. His arms around her, a word of comfort? A journey backward to another summer, when the road belonged to three cousins in a Maxwell, the only automobile for miles.

Bronson turned. He stared at her without recognition, his eyes glazed. His mouth twitched spasmodically.

"It's no use, miss." The woman was younger than she'd looked from a distance, too young to be his mother. She explained in a hushed voice that she was Bronson's nurse, hired by the family. His mind had been affected by the shock of battle. Among other things, he had lost the power of speech.

Viola watched her lead him away, toward the Maxwell parked at the cemetery gate. He climbed in on the passenger side. A moment later his father approached and got behind the wheel.

She never saw Bronson again. He was sent back to England to be looked after by his mother, and in the fall Viola enrolled at the State Normal College. A year later she stood at the front of her own classroom, at Fallentree Primary School.

. . . .

THE PUPILS WERE in high spirits, vacation in the air. The girls filed in, chattering excitedly. Alan Spangler stopped at Miss Peale's desk. He wore a handsome sweater, red for the holiday, cashmere possibly. He sucked a lemon drop. "For my throat," he explained. "You'll be at the concert, won't you?"

"Of course." She had promised to come early to hand out programs for Edna O'Shane's big night.

"I have two solos." Alan grinned, showing his dimple. "I've been practicing for months."

Viola called the class to order, no easy task, and took attendance. Only one pupil, Helen Lubicki, was absent. Looking over the day's announcements, Miss Peale understood why.

"We at Bakerton High are saddened to report the death of Private First Class Peter Lubicki," she read. Helen's brother had been killed in action, his body sent home from Italy. A funeral Mass would be held Saturday at St. Casimir's.

She glanced up from her mimeographed sheet. A few of the girls looked ready to cry, and even the hoodlums were silent. In five short months they would be turned loose into the world, beyond the daily tending of Miss Peale, the protection of Bakerton High.

After the second bell she crossed the hall to Edna O'Shane's classroom. At the school Edna was an oracle of sorts, an authority on town gossip. Peter Lubicki, she told Viola, had not attended Bakerton High. He'd come of age before Roosevelt's law and gone into the mines at fourteen.

"We should go to the wake," Viola said, surprising herself. "To pay our respects. We can stop by after school."

Edna gaped as though Viola had proposed a safari in Africa. "Viola, why on earth?"

It was a difficult question to answer.

"His sister is in my homeroom," Viola said, as though that explained it. That she'd never, in her memory, exchanged a word with Helen Lubicki seemed beside the point.

THERE WERE NO streetlamps on Polish Hill. The only light came from interior windows, the company houses alike as matchsticks. The Lubickis', at the bottom of the dead-end street, was no different from the others, except that the family owned—or had simply appropriated—the land adjacent. In summer they planted every inch of it—not a garden but, with nine children to work it, a small subsistence farm.

The road was unpaved. Viola looked in vain for a flat place to park. Finally she pulled off the road, scattering gravel. There were no other cars in sight.

She stepped out of the car and approached the house. A cluster of men stood smoking, not speaking. Two blue stars hung in the front window: another Lubicki son was serving overseas.

The mean little house was crowded with people—large women serving food, a flock of unruly children underfoot. A wooden casket stood in a corner of the parlor, its lid closed. Two women in babushkas knelt before it, their lips moving silently. Viola knelt beside them and bowed her head in prayer.

. . . .

SHE DROVE HOME carefully, grateful for the empty roadway. Snow was falling, the pavement frozen in spots. The night was moonless, the road lost in shadow. The air seemed filled with ghosts.

A male figure limped alongside the road, heading in Viola's direction. She felt a sudden chill.

The boy held one arm close to his side, as though it pained him. His left arm hugged a large box. The car's headlamps picked out blond hair, a red sweater. Viola rolled down her window and stepped hard on the brake.

"Alan? Is that you?"

He shielded his eyes against the headlamps. In the strange light, his mouth seemed to be covered in blood.

"For heaven's sake, what happened?" She threw open the car door. "Are you all right?"

He nodded mutely, his eyes streaming. Gingerly he touched his face.

"Come with me. You're bleeding," said Viola, her heart racing. "You need to see a doctor."

He got into the car without protest, setting the box in his lap. Viola groped for the light switch. His right eye was swollen shut, his cheekbone scraped, his lip split. She saw that his mouth was covered not in blood but red lipstick. "My God, Alan. Who did this to you?"

"I'm going to miss the concert." He stared straight ahead at the lights of the high school blazing in the distance. "Strange, isn't it? To see the school open after dark."

Viola started the car. "I'm taking you home. Your parents can call a doctor."

"No! My father can't see me like this." His voice broke. "Take me to the store, Miss Peale? I have a key. I can clean up there."

They rode in silence. Alan directed her to an alley behind the hat shop. Viola parked and engaged the brake.

They sat a moment, not speaking. He would not meet her eyes.

"I brought this for you," he said softly. "I was going to give it to you after the concert. It's ruined now."

They both stared at the box in his lap.

"I was walking to the concert," he said. "It was dark. I didn't even see them coming."

"Alan, why?"

The question hung in the air.

"They hate me," he said in a low voice. "They've always hated me."

"Who? Who hates you?"

"Boys."

Viola reached for his hand. "They're just jealous," she said, "because all the girls like you."

Almost imperceptibly he shook his head. "I'm leaving," he said. "I'm eighteen now. I don't need a diploma. I can go live with my sister in Washington and get a job."

No, Viola thought. Alan was a good student, and his family owned a profitable business. Unlike his classmates, who'd be swallowed up by the mines or the steel mills, he had an actual reason to stay in school.

"You can't," she said.

"What choice do I have? I can't live in this town."

The words had the terrible bite of truth.

"Alan, listen to me. If you drop out of school, you'll be drafted immediately."

He shrugged. "Now or six months from now, what's the difference? At least I'd get out of here." He opened the passenger door. "Thank you, Miss Peale. You've been very kind to me. I wish I had something to give you." He held the hatbox to his chest. "I won't even show you what they did to your hat. It would break your heart."

Viola watched him climb the back stairs to the shop.

In a daze she drove down Susquehanna Avenue—past the Polish church, the company store, the sign her cousin Chessie had erected, with typical grandiosity, near the train depot, so that no visitor could avoid seeing it. BAKERTON COAL LIGHTS THE WORLD.

I can't live in this town.

Viola's cousins were the only boys she had ever loved. One August afternoon they'd abandoned her to go swimming. Lonely, dejected, she had taken Edgar's horse on a hard ride. She rode out to the end of Deer Run Road, to where the Maxwell was parked. Through dense trees she'd watched them, naked but not swimming, Bronson and Edgar as tender as girls.

She was unsure what exactly she'd seen, or if she had even seen it, until the day of Edgar's funeral: Bronson standing at their cousin's grave, weeping like a widow.

CLASSES RESUMED THE second day of January. In homeroom Miss Peale took attendance. Two desks were conspicuously empty. Joseph Poblocki had turned eighteen; now beyond the grasp of Roosevelt's law, he'd dropped out to work in the mines. Peggy Schultheis had dropped out, too, to do God knew what on the family farm. It happened every year: seniors disappearing in the final semester, a few short months before graduation; young people pulled away by family obligation or need, constraints Miss Peale would never understand.

To her relief, Alan Spangler was present. His eye had healed, his lip nearly so. He sat a little apart from the pretty girls—off to the side, in the desk abandoned by Peggy Schultheis. At the final bell he rose without speaking, the first pupil out the door.

In May the school year ended, and one by one, the boys were drafted: Henry Eickmeier, Chauncey Hoeffer, Richard Dickey, Jerry Bernardi, John Quinn. Bakerton, more and more, became a town of women—a place that might have suited Alan Spangler, except that he, too, was called up to serve. Like Edgar and Bronson, like Viola, he was a child of the century. Silently Miss Peale blessed him, and hoped.

BROKEN STAR

I met my aunt Melanie in the summer of 1974, an August of high
bright days, so dry that my father had to oil our front lane to
keep the dust down. I was fifteen, midway through high school
and deadened by its sameness. I could scarcely remember what had
preceded it, or begin to imagine what might follow.

"You don't remember me, do you? You were so little when
I left." Melanie climbed into the front seat of our station wagon,
next to my father. It was my mother's usual place, surrendered out
of courtesy since Melanie was a guest. She had arrived with her
stepdaughter, Tilly, on the Greyhound bus from Pensacola, Florida.
Tilly, who was eight, shared the backseat with me and my mother.

"Not exactly," I said, though I had heard about Melanie my
whole life: my mother's sister, the youngest of seven, the midlife
baby who'd surprised my grandmother after two miscarriages. *I was
an "oops,"* Melanie would tell me later, a confession that shocked
and thrilled me. I'd never heard an adult allude to such matters. We
were not that kind of family.

There was a rustling as she rifled through her shopping bags.

"For Regina," she said, handing me a small unwrapped box. Inside was a pair of earrings, the dangling kind I admired, decorated with tiny seashells. These were made for pierced ears, so I wouldn't be able to wear them.

"They're beautiful," I said. "Thank you."

My mother glanced at the earrings. She didn't care about jewelry but feigned interest to be polite. "Very nice," she said. "But Melanie, you shouldn't have."

She greeted all presents this way—*you shouldn't have*—no matter how worthy the occasion or how trifling the gift. It was a habit born of embarrassment. No gift—even one she'd always wished for—was worth drawing attention to herself.

Melanie seemed not to have this problem. On the ride home, she talked nonstop: the difference in weather from Florida to Pennsylvania, the assortment of characters she and Tilly had met along the way. She imitated the bayou accent of the bus driver, so thick that the names of cities where they'd stopped—Savannah, Georgia; Raleigh, North Carolina—were completely unintelligible. My father chuckled appreciatively. My mother giggled like a schoolgirl, covering her mouth with her hand.

MELANIE HAD BEEN gone for twelve years, the only one of my relatives who lived away. *Away,* in my family, meant anywhere outside rural Pennsylvania, the quiet stretch of country, bordered by highways and Amish, where we'd farmed for four generations. Philadelphia was away. Pittsburgh, a grimy city of immigrants and steel mills, was—emphatically—away.

Melanie had left after graduating high school. She attended secretarial school in Washington, D.C., and worked as a typist at the Department of the Interior before marrying Uncle Dan and moving to a naval base down south. I knew her face only from photographs, the half dozen that decorated my grandmother's parlor. One in particular impressed me, her high school graduation portrait: Melanie in an off-shoulder blouse of glamorous black, a color nobody much wore in those days, certainly not young girls. "It's a drape," my mother explained. "They made all the girls wear it. Don't ask me why." She said it in the impatient tone I recognized, the one that meant I was interested in the wrong things.

I never mentioned the drape again, but I thought about it a great deal, Melanie being draped by someone, a photographer presumably. It seemed a reverent gesture, exquisitely romantic. In the photo Melanie's dark hair was spread across her shoulders, her chin tipped at the unnatural angle favored by school photographers. The whole presentation was theatrical, and Melanie smiled as though she knew it but was simply playing along. Her attitude, though I didn't yet know the word for it, was ironic, and it was this quality that delighted me.

Now, in person, Melanie looked much the same as she had in the photo, though she had just turned thirty-one, an age I did not consider young. By thirty, my female cousins were stout matrons: large bosoms firmly corseted, hair cut and permed into helmets of tight curls. Melanie's hair hung nearly to her waist, and she wore the kind of wide-bottomed blue jeans I saw in magazines but didn't own, since they were impractical for farm chores. She looked the way girls my age were supposed to look, while I—in my sleeveless blouse and homemade skirt, the flowered pattern not quite match-ing at the seams—looked like a younger version of my mother.

Night was falling as we left the bus station, an amenity that, until then, I hadn't known the town possessed. I went to high school in town—this involved a half-hour ride on a rickety school bus—but apart from the main streets, I'd spent little time there. The bus sta-tion was located on a side street next to the pool hall. My father had escorted us at my mother's insistence, though he grumbled that it was unnecessary. The neighborhood was perfectly safe.

I was beginning to notice how often they had such conver-sations: my mother asking for protection, my father reluctant to provide it. At home she was a model of efficiency, a take-charge housekeeper who structured my free time around endless daily chores, but in the outside world she was timid. My father had taught her to drive early in their marriage, but she refused to go any farther than the grocery store. She drove slowly, nervously, and only on the back roads. The Pennsylvania Turnpike, with its three lanes in either direction, scared her witless.

Back at the house, my father carried Melanie's suitcase upstairs to the sewing room, where the couch opened into a bed. Tilly would sleep in my room. "Give your cousin the bottom bunk," I was instructed, though Tilly wasn't really my cousin, being Uncle Dan's from a previous marriage. This was how my mother said it: "from a previous marriage," as though there'd been more than one.

I helped Tilly unpack her shorts and T-shirts. She was a skinny little thing, red-haired, with a sharp chin and a dark band of freckles across the bridge of her nose, so that from a distance she seemed to be wearing a Band-Aid. "Why do you have bunk beds?" she asked.

"For sleepovers," I said, though technically that had never happened. In the third grade, I'd been allowed to invite Barbara Vance to spend the night. Homesick, she had cried all evening, until my father drove her the fifteen miles back to town. After that, no more sleepovers.

Tilly considered. "Maybe," she said judiciously. "Or maybe they wanted to have more kids."

"Nah," I said, as though the idea had been discussed and dismissed. In fact, the possibility had never occurred to me.

"Anyway, it doesn't matter," she said, climbing into bed. "They're too old now."

I turned off the light, and in a few minutes I heard Tilly snoring in the bunk below. I lay awake a long time thinking about what she had said. I couldn't imagine my mother pregnant, let alone doing what was necessary to get that way. Like any farm girl, I understood the mechanics of reproduction. I'd once sneaked into my uncle Wilmer's barn while Lassie, a beautiful little mare, was being bred, a polite term that doesn't convey the brutality of the operation. I was squeamish about applying that model to any human couple, let alone my parents. At that age I was more interested in the runway leading up to such intimacies, the kissing and ardent glances, none of which I had experienced myself.

Drifting off to sleep, I found myself thinking of Melanie and Uncle Dan, who had met on the beach at Ocean City, Maryland. I'd been to the shore only once, on a rare family vacation, but I still dreamed of it. Not the ocean itself, but the human tableau running alongside it, the hundreds of strange, bare bodies on display, decorated with bright bathing suits. It was easy to place Melanie on that beach. I'd never seen Uncle Dan, not even a picture; but I imagined him tall and dark, with a hairy chest, like Burt Reynolds.

I was nearly asleep when I heard Tilly sniffling.

"What's the matter?" I whispered. "Did you have a bad dream?"

"I miss my dad," she wailed.

This surprised me, because Tilly seemed older than her years. In fact, she was the same age Barbara Vance had been at the time of our sleepover, and much farther from home.

"It's just temporary. You'll see him soon enough."

"No, I won't." Tilly inhaled wetly. "We're never going back."

"Don't be silly," I said, because that was what my mother would've said.

For a long time Tilly didn't speak.

"Why would you think that?" I whispered. "Did Melanie say that?"

"No," Tilly said. "I just know."

I KEPT QUIET about what Tilly had said. It was easy to do, since I rarely saw my parents during the day. August is busy on a farm, and we were all occupied with separate chores. I would see my mother at suppertime but not my father even then; most nights he had meetings at the Grange Hall, to prepare for the county fair. That year he was a judge in two categories, Swine and Youth Dairy Cattle. He felt out of his depth with the swine—we hadn't raised piglets in years—but with the calves, he was more than confident. I'd heard it said my whole life, by neighbors and uncles and men from church, their grave inflection giving it the weight of a proverb: Bert Yahner knows cattle.

The fair had been a fixture of my childhood, as thrilling as Christmas, as anticipated and beloved. For six days each September there would be crowds and commotion, the Ferris wheel, the sweet greasy aroma of frying potatoes and funnel cakes. As a little girl, I'd walked the midway flanked by my parents. Holding their hands, I kept up a steady chatter, enjoying their nearness, their protection from the unaccustomed crowd. When I got older, I entered animals in the youth competitions. I showed rabbits three years in a row and, at twelve, a Jersey calf named Buttercup, who took second place in her class.

Three years later, my father still pestered me to raise another calf. "Someday," I told him. The truth was, I had no intention of doing it; given the choice, I would skip the fair altogether. I was embarrassed now by the cowboy music, the livestock smell, the farm boys in their stiff new dungarees, hair slicked back as if for church. Last year I'd stayed close to the booth where I sold raffle tickets to raise money for the 4-H Club, keeping a nervous lookout for my schoolmates, the town girls in their sundresses and pretty sandals. How I coveted those sandals! I loved them precisely because they were so impractical, bound to get ruined in the gravel and muck. The girls came in groups of three or four, whispering and sometimes breaking out in loud laughter. They might have been laughing at anything, but I felt with a deep certainty that they were mocking people like my parents. My mother in her housedress and dark lipstick, flushed with excitement, clinging to my father's arm.

"It's about that time, isn't it?" Melanie asked at supper. "The fair. God, I used to love the fair."

"It's a lot of aggravation, if you ask me," my mother said, passing a platter of fried chicken. "Bert will be relieved when it's over."

"I think he likes it," I said.

"It's too much for him. Since his heart attack."

"What about you, Gina?" Melanie had taken to shortening my name, which delighted me. I'd never had a nickname before.

"I probably won't go," I said, avoiding my mother's eyes. "I'll have homework then. It's the first week of school."

"You've got to be kidding." Melanie took the platter. "Won't all your friends be there?"

My mother stared at me in bewilderment. "I don't know what's come over you."

"Don't listen to her, Peg." Melanie heaped her plate with potato salad. For a small person, she had a huge appetite. "She's going to the fair."

MELANIE WAS A late riser. It was ten, ten-thirty by the time she wandered into the kitchen in her nightgown. Even Tilly slept until nine. My mother tolerated this for two days. The third morning she enlisted them to work in the kitchen, putting up bread-and-butter pickles. She and Tilly picked the cucumbers, brought them in from the garden, and scrubbed them at the sink. Melanie had the best job, slicing them into thin rounds, and I had the worst, sterilizing the Ball jars. Using metal tongs, I placed them four at a time in a huge cauldron of boiling water, a steamy, miserable operation that kept me in front of the blazing stove in the August heat.

"Your mother runs a tight ship, Gina." Melanie sat perched on a high stool in front of a breezy window. "Jesus, you'll be glad to go back to school."

"Ten more days," I said, grinning. I'd forgotten—it was easy to forget—that Melanie had been a farm kid, too.

"Do they still make you write that essay? 'What I Did on Summer Vacation'?"

"Some vacation," I said, mopping my forehead with a towel.

"My vacation was just super," Melanie said in a simpering voice. "I watered two hundred head of dairy cattle."

"I hauled manure a quarter mile to the garden," I added.

"I sat by the highway all day in the blazing sun," said Melanie, "and I sold six ears of corn."

I laughed so hard no sound came out, a feeling both delicious and frightening. Through the open window, I saw my mother come up the garden path with another bushel of cucumbers.

"I put up a million quarts of bread-and-butter pickles," Melanie continued. "For God's sake! Does anybody like bread-and-butter pickles?" Then she noticed my expression. "Gina? What's the matter?"

My mother stood in the doorway, her cheeks flaming. The screen door spanked shut behind her. She glanced around the kitchen: the steam rising from the stove, the counters, covered with old towels, where I'd set the jars to dry. "You don't have to help if you don't want to," she said, an odd tremor in her voice.

"Peg," said Melanie, turning to face her. "We were just having fun."

My mother set her basket on the table. "Don't bother with these. I guess we have enough."

. . . .

"HOW LONG IS Melanie going to stay?" I asked my mother.

We were preparing Sunday dinner—roast beef, potatoes and carrots, a relish plate of pickled beets and my mother's vinegar cabbage, which we called chowchow. It was the standard menu for when the relatives came to dinner. For summer visits like this one, a platter of cut vegetables was added, whatever was ripening in the garden, but otherwise my mother made no concession to the season. Even today, maybe the hottest of the year, she didn't consider a barbecue or cold supper, to avoid firing the oven all afternoon.

"You never know with Melanie. You can't pin her down." She opened the oven door. A wave of heat smacked my bare legs.

"But doesn't Tilly have school?" My own classes would begin in a week, an event I looked forward to with a mix of excitement and dread.

"Not for another month. The Florida schools start later. The heat, I suppose."

The screen door slammed and my father appeared, still dressed in his church clothes. His sleeves were rolled above his elbows. Sweat rings showed under the arms of his white shirt.

"Makes sense, if you ask me." He turned on the faucet and scrubbed his hands and forearms, streaked with farm dirt. My mother frowned but said nothing, just watched the filthy water pool in the sink.

I persisted. "A month, then?"

"Goodness, no. I'm sure Dan will want her back before then. A week at the most."

My father raised his eyebrows. "A week is a long time."

"Don't be silly. She's my baby sister. Who knows when we'll

see her again?" My mother arranged tomato slices on a plate. "It won't kill Regina to share her room for a week. When I was a girl, we slept three to a bed, except for Carl."

This was not new information. I'd heard my whole life that I'd been spoiled by having my own room. (My uncle Carl, the one boy in his family, had been similarly pampered, a privilege he'd apparently paid for by being killed in the war, long before I was born.) I was often treated to sermons on the value of sharing, wearing hand-me-downs, and waiting in line for the bathroom—lessons I, the first only child on either the Yahner or Schultheis sides of my family, had failed to learn. I didn't have the nerve to protest that I hadn't chosen to be an only, that my parents, who'd married late, were to blame. An eldest son, my father had spent his younger years running the Yahner farm, supporting his siblings and widowed mother. Even if he'd wanted to marry, my mother often said, where would he have found the time? Her own reasons for waiting were less clear and more delicate. Plain and awkward, she had always been a homebody. Because of her shyness, school had been torture; when she dropped out of the twelfth grade, her sisters were amazed that she'd lasted so long. My aunts agreed on this point: Peg was lucky to have found a husband, even one twenty years older. That was repeated throughout my childhood, so often that it never struck me as cruel: *Peg is lucky to have a husband at all.*

My aunts—Rosemary, Velva, and Fern—were brisk, no-nonsense women who'd married in their teens and raised large families. Their children were grown now, with babies of their own. These grandchildren were the subject of much discussion. *Two and a half and still in diapers. Marcia lets him sleep in bed with her and Davis.*

I can't see why he puts up with it. Occasionally one of the aunts would notice that I was listening as I stirred the gravy or fetched bottles of root beer for the men. *Remember this when you have babies, Regina. Before you know it, you'll be toilet-training your own.* These comments thrilled and perplexed me. To my knowledge, no boy had ever looked at me twice. What made my aunts so certain that, *before I knew it,* one would want to marry me? Explain this, I wanted to say. Explain how it happens.

It seemed to me then, and still does, that my aunts were made by marriage, that every defining feature of their lives—the children and grandchildren, the canning and cooking and crafting skills each possessed—was intimately connected to that long-ago moment of being chosen. My uncles Wilmer, Dick, and Bill were like all the men I knew then, soybean and dairy farmers who spoke rarely and then mainly about the weather. Yet unlikely as it seemed, I accepted that these men had the power to transform. My aunts had been pretty, lively girls—one stubborn, one mischievous, one coquettish, according to my mother — though somehow all three had matured into exactly the same woman: plump, cheerful, adept at pie making and counted cross-stitch, smelling of vanilla and Rose Milk hand lotion. That I would someday become that same woman terrified me. My only greater fear was that nobody would choose me, and I would become nothing.

The aunts and uncles arrived promptly at two, a strange time to eat a large meal—too late for lunch, too early for supper—but this was a Schultheis Sunday tradition. After spending all morning in church, the hostess needed a few hours to get the cooking under way.

"Hi, stranger," said Aunt Velva, giving Melanie a squeeze.

"Didn't you look pretty this morning? I just love that white dress."

"Thank you." Melanie winked at me over Velva's shoulder. She had borrowed the dress from my closet, after coming to the break-fast table in a printed sundress that tied behind her neck like a halter top, leaving her back and shoulders bare.

"Melanie, you can't," my mother had protested.

Melanie shrugged. "It's this or blue jeans. It's the only dress I brought."

"Wear something of mine," my mother suggested, though nothing in her closet was likely to fit. She wasn't fat but tall and large-boned, with broad hips and shoulders. "Or Regina's."

"I don't mind," I said. "You're welcome to wear anything you like."

Melanie followed me upstairs. "I forgot all about church," she said with a conspiratorial laugh, as though this were a private joke between us. "Honestly, I haven't been in years."

I stared at her in wonderment. It's hard to credit now how exotic I found this, as if I'd just discovered that Melanie could fly. "Really? Never?"

"Nope. And God hasn't struck me dead." She threw open my closet door and rifled through the dresses and blouses, stopping to admire a skirt I'd made that summer. "This is pretty, but I don't think it will fit."

"You're skinnier than I am," I said, though that didn't describe it. Melanie had small breasts, a narrow waist, sharply curving hips. My body had the same features, or was beginning to, but these were recent developments. I wasn't used to seeing myself that way.

She gave me a playful shove. "No, silly. We're the same size. You wear your clothes too big."

I blinked. My mother bought patterns in size fourteen when she could have worn a twelve. I'd never realized I did the same thing.

Melanie chose a simple white dress that I'd never liked, feeling exposed by its plainness. I turned my back politely as she untied her sundress. "You'll need a slip with that," I told her, digging through a bureau drawer. I couldn't bring myself to say, You'll need a bra.

Now she had changed back into blue jeans, though the rest of us were still in Sunday clothes. Even Tilly wore the dressiest outfit Melanie had packed for her, a denim skirt and blouse.

"And who is this little princess?" Aunt Fern asked, patting Tilly's head. "Honey, we're so happy to have you here. We've been hearing about you for ages."

That was a blatant untruth. Though Melanie's name came up often in family conversations, no one ever spoke of Uncle Dan, let alone his daughter.

Tilly blossomed under the aunts' attention, guzzling cream soda and eating Velva's lemon drop cookies. Watching her, I felt lonely for my childhood, when the aunts had been at the center of my small universe. I had especially adored Elsie, the oldest aunt, who, until she died of kidney failure, had spoiled me with small presents—knitting needles, beautiful buttons—prompting protests (*You shouldn't have*) from my mother. Recently the aunts had become less interesting to me, their company less dear. They had always fussed over me, the youngest of the girl cousins, but it was no longer the type of attention I craved. I wanted them to notice the ways I differed from JoAnn and Prudence and Theresa and Ruth:

my love of reading, my high marks in school. Of course, those dif-
ferences weren't visible, and I was too shy to speak of them. But at
the time that didn't occur to me.

THE FAIR OPENED on a Monday, with a horse show and equipment
expo, nothing I cared about. Tuesday would be barn games and
harness racing; Wednesday, the milking contest and tractor pull.
This year I begged off, complaining—in whispered tones, to my
mother—of menstrual cramps. "I'll be better by the weekend," I
told her. The most popular events would be held then—the Beef
Cattle judging, the aerial show. Saturday night was the grand finale,
an outdoor dance with a live band on the stage behind the Ag Hall.

We drove there in the pickup, my father, Melanie, and I. My
mother had gone ahead of us, taking Tilly with her, to sell baked
goods and preserves at the Church of the Brethren tent. My father
left us at the main gate and we wandered into the Ag Hall, past
booths showing pies and needlecrafts, macramé and ceramics,
hooked rugs and intricately pieced quilts.

"Wait. Look at that," Melanie said.

The winning quilt hung against a makeshift wall, a blue ribbon
pinned to its corner. The pattern was classic, an eight-pointed star
on a white background, surrounded by a jagged border. It was the
border that was most difficult to execute: sixteen sharp points, folding out from the original star like a paper snowflake. The design
was pieced with snippets of blue fabric—ginghams and plaids and
paisleys and sprigged muslins, all in shades of blue.

"It's beautiful," Melanie said. She ran her hands over the quilt, admiring the delicate stitching. Only then did I notice the name on the entry tag.

"That's Mom's. She makes one every year. It's an old pattern. Broken Star." I stared at the quilt, ashamed that I hadn't recognized it. For most of the summer, my mother had spent evenings alone in her sewing room. She'd been working on the quilt for months, and I had never bothered to take a look.

"Peggy's amazing," Melanie said softly. "She can do anything."

This stunned me. I had never thought of my mother that way.

Over Melanie's shoulder, I saw a group of boys trotting through the expo hall. "Pretend like we're talking," I told her.

"We *are* talking." She lowered her voice to a whisper. "Why? Did you see somebody you know?"

"Those boys are in my class. Don't look."

"I won't." She leaned toward me as if whispering something in my ear. Then she laughed loud and bright, a perfect imitation of the town girls in my class.

The boys approached us. "What's so funny?" said the tall one, Darren Wolf. For two years he'd sat in front of me in homeroom, the luck of alphabetical order. I knew all his shirts, how the rear seam followed the shape of his shoulders, how his blond hair curled over the collar. I couldn't recall him ever looking at me or saying a word.

"None of your business," Melanie said tartly. "Gina, don't tell them."

"Hi, Regina," said the other boy, Philip Schrey. We were in the same geometry class. I was surprised he knew my name.

"Regina," said Darren Wolf. "Is this your sister?"

"Sort of," Melanie said.

"Do you go to Bakerton?"

"Did. I graduated."

Darren Wolf nodded as though he'd suspected as much. "You girls going over to the dance?" he asked, though he was clearly asking Melanie.

Yes, I thought. Just say yes.

"In a minute," she said. "We're waiting for some people. We'll see you over there."

"Okay, then," said Darren Wolf.

"See you," said Philip Schrey.

When they were safely away, Melanie grabbed my hand. "Do you go to Bakerton?" she asked in a gruff voice.

We both shrieked with laughter.

AUGUST COOLED INTO September. A dusting of yellow appeared on the trees. Each morning I trudged down the lane to wait for the school bus. Some nights I had long conversations with Philip Schrey, who'd asked for help with geometry homework and had begun calling me on the phone. Usually my mother answered. She handed me the receiver without comment but later peppered me with questions: *Who's that boy? The same one as before? Why does he keep calling?*

It's just homework, I said. But these phone calls—the waiting and planning, the delight when they occurred and the crushing disappointment when they didn't—occupied all my attention. Asleep or awake, I was thinking of Philip Schrey. My dreams were full of ringing telephones.

One morning I woke to find Tilly's bunk empty. Downstairs I

found my mother at the stove, frying eggs and bacon. Fresh coffee bubbled in the percolator.

"Where's Tilly?" I asked.

"She's spending the day with Fern. Melanie, breakfast!" she called, scraping eggs onto a plate.

I heard loud footsteps above, the clatter of Melanie's wooden sandals on the stairs.

"Good morning!" she said breathlessly, giving my shoulder a squeeze. To my astonishment, she was fully dressed, a poncho slung over her arm. She sat at the table and tucked in to her breakfast.

"Regina, drink your milk," my mother said. I noticed then her high color, her cheeks flushed with agitation or excitement.

"What's going on?" I asked.

"We're going to Pittsburgh," Melanie said.

"You and Mom?" To my knowledge, my mother had never been to Pittsburgh in her life.

In my half-asleep state, I watched Melanie eat, stung by the unfairness of it all. Once, as a little girl, I was allowed to stay up until midnight on New Year's Eve, to watch the celebration on television, but I fell asleep before eleven. I awoke hours later in my own bed, where my father had carried me. I lay awake until sunrise, fuming at the injustice, heartbroken that I had missed my chance.

"Can I come?" I finally asked.

"Regina, don't be silly," said my mother. "It's a school day."

"I don't care." I felt suddenly alert, shocked awake by my own bravery. "We never go anywhere." I held my breath because there was more I could have said: Because you're afraid of everything. I'm stuck here because of you.

Melanie took her plate to the sink. "Peg, let her come. She can go to school anytime." My mother started to speak, but Melanie interrupted her. "Please, Peggy? I want her to be there."

My mother studied me for a long moment. She seemed to be deciding something. Then a remarkable thing happened.

"All right, then," she said.

Later I would understand her reasons, but at the time I was too excited to care. We set out in the station wagon, driving south and west. The air had turned cold overnight. Steam rose from the Yaegers' bean fields on either side of the road, a ghostly haze that parted to let us pass. Melanie drove with a speed and joyful carelessness that exhilarated me: the windows open, her long hair billowing in the breeze. She sang along with the radio, an AM station crackling with static: *You can't talk to a man with a shotgun in his hand.* My mother sat beside her, clutching the door handle. If my father had been driving, she would have scolded him: *Bert, slow down. You'll get us killed.* To Melanie, she didn't say a word.

We approached Pittsburgh at just before noon, which surprised me. I'd imagined it much farther away. The city itself was a revelation—the tall skyline, the Allegheny busy with boat traffic. We exited the highway and made a series of turns down busy boulevards. As we neared the city center, Melanie pulled over to look at a map.

"Let's stop here," I suggested, staring out the window. Across the street was a public park, crowded with people enjoying the midday sun.

"Sure," said Melanie, cutting the engine.

"Melanie, really," my mother said.

"There's an ice cream stand." Melanie pointed. "I want an ice cream."

We got out of the car and crossed the street, my mother hugging her purse to her chest.

"Three strawberry cones," Melanie told the man at the window. She reached into the pocket of her jeans.

"Save your money," my mother said, opening her purse.

I spotted an empty park bench. Melanie sat in the middle, her legs tucked up under her. I did the same.

"Sit like a lady," my mother told me. "Melanie, you're a bad influence."

Melanie laughed. "It's comfortable this way."

We sat watching people pass: men in suits, smoking cigarettes; well-dressed women toting shopping bags; black maids in uniform, pushing baby carriages. They were the sorts of people I didn't see in everyday life. I could have sat there for hours.

"It's getting late," my mother said.

Melanie licked her fingers. "I could eat another one," she said. "Gina, could you eat another one?"

"Definitely," I said.

"We could, you know." She laid her head on my shoulder. "We could eat ice cream all day long."

"Melanie!" my mother said, so sharply that heads turned in our direction. Her anger startled me. I couldn't remember the last time I'd heard her raise her voice.

"Just kidding," Melanie said, rising. "Jesus, Peggy. It was a joke."

We crossed the street and got into the car. Melanie drove down a narrow street and then another, barely wide enough for one car. The closeness frightened and delighted me: the houses and storefronts abutting, with no space between buildings, the pedestrians—a different crowd now, young and long-haired—crossing at random, mere feet from our car.

"Where are we going?" I asked for the first time.

Melanie didn't answer. Finally my mother spoke. "Your aunt has an appointment." Something in her tone, her way of referring to Melanie—*your aunt*—warned me. I didn't ask again.

"Look for number one-twenty," Melanie said. "It should be on the left."

I was the first to spot the building, a narrow brick house with a dilapidated porch. Melanie parked and we went inside. We climbed a graceful old staircase to the second floor. The steps were covered in hexagonal tiles no bigger than quarters. The spaces between the tiles were filled in with grime.

At the end of the corridor we went into an office. A brass plate on the door read INTERNAL MEDICINE. We stepped into a dilapidated waiting room: mismatched chairs covered in green vinyl, outdated magazines—*McCall's, The Saturday Evening Post*—piled on a table in the corner.

I'm not sure how long we waited after Melanie's name was called. My mother paged through a *Ladies' Home Journal* from front to back. Then she started over again, reading it back to front.

OUTSIDE, THE AIR had turned colder, the sky darkly clouded, as if the brilliant morning were something I'd dreamed. Slowly we crossed the street to the car, Melanie leaning heavily on my mother. I followed behind. They seemed to have forgotten I was there.

I watched as Melanie lowered herself into the driver's seat. When she turned the key in the ignition, the radio came on, a patter of muted trumpets. My mother reached to turn it off.

"No," Melanie said. "I like that song."

She drove us out of the city and onto the Turnpike. No one spoke. Then, suddenly, she pulled over to the side of the road.

"I'm bleeding." Her voice sounded strange, low down in her throat. "I can feel it. Peggy, you'll have to drive."

My mother stared at her, wide-eyed. "Melanie, I can't."

"Why not?" Melanie turned to me, her eyes pleading. "Gina?"

I shook my head mutely, shamed by my uselessness. I wouldn't be sixteen for two months. My father had promised to give me driving lessons, but so far I hadn't so much as turned the key in the ignition.

"Peggy, please." Melanie got out of the car, her hand low on her belly, and opened the rear door. I climbed out and took the passenger seat up front. I will never forget the look on my mother's face as she took the wheel. She found the lever beneath the seat and slid herself forward so that her face was inches from the windshield. Then she shifted into first gear and we rolled into the right lane. A shrieking sound as the car behind us slammed its brakes. My mother gasped.

"It's okay," I said. "Just give it some gas. You're doing fine."

In the left lane, cars whizzed past. My mother didn't answer. She kept a tight grip on the steering wheel, her eyes on the road.

"It'll be okay, Mom," I said. "Just keep driving."

For a long time neither of us spoke. Once, twice, Melanie moaned softly from the backseat.

"Is she all right?" I asked.

My mother shifted into third, grinding the gears. An eighteen-wheeler screamed past us, its headlights blazing. She shielded her eyes.

"It's hard to look," she said. "Regina, I'm so scared. I just want to close my eyes."

IT WAS DARK when we arrived back at the house. My father's truck was gone. Melanie went immediately to bed, my mother to the kitchen. She filled the percolator and took carrots from the refrigerator, a couple of pork chops.

"I'm not hungry," she said abruptly. "Are you hungry?"

"Not really," I said.

When the coffee was ready, she poured me a cup, something she had never done. Across the kitchen table, she explained how Melanie felt trapped with Uncle Dan, who had a terrible temper and sometimes hit her. "He's an animal," my mother said.

I was as shocked as if she'd spoken an obscenity. I'd never heard her say an unkind word about anybody.

"That's no way to raise a child. Can you imagine? Seeing his father behave that way. It's for the best," she said softly, the last words I'd hear her say on the subject.

My father's truck pulled into the driveway, and my mother busied herself at the stove, laying the pork chops in a pan. I poured my coffee down the sink. The smell nauseated me. I have not drunk coffee since.

When I came home from school the following day, Melanie and Tilly were gone.

IT WAS TIME, my mother explained. They'd been staying at our house for nearly a month.

A change came over her after Melanie left. For two days, three, her bedroom door was closed when I came home from school. "She's feeling poorly," my father said when I asked. "A humdinger of a headache." Baking and canning seemed more effort than she could muster. The last of the tomatoes rotted on the vine.

I could have lent a hand in the garden, but I didn't. I was preoccupied with my own concerns. I went with Philip Schrey to see *The Towering Inferno* at the Rivoli Theater in town. We ate lunch together every day in the school cafeteria. We went to football or basketball games on Friday nights. This new dimension of my life occupied me completely. My mother's difficulties didn't interest me at all.

We never spoke of the trip to Pittsburgh. My mother didn't mention Melanie for months. A card arrived at Christmas with a Florida postmark. Inside was a single handwritten line:

Thanks for everything. Love, Melanie, Dan, and Tilly.

YEARS PASSED, AND I stopped thinking about that summer. Soon the slow August days were lost to me forever; it seemed, often, that I had no time to think. I went to college, worked, married a much older man, and moved to a different country, feeling always that the world moved too fast for me, that I'd been raised to live at a gentler pace. In my late thirties I looked up and noticed that my parents were gone, the farm sold. Every year I considered sending a hundred Christmas cards via airmail to the dozens of Yahner and Schultheis relatives, but I never actually did this. My reasons were laziness and lingering guilt. I had neglected to invite my aunts to my wedding, a slight that, if they'd known about it, would have hurt them. I understood this just as I understood that nothing— certainly not a secular city hall wedding—could have induced Velva or Fern to travel to New York. Thinking of them made me sad and ashamed, so I stopped thinking of them. It wasn't hard to do. My interest in family had died with my mother. Without her, I didn't see the point.

My first book was published the year we returned from Sweden—a slender collection of short stories that seemed, and was, destined for the remainder bin. My publisher made a brief effort at promoting it with a handful of signings at bookstores in the South and Northeast. It was at one of these signings that I saw a familiar face, though I couldn't place it immediately. The woman was slight and red-haired, my age or a bit younger. "Regina," she said. "Do you remember me?"

I looked at her closely. Through her heavy makeup, I could discern a dark band of freckles crossing her nose like a bandage.

Tilly lived in Atlanta now, married to a linesman for Georgia Power. They had two daughters. She'd seen my photo in the arts section of the newspaper and recognized me at once, despite my unfamiliar last name. "I'm so proud of you," she said. "Melanie would be so proud."

Melanie. After all these years her name affected me strangely, like the name of my first love. "How is she?" I asked.

"She died," Tilly said.

Over tea in the bookstore café, Tilly told me how Melanie had battled polycystic kidney disease, the illness that had killed my aunt Elsie. "It runs in the family," said Tilly. "You should have yourself checked."

I nodded, not trusting myself to speak.

"I'm sorry to lay this on you," she added. "She was ill for such a long time. We looked everywhere for you. We thought maybe you could help."

"I was living in Sweden," I said automatically, not comprehending her meaning. "With my husband. I got married."

"I guess that's why we couldn't find you. We didn't know your married name." Tilly stared off into the distance. A bookstore employee was making a racket, stacking plastic chairs. "We tried her aunts, but Rosemary was too sick. And Velva wasn't a match."

"*My* aunts," I corrected her. Tilly wasn't really part of the family; it was understandable that she'd get confused. "They were Melanie's sisters."

Tilly covered her mouth with her hand.

AND SO IT was Tilly who told me that Melanie was not my aunt. She was my sister. Melanie, dying, had needed a kidney, and the family had tried desperately to find me. They were certain that I'd be a match.

"I'm sorry," Tilly said that day in the bookstore. "We all assumed Peg had told you."

But Peg, my mother, had not.

The baby was born in May, the year my mother turned eighteen. A few years before, *Gone with the Wind* had opened in theaters, with Olivia de Havilland in the role of Melanie, a beautiful woman who also died young. It was my mother's favorite film. She saw it four times at the Rivoli Theater. That was before she quit school and became a homebody, canning and cooking and helping my grandmother with the new baby.

I imagine a boy from a neighboring farm, in love with my mother—a girl who lived for the movies, tall and red-haired and less shy than I'd been led to believe. Who was that boy, I wonder, and who was that girl? I have pieced together as much as I can. My mother and my aunts are gone now. There is nobody left to ask.

I've thought often of that trip to Pittsburgh, my mother opening her pocketbook to pay for our ice cream. For her it was a day of silent, anguished giving: to one daughter, a searing lesson; to the other, a second chance.

Peggy can do anything.

I can still see Melanie that day in the Ag Hall, her hands oddly gentle as she admired our mother's quilt.

Is this your sister? the boy asked her.

Sort of, she said with the smile I now think of as secretive. Did she know the truth then or find out later? I missed my chance to ask her. I was in Sweden for three years with my husband. I wasn't here to help.

A PLACE IN THE SUN

They drove east through the desert towns: Hesperia to Victorville to Barstow to Yermo, past the dusty bed of Soda Lake, dry now, a ghostly crater waiting for rain. The route was familiar, a memory stored in his bones. The return trip, Sandy had driven in every condition—exhausted, panicked, blind drunk, sick with shame. But the eastbound journey occurred, always, under controlled conditions. They'd left L.A. at three in the afternoon. *You're crazy,* said Myron Gold, whose car he'd borrowed this time. *It's the hottest part of the day.* But the timing was no accident; it was part of the protocol: rolling into Vegas at first dark, slipping away (this was the hope) before dawn. Vegas at noon would look stripped and diminished, like a Christmas tree in daylight. It was no place he wanted to see.

He glanced over at Marnie, curled up in the passenger seat, her breathing slow and deep. She had never been to Vegas. *It's your birthday,* she'd pointed out. *We should be together on your birthday.* Bringing her was a mistake, he knew it already: a clear breach of protocol. A month ago his *no* would have been easy, automatic. But she loved him too much, had lost too much. Now he couldn't refuse her anything.

In the rearview mirror the white sun was nearly blinding. Years ago, crossing the desert in his Pontiac convertible, he'd kept the top up and sweated through his shirt. Later he'd borrowed girlfriends' cars, a Chevy Bel Air, a Mustang. He remembered both distinctly, more clearly than he did the girls. The trips, too, ran together in his memory—the radio stations that petered out every ten minutes, the stops in Barstow or Baker for cold sodas and gas. The desert heat had been a constant, a character in the story. But Myron Gold's Eldorado had air-conditioning, an unsettling development. When Marnie turned it on full blast and bent her face to the cold, Sandy had snapped to attention: another break in the protocol. His nerves prickled, a flash of alarm.

The protocol was scientific, based on experience. He'd learned through trial and error—expensive, devastating error—which conditions produced the desired result. In Vegas he'd have a light supper at the Boxcar, scrambled eggs and coffee; then a single drink to smooth him out. Nerves were the enemy. He'd seen it plenty of times, from both sides of the table: the anxious player under a toxic cloud, fear rising off him in waves. One drink was enough to dispel it, but two was risky. Three and you might as well leave your wallet on the table, a lesson it had taken him years to learn.

HE'D LEFT VEGAS—FOR good, he thought—in the summer of '60, grateful to get out with his skin. In the Pontiac convertible, watching the desert fly past, he'd made a series of resolutions.

Three squares a day, bed at a decent hour.

A daytime job—steady, respectable.

No cards or dog track or lottery tickets, no slots or craps or betting on sports.

It was a pledge he'd modify later, in the dazzling season of '62, Vince Lombardi's Packers an irresistible sure thing. But the central promise, the critical one, he adhered to strictly: he did not set foot in a casino.* Since then he'd ventured back only when necessary, when his material circumstances left him no choice. Now, for instance: his phone shut off again, the landlord clamoring for rent. He owed thousands to Myron Gold, hundreds to his relatives back in Pennsylvania. *Try to cut back on your expenses,* his sister Joyce had suggested in a letter, Joyce the prim schoolteacher who wrote him faithfully once a month whether he answered or not, and tucked a ten-dollar bill into the envelope. Because Joyce loved him more than anybody did or should, he tried to follow her advice. He smoked fewer cigarettes. Finally he sold the Pontiac at a price that sickened him, and rode the bus to work.

Work, he knew, was half the problem. Tending bar kept him out and circulating. If a card game was happening somewhere in North Hollywood, it was impossible not to know. But his various day jobs (driving a bread truck, selling vacuum cleaners) had ended badly. The last one—short-order cook at Myron Gold's diner—had proved more dangerous than bartending. Gold's wife had taken a shine to him, a development that could only end in disaster.

She had hired him off the street. Bleary, hungover, he'd wan-

---

* Until he had to: the Thanksgiving Day debacle, Detroit over Green Bay, a rout no one could have predicted.

dered in for breakfast after an all-night card game. A sign in the window said HELP WANTED. *Can you cook?* Vera Gold asked.

He looked down at his greasy plate. *Better than this? Sure. You bet.*

For months they'd worked side by side, through lunch rushes and long empty afternoons. Her husband had bought the diner on a lark—*It's smart to have a cash business,* he told Sandy later. Vera kept the place running. She hired and fired and ran the register. On Friday afternoons her husband appeared, heading straight for the back room. He emptied the safe into a zippered vinyl pouch.

He had noticed Sandy immediately. *Who's the pretty boy?* he asked Vera, loud enough for Sandy to hear. A moment later he barreled into the kitchen, a short, squat man in Clark Kent eyeglasses and a bristly gray crew cut.

Where'd she find you? he demanded.

I came in for breakfast, Sandy said. *Where'd she find you?*

And just that easily they were friends. Every Friday afternoon, Gold spent a few minutes in the kitchen with Sandy, dispensing filthy jokes and business advice. Vera rolled her eyes good-naturedly; she had heard it all before. For work she dressed in clinging dark dresses. All day long Sandy was aware of her body—behind the lunch counter, at the cash register, her high heels clicking across the floor. Without even looking, he sensed exactly where she was. Her whole life, probably, she'd affected men this way—a bombshell, tall and red-haired.

You mean it's not natural? he asked later, when this fact had become apparent.

Smart aleck, she said, laughing low in her throat.

They were lying in bed at Gold's house in the hills—their first time or second, half smashed on Bloody Marys Vera mixed by the pitcher. In the afternoon light, her face was etched with lines, her makeup kissed away.

Her exact age was a mystery. He'd never had the brass to ask. She was Gold's fourth wife—*my child bride,* he called her—but that could mean anything; the man was seventy if he was a day. He'd made a fortune in his youth, lost and then remade it. Somewhere along the way he'd invested in the pictures. Vera had been a contract player at MGM, a rising starlet with a big future, until the war came.

Go ahead, do the math, she told Sandy. *Count on your fingers if you need to.*

(In fact, math was the only subject he'd ever excelled at, the one part of his schooling that seemed to have a point.)

She was a voracious lover, nothing like the girls he was used to, pure or pretending to be, waiting to be coaxed. From his high school sweetheart, who really was one, to the fastest showgirl, each had acted like a virgin, a charade he was expected to uphold. But with Vera there was no playacting. She wanted him openly, fervently—as, against his better judgment, he wanted her.

When he finally came to his senses, she dismissed him with a shrug. *You'll be back,* she said.

Fearing she was right, he quit the diner and got hired at the Beehive. It wasn't hard to do. He could mix anything, make conversation with anyone.

Are you an actor? At least once each shift, a customer would ask. In North Hollywood it was a reasonable question. Half the guys under forty and all the pretty girls wanted to be in the movies.

Nah, he said each time. *I just pour drinks.*

He knew it wasn't true, that in some way the bar back *was* his stage, a showcase for his best qualities, his wit and style and instincts and speed. It was an act he'd mastered long ago, running the most popular table at the hottest casino in Vegas, which involved more than dealing cards. Tending bar was no different. Any clown could pour a drink, but Sandy's customers became regulars. Men liked to be remembered: Rams or Dodgers, vodka or gin. A plain girl fed on flattery, a pretty one on judicious appraisal—an appreciation of her unseen qualities, her intellect and taste. In Hollywood everyone, when you got down to it, just wanted to be seen.

In that way it was the opposite of Vegas, where taking a snapshot could get you bounced from a casino. Bartenders, drivers, dealers, stickmen: in Vegas you learned when to look away, to keep your eyes on the floor.

THE SUN WAS setting right on schedule, a fiery backdrop for the famous horse-and-rider sign. The Hacienda was a tourist trap catering to retirees. A mile ahead, the Tropicana marked the beginning of the Strip. Sandy would never forget his first sight of it, the tulip-shaped fountain dancing with light. To a snot-nosed kid from Bakerton, Pennsylvania, it had seemed the height of splendor, the swankest joint in town. Ten years later—an eternity in Vegas time—it had been eclipsed by flashier acts: the Stardust with its elaborate signage, a panoramic view of the solar system; the new Caesars Palace, *Ben-Hur* with showgirls. But to Sandy, the Trop still sparkled—an aging siren, glamorous and wicked, and rife with possibilities.

Against his will, he thought of Vera Gold.

Beside him, Marnie stirred. "Wake up, baby," he murmured, touching her shoulder. "You don't want to miss this."

She sat up in her seat, disoriented. "We're there already?"

"Four hours door-to-door. Just like I said." He drove too fast, he knew he did, but cops were rare on this stretch of freeway. He hadn't gotten a ticket in years.

She stared out the window. The Strip unrolled before them, a throbbing assault of shimmering, bubbling neon. Same old Vegas, though changes were visible if you knew where to look. The Tally-Ho was now the Aladdin, where Elvis Presley had just married his Priscilla. The Sans Souci had become the Castaways, recently bought—like half the Strip—by Howard Hughes.

"Is that a *church*?" Marnie asked.

"Wedding chapel. An old one. The new ones, you can drive through." He signaled to change lanes. The Eldorado responded smoothly, a hell of a car. "There are a couple dozen more up the road."

"Is this real?" she murmured.

"Sort of," he said.

She rubbed her eyes, patted her stiff blond hair. She'd had it cut recently, teased into a stylish bouffant. Still her hand went often to the nape of her neck, where her ponytail had been, as though she couldn't believe it was gone. They had known each other four months, longer if you counted the run-up, when she'd appeared at the Beehive with an actor named Donny Valentine. *My boyfriend,* she'd called him, and no one had the heart to correct her, though everyone knew Donny was queer. To Sandy, her innocence was touching and a little alarming. He had no business messing with a girl so easily fooled.

"Wayne Newton is playing tonight," she said. "I saw it on TV."

"Old news, baby. He was headlining back when I lived here."

"Did you ever go see him?"

"Nah. That's for the tourists." Sandy's shift had started at eight, the precise moment when curtains were rising all over town. He'd been working the night Sinatra and Dean Martin first played the Copa, an act he wouldn't have minded seeing. But he had never watched a show of any kind. "That's where I used to work," he said, pointing. The familiar sign filled him with an old longing, the looming S with its tall graceful curves.

The Sands
A PLACE IN THE SUN

"Is that where we're going?"

For a moment he was tempted. The town had a short memory, and seven years had passed. Still he wouldn't chance it. He'd been known there, known and recognized: Sandy from the Sands. It wasn't worth the risk.

THEY FOUND A cheap motel a block north of Fremont. Alone, he wouldn't have bothered. He could stay awake for days if he had to, drive home high on adrenaline and caffeine. But with Marnie, gentle measures were called for. He'd make sure she got to bed by midnight. He owed her that much and more. (Loyalty? Protection? He wasn't sure. He knew only that he was inadequate to the task.)

Now, for instance. The drive up the Strip had juiced him. He was ready for his eggs, his drink. Instead he willed himself to be patient as Marnie unpacked her small suitcase into the crappy particleboard dresser, lingered at the bathroom mirror in her stockings and slip. Sandy lay on the bed watching her: the round freckled shoulders, the small ripe breasts. He hadn't gone near her in weeks. *I'm still sore,* she said the one time he'd tried. Ashamed of himself, he hadn't touched her again.

"It might be a late night for me," he said. "You can take a taxi back here when you've had enough."

"Are you kidding? We're in Vegas! And it's your birthday. I want to stay up all night." She turned, her bright face startling. Like all actresses, she was an expert with makeup. Barefaced, she looked like what she was—an exceptionally pretty twenty-year-old, the flower of her father's dairy farm in southern Ontario, raised on milk and apples. Now her freckles were gone. In false eyelashes and pancake, she was just a Hollywood beauty, like so many others.

She blotted her lipstick. "Come on. This will be fun."

Not fun, Sandy thought. The exact opposite of fun. Vera had understood the difference. The night before a trip, she could sense his sober mood.

You're a barrel of laughs, kid. Like a banker leaving for the office.

That's right, baby. I'm all business.

"The thing is, I'd like to win some money," he told Marnie. "Need is more like it. I *need* to win some money." The confession pained him. Myron Gold had loaned him another five hundred but made him beg first. Behind the Clark Kent glasses, his eyes narrowed ominously. *I'll put it on your tab,* he said finally, handing over the keys to the Eldorado. *I'm starting*

to think you're a bad investment. You know what gonif *means? No?*
Look it up.

"Oh, I almost forgot!" Marnie reached into her pocketbook and brought him a small gift-wrapped package. "This is for you."

Shame burned his cheeks. He was sorry he'd told her about his birthday. He hadn't told anyone else, so only his sisters had remembered. Dorothy's card promised a month of prayers by the Carmelite Sisters of Loretto, Pennsylvania. Joyce was more practical, or maybe she simply knew him better. Her card contained two twenty-dollar bills.

Marnie sat on the bed beside him, leaned close to his shoulder. Her hair smelled of sugar and flowers.

"You didn't have to get me a present," he said.

"Well, sure I did. Thirty-three is special. You're the same age as Jesus."

"Jesus who?" he said, a smart-aleck moment he instantly regretted.

(*You don't believe in God?* Vera asked him once.

I believe in math, Sandy said.)

"You shouldn't joke about Jesus," said Marnie.

He gave her a squeeze. "Sorry. Thirty-three, huh? Seems like he's been around longer than that." He ran a hand over the shiny gold wrapping and pictured Marnie in her tiny rented room, cutting and scotch-taping; measuring, probably, to conserve the pricy paper. It seemed wrong to tear it open, untender, a violation.

"Thanks, baby," he said, kissing her. "You're the best."

. . . .

THE LARIAT WAS a sawdust joint, built fast after the war by a character named Buster Kilgallon, who saw it all coming and put up his Texas ranch to buy two properties on Fremont—a narrow cow path then, before it became Glitter Gulch. The Lariat and its sister casino, the Lasso, sat kitty-corner at a busy intersection. Their matching signage—two huge whirling ropes, one red, the other green—had been visible for half a mile, until the neighboring casinos built taller and brighter. Same old story.

The place was busy for a Tuesday night. Men in hats and string ties drank cheap beers. Fleshy women in capri pants hunched over the slots. It was an older crowd, locals mostly—tourists rarely left the Strip. The old sawdust floor had been replaced with carpet, the main room tarted up with chandeliers, yet the Lariat had remained low-profile, one reason he'd chosen it. Certain people were unlikely to venture here. Another reason, equally important: its blackjack tables ran on Strip rules. The dealer drew to 16, and stood on a 17. The rest of downtown played old-style—the dealer hitting a soft 17, a shady rule that favored the house.

Sandy sipped methodically at his martini, stirred, two olives, dry and cold. He had given precise instructions, like the customers he himself hated, the turkeys who rattled off entire recipes as though the barman had never mixed a drink. But tonight he had no choice; the drink had to be perfect.

Protocol.

Drink in hand, he scoped out the floor. Ten blackjack tables against the far wall, four cameras trained on them from above. Just as he remembered, the corner table was in a blind spot. He hadn't played the Lariat in years, but his memory was precise in these matters. If he stationed himself at the far end, his face would be hidden in shadow. An unnecessary precaution, maybe, but he played better when he wasn't being watched.

Gonif: a thief, a swindler. He had looked it up.

He reached into his jacket for the new wallet from Marnie, soft blond leather with rawhide stitching, heavy against his heart. Inside was his bankroll from Myron Gold and, tucked into a hidden compartment, the two twenties from Joyce. Her birthday card had come a day early, his sister punctual to a fault. Her baby, too, would arrive on time, if it hadn't already. (The actual due date had slipped his mind.) But a first baby at Joyce's age was risky, something he hadn't understood until Vera Gold explained it. Now he found himself worrying about Joyce, a strange reversal. It was Joyce who'd always looked after him. Who'd looked after them all: Lucy, their baby sister; Dorothy, their crazy one. Sandy's worries were confusing and, he hoped, unnecessary. Joyce had more reliable people to lean on. Her husband—solid, dependable Ed—was surely up to the job.

To Joyce. To her health, he thought, raising his glass. It was as close as he could come to prayer.

THE CORNER TABLE went hot, cold, hot. Sandy settled in, his nerves humming. The cards revealed themselves in canny combinations, tens and threes, threes and tens. It took him a moment to grasp the connection: the third of October, the beginning of his Jesus year.

By eleven o'clock he was down a hundred. Again and again he hit on 13; again and again the face cards found him, inscrutable queens and smirking jacks.

(The king looked somber, disappointed. *Gonif.* Of course, he wasn't talking about money.)

"You're killing me," Sandy muttered to the dealer. In an hour it would be the fourth of October. If the pattern shifted, he'd be even further screwed, forced to hit on 14.

He found the thin metal disk in his pocket, kept there for emergencies. It was smooth and flat, smaller than a quarter. Carefully he nursed his drink. His fellow players were two gruff men in Western wear—strangers, probably, but alike as brothers. Beside them sat an old babe, Spanish-looking, and what might have been her daughter, both heavily made up and enormously fat. Downtown: no sharks in suits, no beauties showing cleavage. Nothing here to rattle him, no distractions from the game.

Then, suddenly, the juice found him. He drew one sweet hand and then another. Face cards arrived in decorous pairs, like dinner guests.

King and queen.

Queen and jack.

He was about to pony up again when he glimpsed Marnie across the room. He'd left her at the bar with a rum and Coke, hoping the scene would bore her into surrender, until he could put her in a taxi back to the motel. Now she was attracting lots of attention, from the men, anyway. Nothing could distract the old babes at the slots. In her strapless dress, she belonged at the Sands or Caesars. For the chintzy Lariat—its chandeliers dusty, its walls dark with cigarette smoke—she was like visiting royalty, the best-looking girl the place had seen in years.

Sandy turned his back slightly, hoping she hadn't seen him. To his dismay, she headed in his direction, teetering on high heels.

Not now, he thought, counting furiously. Please, not now.

A moment later she lurched toward him. "There you are. I lost you," she said thickly. Her eyes were bleary, her makeup smeared.

He spoke in a low voice. "Baby, are you okay?" Could she possibly be this tight on one rum and Coke?

"I drank too much. Some guy kept buying me drinks." She glanced over her shoulder. At one of the baccarat tables, a man in a Western hat was watching them intently. It was a look Sandy recognized, known to bartenders everywhere: the hillbilly stinkeye. A drunk itching to pick a fight.

"Oh, Jesus." Sandy ran a hand through his hair. Now, of all times? The juice surging, the whole table waiting on him. And yet he owed her.

The count fell out of his head.

"Cash me out," he told the dealer. "Sorry, buddy. I gotta go."

OUTSIDE, HE LED her to the taxi stand. "I'm sorry," she said, her hand low on her belly. "I ruined everything."

He could not disagree with this.

"Do you feel sick?" he said.

"I'm so tired. Aren't you tired?" She leaned against him briefly, her hair fragrant, as though the stale casino air had not touched her. Sugar and flowers. "Let's go back to the hotel."

Well, he was up—a little. He could walk away with cash in his pocket: five hundred bucks to catch up on some bills, plus enough for a nice dinner. He could end his birthday in bed with Marnie, the girl who loved him. What was wrong with that?

Marnie sighed. "Can't you just quit?"

It was a question he'd been asked many times—by Vera Gold, his brother, George. Tonight, like every night, walking away was theoretically possible. But he'd spent three hours at the table, sweating, his pulse racing. He had invested other people's money, his own time and anguish; lost everything, then won it all back. It seemed worse than foolish, it seemed somehow *wasteful*, to leave holding exactly what he'd brought.

And back in L.A., Myron Gold was waiting: Gold the human cash register, tracking every cent he'd borrowed, no longer so blind, maybe, to the precious thing he'd stolen outright. Booby traps were everywhere—hidden pits of quicksand, the ground sinking around him. And yet, at the table, Sandy had beaten the odds. In just a few hands, he'd won back all he'd lost and more. If he could accomplish that much in a matter of minutes, what did the rest of the night hold?

"Baby, I can't," he said. "You understand, right?"

She nodded almost imperceptibly and stepped into the taxi. From the window she waved goodbye.

THAT FIRST NIGHT at the Beehive, he'd noticed her immediately, though Donny Valentine did his best to hide her. The two sat, always, at a secluded corner table. Donny came up to the bar and ordered their drinks. Then one night Donny kept her waiting, and Marnie herself approached the bar. She ordered a rum and Coke and fished a dollar in quarters from a little straw purse.

"I'll need to see some identification," Sandy told her sternly, a game he played with the young ones. "Just kidding," he whispered when the color drained from her face. "I'll make you anything you want."

In a single night he knew everything about her: her teenage reign as Dairy Princess; the conviction of all Winthrop, Ontario, that she was destined to be a star. Her very knowability charmed him. In the year he'd been Vera Gold's lover, she'd confided almost nothing. Her dark complexity fascinated and repelled him. With Vera, nothing was what it seemed.

Yet a few crucial things had been simple. Without consulting him, Vera had taken precautions, or perhaps at her age, none were necessary. He'd grown used to the freedom and, with Marnie, was careless. For weeks he crept out of her room at dawn, careful not to wake the landlady, as though it were the worst that could happen.

INSIDE, HE FOUND a phone booth and lit a cigarette. Vera answered on the first ring. Television in the background, Vera nursing a highball in front of the late news. Like Sandy, she was nocturnal. Her husband slept like a bear.

"Are you up or down?" she asked. "Dumb question. If you were up, you wouldn't be on the phone."

"Marnie lost the baby." *On purpose,* he could have added but didn't. He had never said it aloud.

With Vera, he didn't have to. As always, she heard the words he was too cowardly to say. "Ah, geez. Listen, Sandman: what else could she do?" The line went quiet, Vera switching off the television. "Think about it. Poor kid still thinks she can make it in this town. Hell, maybe she can. What do I know?" Ice cubes clinking in a glass. "But not with a baby, she can't."

Sandy had never thought of it in those terms. "I didn't tell her to do it," he said.

"You didn't tell her not to."

"It could have been different," he said.

"Tell me how." A click, a slow inhale: Vera lighting a cigarette. "What, you were going to marry her? Take her back to Bakersfield?"

"Bakerton." The town he'd fled, whose mines had killed his father; the bleak small-town life a prison from which no one escaped. And yet he had considered it: driving back east with his bride beside him, having stopped off in Vegas for a different purpose entirely. It was a task easily managed—no blood test, no waiting, the ceremony over in minutes and cheaper than breakfast. For a time it had seemed a real possibility, the right thing to do.

"I couldn't make up my mind," he said. "I guess she got tired of waiting."

"Smarter than she looks," Vera said.

BACK AT THE table, the tide had turned. Sandy felt it immediately, the juice seeping from him like blood from a wound. He bet big and then bigger, a strategy that sometimes worked. The juice was fickle; she punished you like a pouty girlfriend. Sometimes you could win her back with a show of bravado. It was worth a try.

He fingered the cheap silver-plated medal in his pocket—

Saint Anne, patroness of miners—his father had been wearing when he died.

The juice was jealous. Like an angry lover, she knew when his attention was elsewhere. And tonight his mind was crowded with other women. Marnie passed out in the cheap motel room; Vera Gold sleepless in the Hollywood Hills, lying next to the husband who owned his soul. Back in Bakerton, the sister who loved him more than anyone, dying in childbirth, for all he knew.

In his new wallet were the two twenties, Joyce's gift to the brother who rarely called and did not visit, who always had something better to do. Money sent without her husband's knowledge: it was, he knew, the only lie in his sister's marriage, the only secret she kept from Ed.

It was enough to cover the motel, a tank of gas to get them back to L.A., expenditures Joyce would approve.

Forty bucks was enough, probably, to pay for a wedding.

It was ten to midnight, the last breath of his birthday. Sandy Novak was thirty-three, the same age as Jesus. The two twenty-dollar bills were all he owned in the world.

WITH THE TIME difference, it was three in the morning, a fact he put out of his head.

"Ed," he said into the phone. "It's your brother-in-law in California. How the hell are you?" His voice sounded manly, confident. With money in his pocket, his shame had receded. At the roulette table, he'd bet straight up, the whole forty bucks on thirty-three. *Happy birthday, pal,* he said, to himself or Jesus.

The wheel spun.

"Sandy?" Ed sounded groggy, confused. "Is everything all right?"

"Everything's great, Ed. Couldn't be better." In a single spin—a straight-up bet that paid thirty-five to one—the juice had come back, filling his veins like blood. Joyce's forty bucks had become fourteen hundred. "Is my sister awake?"

"She's not here, Sandy." A pause that seemed endless. "She's in the hospital."

A flutter in his chest, his heart skipping. "Oh, Jesus. Is she okay?"

"She's fine. A little tired." Another pause. "She had the baby. Rebecca Rose. We have a little girl."

It took Sandy a moment to find his voice. "That's great, Ed. Congratulations. That's—" His throat ached. "When?"

"This morning."

Again something stirred inside him, a feeble creature no bigger than a moth. His soul fluttered blindly toward the power that made it, the only power he believed in.

He did the math.

His niece had been born on his birthday. The odds against it were staggering, a split bet times ten. Three hundred sixty-four to one.

For the second time that night, he stepped out of the phone booth. Outside the glass doors, wheels were spinning. Cards passed like water through dealers' hands. He heard a brash shower of metal, a jubilant whoop: one of the old babes had won at the slots. For just an instant his body was filled with it, a roiling storm of sound.

It was a feeling he'd remember forever, a rare and blinding flash of clarity as he crossed the carpet desert. The longest walk of his life, a journey he'd never made before and would not make again.

In midstream, the juice still flowing, he cashed in his chips and walked out the door.

FLASHES DON'T LAST, of course, and that one didn't. After his Jesus year had come and gone, after Marnie went back to Canada and Myron Gold was looking for him and it wasn't safe for Vera to take his calls, he would remember his one moment of grace. The wallet swollen in his pocket, a feeling nearly sexual, as he crossed the street to Western Union and wired fourteen hundred dollars, the sum total of his earthly wealth, to Rebecca Rose Hauser, the mathematical miracle. The baby girl who shared his birthday.

Welcome to the world.

TO THE STARS

Saxon County has an airport. Joyce Hauser has lived here her whole life and never knew. Though *airport* is perhaps too grand a term; *airfield* is more like it. There is a single bare strip for a plane to land, lit at either end by colored lights: red, amber, blue.

In the parking lot she cuts the engine. A small plane buzzes in the flat blue sky. Watching it, she thinks: Is that you? As though the plane were her brother himself and not merely carrying what's left of him. She imagines the view from above, the fall foliage peaking, a wash of color over the hills. Except for some scattered sumac, there are no red leaves, none of the brash sugar maples she and Ed saw years ago in New England, where they'd driven on their honeymoon. In western Pennsylvania the fall is pure gold.

She rolls down the window and sits a long time, listening to the quiet. The car is a wood-paneled station wagon, five months old, still smelling like its vinyl seats. It's the first time Joyce has driven it alone. Her son and daughter are three and seven, and always one child or the other must be delivered somewhere. Ed makes do with their old car, a Chevy Nova with rattling windows, prone to over-heating. He doesn't mind the ribbing he gets at work, the principal rolling up to Bakerton High School in a rickety jalopy. It is Joyce who drives their son to his doctor's appointments, some as far away as Pittsburgh. She needs a dependable car.

She is startled when the hearse pulls in beside her and rolls down its window. "Mrs. Hauser?"

It takes her a moment to recognize Randy Bernardi, in his twenties now. Like all the Bernardis, he is handsome: curly hair, square shoulders, dark eyes full of mischief. He was her pupil several years ago at the high school. Like many adults in Bakerton, he can't seem to call her by her first name.

Joyce steps out of her car, and for a few minutes they discuss the weather. Randy, once a shy boy, has learned to make small talk. In his profession, she imagines, it is a necessary skill. The Bernardis are the town undertakers—Randy's father and grandfather, his many uncles.

"It's quiet here," says Joyce. "Is it always this quiet?"

The airport is used mainly by the National Guard, he explains. To get a commercial flight, you'd have to drive to Pittsburgh, three hours south and west. Occasionally a crop duster lands here, or a cargo plane.

"Cargo," Joyce repeats, as if coaxing a reluctant pupil. She is conscious of prolonging their conversation. As long as she is standing in the parking lot with Randy, the next thing will not happen. She will not see the box brought all the way from California, her brother packed inside.

Cargo.

Randy shrugs. "Most everything is shipped by truck these days. Unless it's, you know, urgent."

Joyce nods. She can think of many things Saxon County needs urgently: decent jobs, better roads. Coal operators responsible enough to backfill the land ruined by strip-mining, the sooty moonscapes left behind. None of this is likely to be delivered by cargo plane, from points far away.

"Thank you for doing this," she says. "On a Sunday morning, yet." It doesn't sound quite right, though she means it; she is grateful for his presence. Nothing in her life has prepared her for this day. Randy, though young, is a Bernardi and will know what to do.

"I haven't been out here in a couple years. For a while I was coming all the time. Soldiers," he explains.

He leads her across the parking lot to the terminal. He seems to sense her resistance; his hand hovers at her lower back. The building is quiet inside, a single large room, sun-filled. The plate glass windows are streaked in the morning glare.

"Wait here, Mrs. Hauser." Randy lopes across the floor to confer with a stooped man behind a counter. A moment later he returns. "They landed early. This way." Again he presses her lower back. His presence is reassuring, calm and practiced. She wonders how many women he has guided through this airport—mothers of fallen soldiers, boys his own age back from Vietnam.

She follows him through a swinging door, through an empty back room smelling of diesel. Through an open hatch, they walk out onto the tarmac. A small plane sits with its engine idling, propellers quivering. A uniformed pilot stands smoking with a man in coveralls, who spots them first. He shades his eyes. "Randy, man, is that you?"

"Yeah. I'm parked out front."

"Well, come on around. You can help me unload him."

Joyce hugs her arms around her. The mornings are cold now. Fooled by the bright sunshine, she left her coat in the car.

The man in coveralls turns to her. "What about the passenger?"

Joyce stares at him dumbly.

"You're the family, right?"

She nods.

"There's a lady on board. I'll go get her."

He climbs the stairs into the plane and comes back carrying a Pullman suitcase. Behind him is a woman in dark glasses and a long pink coat. Her red hair blows in the breeze.

"You must be Joyce." She offers a clawlike hand, bony, heavy with jewelry. "We spoke on the phone. I'm Vera Gold."

SANDY NOVAK DIED on the second of October, the day before his fortieth birthday. This is the fact of the matter, the only one the family knows for certain. He left them so long ago, went so far away. For years he told them little about his life, and not everything he said was true. After high school he worked on an assembly line in Cleveland; later he sold cars and cleaning products and sets of encyclopedias. He was a fry cook, a bartender, a blackjack dealer, a limousine driver. He spoke of meeting famous people: the governor of Nevada, a boxing champion, the actress Annette Funicello. Once he drove the daughter of Frank Sinatra. On several occasions he was chauffeur to the stars.

For twenty years he followed a jagged path westward: Cleveland, Chicago, Las Vegas, Los Angeles. He occupies a full page in Joyce's address book, the entries crossed out every few months and replaced with new ones. That his journey ended in California—a place that had fascinated him since childhood—seems somehow correct, as though he planned it that way all along.

His final address was a basement apartment in a low stucco building in North Hollywood. Joyce has never seen it herself. Her older brother, George, in Los Angeles on business, once visited him there. When George rang the bell at noon, Sandy was still asleep. He answered the door groggy, in undershorts. George hadn't called ahead, couldn't have if he'd wanted to. Sandy rarely had a working phone.

It wasn't much of a place, George told Joyce later: a single room with an electric hot plate, a mini refrigerator, a Murphy bed. Sandy shared a bathroom with the tenant next door.

"Is he eating properly?" Joyce asked. "Where does he do his laundry?"

She could tell by George's face that he hadn't considered such questions.

"Never mind," she said. "How did he look?"

"Like Sandy," George said. "Like a million bucks."

THE MEN SLIDE the box into the rear of the hearse. Joyce and Vera Gold watch in silence. The box resembles a shipping crate, long and narrow. Stamped at one end are the words *Stern Brothers Mortuary, North Hollywood, California.* He's in there, Joyce thinks, but it seems implausible. At Bernardi's his body will be transferred to a different box, the handsome coffin she chose from a catalog.

Randy leads the women to the terminal, carrying Vera's suitcase. "I guess that's it," he says, pressing Joyce's hand. "We'll see you tomorrow, Mrs. Hauser." The autopsy, the flight from California, have left no time for a wake. The funeral Mass will be held Monday morning, Sandy's body rushed into the ground.

"I'm parked out front," Joyce tells Vera, and for the first time she thinks of the ride ahead, an hour in the car with this strange woman, delivered to them along with Sandy's remains.

At first they ride in silence. Vera stares out the passenger window, her hand over her mouth. Her long red hair is dyed. She fills the car with a spicy perfume. She is older than Joyce. How much older is hard to say.

Do you know a person named Sandy Novak? she asked when Joyce answered the phone yesterday morning. *I found this number in his wallet.*

Joyce, stunned, could barely formulate the questions.

Friday, they think. He was lying there awhile.

Sleeping pills. They found an empty bottle.

Yes, honey. I'm sure.

Only now does Joyce wonder: How did you know my brother? For God's sake, why did you come?

As if sensing these questions, Vera turns to her. "Sandy told me so much about you."

Joyce thinks, He told us nothing about you.

"We were great friends." Vera smiles wanly. "When he first came to L.A., he worked for my husband. We owned a diner. I'm a widow."

Joyce takes a moment to ponder this. She dimly recalls Sandy working in a restaurant several jobs ago.

They take the back road through Kinport, through Fallentree. The sun is nearly blinding. A gentle breeze blows; the golden leaves shimmer in the clear morning light. When they make the turn onto Deer Run, Vera removes her sunglasses. Her eyelids are red and swollen, smeared with makeup. "What's that?" she asks, pointing.

"A coal mine. It's closed now. There was an accident years ago."

Vera studies it, shading her eyes with her hand. "Sandy told me about the mines. His father worked there."

"Yes."

Vera roots through her purse for a handkerchief and dabs carefully at her eyes. "It's beautiful here," she says softly. "I didn't picture it this way at all."

FINALLY THEY ARRIVE at the house. Joyce feels an overpowering urge to warn Vera—*my sister's housekeeping isn't what it used to be*—but resists the impulse. If she'd known a visitor was coming, she'd have persuaded Dorothy to redd up.

"Here we are," Joyce says. Like all others on this street, it is a company house: three rooms upstairs, three rooms down. The family bought it years ago from Baker Brothers. Dorothy, who never married, lives here alone.

Vera stares in wonderment, as though the mean little house were a historic monument. "Polish Hill. I've always wanted to see it." Her lips tremble with emotion.

Why, she loved him, Joyce thinks.

She parks and engages the brake. A moment later Dorothy appears on the front porch. Her sister's face is as familiar as her own, but now Joyce sees her as a stranger might: the pilling cardigan, the ankle socks and stained housedress, her graying hair pulled back into a messy ponytail. The sweater, once white, is grimy at the cuffs. Oh, Dorothy, Joyce thinks, hot with shame.

"I thought you were Georgie," Dorothy calls. "He should be here any minute."

When Vera steps out of the car, Dorothy's eyes widen. She has never been comfortable with strangers.

Joyce climbs the porch steps, which are a little rickety. The shabbiness of the house is suddenly overwhelming, its flaws exposed. "This is Vera Gold," she says. And then, for lack of a better explanation: "Sandy's friend."

At that moment a car climbs the hill, a newish Cadillac scattering gravel.

"There's Georgie," Dorothy says with audible relief.

"Our older brother," Joyce explains.

Dorothy squints into the distance. "He's alone. I can't believe it. I thought for sure she'd come." George has been divorced for two years, but Dorothy, ever romantic, holds out hope. In Joyce's view, it's a subject best avoided. To most of Bakerton, divorce is still a rarity. To Joyce, herself: her brother is, in point of fact, the first divorced person she has ever known.

He parks and steps out of the car, a handsome man of fifty with a full head of gray hair. To Joyce, he looks well groomed and prosperous in his stylish trench coat.

Dorothy clatters down the porch steps to embrace him. "Georgie! You made it." It seems excessive, a hero's welcome, as though driving across Pennsylvania were some epic feat. But this brother is hers, her idol since childhood. He belongs to Dorothy the way Sandy had belonged to Joyce.

Arm in arm, they climb the stairs. "Whoa, careful," says George. "These boards are a little loose."

Joyce accepts his kiss on her cheek, struck, as always, by his resemblance to their father. She makes what is now the standard introduction: Vera Gold. Sandy's friend.

Inside, the radio is playing. The local AM station broadcasts a weekly Mass for Shut-ins. Dorothy, who is not a shut-in, listens anyway, though she's already been to Mass at St. Casimir's. Joyce ducks into the parlor and unplugs the radio. The dials are long missing, and this is the only way to turn it off.

Dorothy follows her. "Where is she going to sleep?" she whispers.

"Don't look at me. You're the one with all the empty bedrooms. She can have my old room, I guess. Or Sandy's." Joyce wonders, but does not ask, the last time Dorothy dusted or changed the sheets.

The kitchen is sunny and very warm, the refrigerator packed already with covered dishes. After Sandy's obituary appeared in the paper, an army of neighbor women showed up with casseroles. Joyce puts on a pot of coffee, wiping the counter as she goes. It isn't easy to do, with all the clutter. Near the sink are rows of clean empty jars—mustard, jelly, pickles—Dorothy has set out to dry. Eventually they will join the hundred others in boxes in the basement—for what purpose, Joyce couldn't possibly say.

George and Vera sit at the big Formica table. "We're still in shock," he tells her. "You can imagine."

"Of course." Vera's voice is low and gravelly, a smoker's voice.

"He came back three years ago for my son's wedding. Before that it was ten years, at least."

Cups are passed, the sugar bowl, the can of evaporated milk. George and Dorothy drink their coffee light and sweet. Joyce and Vera take it black. Brown, really: the family brew is Maxwell House boiled in a percolator, so weak Joyce can see the flowered pattern at the bottom of the cup.

"He wanted to visit. He talked about it all the time." Vera sips her coffee, her rings clinking on the china cup. "It was always a question of money."

"I would have bought him a ticket," George says.

"He wouldn't have let you. He'd be too ashamed." Vera hesitates, as though there's more she could say.

"He was always hard up," George says. "I never understood it. He couldn't seem to get on his feet."

I gave him money, Joyce thinks. We all did. It's a subject she has never discussed with George or Dorothy, but she knows, suddenly, that this is true. He called at strange hours: though he'd spent fifteen years on the far edge of the country, he paid no attention to the time difference, as though it were an unsubstantiated rumor he didn't quite believe. Loans, he called them, though he was casual about repaying. He was casual in all things. Joyce remembers his shirts always wrinkled, his blond hair shaggy before that look was popular, back when other boys were wearing crew cuts. The scruffiness suited him. He was so good-looking, he'd have seemed almost feminine without a day's growth on his chin.

The coffee finished, George walks Joyce out to the car. Her

husband has been alone with the children all day. By now Teddy will be clamoring for his mother.

"Who is she, anyway?" George asks. "His girlfriend?"

"No, I'm sure not," says Joyce, who isn't at all sure. "A friend, she says. She's the one who found his body." She hugs her coat around her. "Honestly, Georgie, I don't know who she is."

"She must have been a knockout in her day." He fumbles in his pocket for a cigarette. You're smoking again? Joyce wants to say but doesn't. She is trying to be less critical.

"I finally reached Lucy," she says. "Leonard, actually. They couldn't get a flight out until Tuesday, so I told him not to bother. What would be the point?" Their younger sister is a medical missionary in a remote village in Madagascar. She and her husband run a small hospital, the only nurse and doctor for miles.

"I missed Daddy's funeral," says George. "I never forgave myself."

Here we go, Joyce thinks. It's a story she's heard too many times. During the war George served on a minesweeper in the South Pacific. By the time he learned of their father's death, the body was already in the ground.

"I remember his face so clearly," says George. "More clearly than I remember Mother's, if you want to know the truth." He exhales in a long stream. "Remember my violin?"

It's another old family story, oft-repeated: the time their father spent his whole paycheck to buy George, then eight years old, a secondhand violin. George's version of the story is tender, sentimental. Their mother, charged with feeding four children on groceries wheedled from the company store, had remembered it less fondly.

"I told Sandy that story," he says. "When I went out to California that time. And do you know what he said to me? *I don't remember him at all.* That killed me, Joyce. *I don't remember him at all.*"

"Well," says Joyce, "he was young when Daddy died."

"He was ten. A ten-year-old remembers." George flicks away an ash. "I'm telling you, it affected him. He was traumatized by it." He is a man of certain opinions. In that way he is the exact opposite of Sandy, who believed in nothing at all.

SHE REMEMBERS CLEARLY the last time she saw him. They were riding in her car to the airport in Pittsburgh—Sandy behind the wheel, his suitcase in the trunk. His face was pale that morning, a little drawn. He'd had a late night and too many drinks at their nephew's wedding, the reason for this visit. For years he'd seemed preternaturally youthful, but that day she noticed his hairline receding, faint lines at the corners of his eyes. For the first time he looked his age.

At the wedding he'd put on a good show—dancing and joking, charming neighbors he couldn't possibly remember, old miners and miners' widows who still lived on Polish Hill. The Novak boy, gone a decade, had been welcomed like the prodigal son. *He's so handsome,* Joyce was told again and again. *He always had a way about him.* She accepted the compliments graciously, as though she herself had been praised.

His homecoming had been an unqualified success until the final morning, when—despite Dorothy's wheedling, her lectures, and finally her tears—he had refused to join the family at Sunday Mass. *It would be a lie,* he said simply. *I don't believe.*

"People like to think there's a plan," he told Joyce. "Some

point to it all." He changed lanes smoothly, with barely a backward glance. "So they've made up all these elaborate explanations."

"You don't mean that."

"Fairy tales, Joyce. They're nothing but fairy tales."

She stared at him, appalled. "You don't believe in God? In heaven?" To her it was the essential point: the ultimate reunion with her parents, Rose and Stanley waiting for her on the other side. The alternative—that she would never see them again—was inadmissible, a sorrow she couldn't bear.

"Sorry, doll. Heaven is here on earth."

They drove awhile in silence.

"So you're an—atheist?" The word felt foreign in her mouth, wicked as an epithet. She knew such people existed but had never met one. *Fairy tales.* Nobody she knew—herself included—would dare say such a thing aloud.

Sandy parked at the terminal and stepped out of the car. With a crooked grin, he handed her the keys. She can see it now, the smile crinkling the corners of his eyes. The memory shatters her.

ON MONDAY MORNING the house smells of pancakes—a weekend treat, usually, but her husband has made an exception. Ed is an early riser, and he and Rebecca have already demolished an entire stack. Joyce has no appetite and neither does Teddy, who is running a temperature. She lay awake half the night, listening to him cough.

She drinks her coffee as she dresses for the funeral. "I hate to leave him," she says, helping Ed with his tie. Her friend Eleanor Rouse, the school nurse, has offered to sit with the children while she and Ed are at church. Joyce wouldn't—realistically, she couldn't—leave Teddy with anyone else.

"Where are you going?" Rebecca asks.

She stands in the doorway of her parents' bedroom, watching Joyce put on panty hose. On her head is a pink paper cone left over from her birthday. On Saturday morning, in the Hausers' basement rec room, Joyce served ice cream and cake to a dozen second-graders. It seems a long time ago.

"To the funeral home," she says. "That building I showed you, uptown behind the A&P."

"The red one," says Rebecca, adjusting her hat.

"Yes," Joyce says.

They have discussed the best way to explain Sandy's death to the children. Teddy is too young to ask questions, but Rebecca, who is seven, has been told that her uncle has gone to heaven.

Is that closer than California? she demanded.

Farther, said Joyce.

Ed said, *No one knows for sure.*

THE MORNING IS cold and bright. An iridescent grit coats the windshield, the first hard frost. By unspoken agreement, Ed takes the wheel. Though exceptions are made—for disabled veterans, men crippled in mine accidents—it is local custom for the husband to drive.

At the funeral home Ed parks beside the hearse. They are early, a chronic condition in their marriage. Joyce, with her abiding fear of lateness, hustles him out the door with the insistence of a drill sergeant. At church or movies or family gatherings, they are always the first to arrive.

"Sandy's friend," he says. "The woman from California. She didn't tell you anything?"

"No," Joyce says. "The autopsy report will take a couple of weeks."

Ed reaches for her hand, Ed who did not love her brother. Who remembers him as a teenage delinquent, a troublemaker and a truant. Ed, the high school principal, took a personal interest in Sandy Novak. He bent the rules to let the boy graduate—to score points, he later admitted, with Sandy's sister. A week after commencement, Sandy piled into a car with some buddies headed for Cleveland and wasn't seen for many years. That Ed's favor was never acknowledged is a sore point they do not mention. Ed himself spoke of it just once, after one of Sandy's late-night calls.

It was twenty years ago, Joyce pointed out. *What do you want him to do? Thank you every time he calls?*

I want him to make something of his life. I want him to stop disappointing you.

Broken promises, visits canceled for no reason. Ed was too kind to remind her that Sandy had missed their wedding, that George had stepped in at the last minute to give away the bride. That Sandy had refused—twice!—to serve as godfather. Instead, when Rebecca was born, he wired a large sum of money for the baby's college fund. A week later he'd declined to visit, claiming he couldn't afford a plane ticket. Like most of his excuses, it made no sense at all.

. . . .

THE FAMILY RIDES in two cars. Joyce's wagon and George's Cadillac line up behind the hearse, leading the slow parade to the church.

The Gospel is a familiar story, the raising of Lazarus, Martha's anguished cry to Jesus: *Lord, if thou hadst been there, my brother would not have died.* Joyce closes her eyes, imagining Sandy beside her, the smile crinkling the corners of his eyes.

Fairy tales.

To her surprise, the church is crowded. Sandy was gone twenty years, but Bakerton has not forgotten. Afterward, on the church steps, she is waylaid, questioned, hugged. Sandy was popular in school, she is told, a clown and a cutup. Everyone liked him, the girls especially. They can't believe he is gone.

Again and again she answers the question: "Heart failure. It was very sudden."

The story is her invention. Certainly it is kinder than the truth, welcome as a rodent: *He swallowed a bottle of pills. He took his own life.* Like all the best lies, it contains a grain of truth. What is despair, really, but a failure of heart?

THE FUNERAL LUNCHEON is held at Dorothy's house. Again Joyce and Ed are the first to arrive. She gives the kitchen a lick and a promise, washes the breakfast dishes floating in the sink. The donated casseroles will be served buffet-style, the usual hodgepodge of mismatched food: trays of cold cuts, stuffed cabbage, a lasagna, cakes and pies. A few neighbors—the Poblocki twins, Chuck Lubicki—will arrive with bottles or six-packs, the custom on Polish Hill.

From the window she sees George's Cadillac park on the street.

He opens the passenger door and Vera Gold steps out, nearly his height in her towering heels. That morning every head turned in her direction as she swept into the church. Her black dress is suitable for a nightclub, cut low in front, showing deep cleavage. "Sandy's friend from California," Joyce explained a dozen times, fighting an urge she has felt her whole life: to protect Sandy, his reputation, her family's. It is a habit she will never break.

The guests arrive in waves. She welcomes neighbors and distant cousins, Ed's colleagues from the high school. "Heart failure. It was very sudden." The lie is smooth in her mouth, blameless white, lustrous as a pearl.

She agrees that the service was lovely, that Sandy is in a better place now. She accepts condolences and prayers. It is her role, always: the public face of the family. Dorothy, whose backwardness is known and accepted, busies herself in the kitchen. George is nowhere to be found.

"Have you seen him?" Joyce whispers to Ed.

"Back porch," he says.

Joyce slips into the dining room and glances out the window. George is standing on the porch with Vera and several neighbors—a Stusick, a Lubicki, both Poblockis—in a cloud of cigarette smoke. Joyce feels a flash of irritation and then gratitude. Her brother is performing a useful service, as practical as dishwashing, by keeping Vera occupied.

"Joyce."

She turns. It takes her a moment to place Dick Devlin, bald now, one of Sandy's buddies from high school. After graduation the two shared, along with Dick's brother, an apartment in Cleveland, where they'd been hired at Fisher Body. Eventually the Devlin boys returned to Bakerton, married and raised families; and Sandy moved further and further west.

Dick bends to kiss her cheek. "Joyce, I'm so sorry. I'm sorry now that I lost touch with him. I had no idea he was in such bad shape."

Joyce feels her heart working. "What do you mean?"

Dick looks down into his feet. "To—do what he did. He must have been in a bad way."

She glances over her shoulder into the crowded parlor. "Who told you that?" she says in a low voice.

"Vera. His girlfriend."

Joyce's face heats. She thinks of Vera in the car, her chin trembling as she studied the house. *Polish Hill. I've always wanted to see it.* Vera, ten years older than Sandy, fifteen maybe, holding court on the back porch, dressed like a cocktail waitress and surrounded by men.

"Who told you she was his girlfriend?"

Dick shrugs, coloring. "I just assumed. He always had girlfriends. And she's, you know, his type."

This is news to Joyce, who met none of these girlfriends. Sandy never mentioned any, and she never asked.

"Anyways, I'm sorry." Dick hesitates, groping for words. "Sandy wasn't like the rest of us. He did whatever the hell he wanted. We were just working stiffs."

Joyce feels her eyes tear.

"We had some times out in Cleveland," says Dick. "I never had a better time in my life."

. . . .

AS A CHILD Sandy slept in the back bedroom, small and square, its only window overlooking the woods. Joyce closes the door behind her and stretches out on the narrow bed. "Where are you?" she whispers. "Why did you go?"

She is thinking not of his death but of that earlier departure, his disappearance like a magic trick, as dizzying and complete. His manic and determined flight from Bakerton, from the family, from her.

On the one hand, she almost understands it. Family life, on the whole, does not fill her with joy. Her lively daughter delights but also exhausts her, and Teddy keeps her in a nearly constant state of panic: his fevers and infections, his cystic lungs that will never clear. Her sister, more and more, is a like a grown-up child, unwilling or unable to drive a car, maintain the house, or pay her bills on time. And yet Joyce could never leave them, run off to California or to Africa, as her younger siblings have done. Freedom is, to her, unimaginable, as exotic as walking on the moon.

She hears footsteps in the hallway, a knock at the door.

"Can I come in? I need to get something." It is a woman's voice, low and honeyed. Only then does Joyce notice the Pullman case lying open on the floor.

Joyce sits up quickly. "Of course," she calls, swiping at her eyes.

Vera Gold opens the door. "Sorry. I need my cigarettes." She kneels and rifles through the suitcase. "Damn. I thought I had another pack." She glances up at Joyce. "Oh, honey. Are you okay?"

"This was Sandy's room," Joyce says, her voice trembling. "He had it to himself after Georgie went overseas. I can barely remember him living here. It seems so long ago." Why did he leave us? she wants to ask. For God's sake, what did we do?

Vera sits beside her on the bed. A sweet, dirty fragrance—perfume and cigarettes—surrounds her like a cloud. "He was always afraid of missing something. Even in L.A. he got restless. And this place broke his heart."

The words hit Joyce like a slap. "But *why*? It's home."

"That's why."

(*Heart failure.* Her brother's unknown heart.)

"You told Dick Devlin," she says softly. "What Sandy did. Why on earth would you tell him a thing like that?"

"I'm sorry," says Vera. "He was Sandy's friend. I didn't know it was a secret."

"This is a very small town."

"Sandy told me that. He said everybody knows your business." Vera looks down at her hands, the collection of gold rings. In the dim light, her face looks smooth as a girl's. "He thought about coming back here to live. I guess he told you that."

Joyce stares. He told her nothing of the kind.

"It was a fantasy, really. Whenever he got into trouble, he figured he'd always have this place to come back to." Vera smiles sadly. "He never could have done it, though. He would have felt like a failure. More than anything, he wanted you to be proud of him." She gets to her feet. At the door she pauses a moment, like an actress making an exit.

"The church today—it was a beautiful service, Joyce. But it isn't what Sandy would have wanted. That wasn't for him. It was for Bakerton, and for you."

She closes the door behind her. The click of her high heels fades down the stairs.

. . . .

IN THE KITCHEN Dorothy is putting away the leftovers. Joyce goes out to the back porch, where a Poblocki twin stands alone, smoking. "Have you seen Georgie?" she asks.

"Vera ran out of cigarettes. He's driving her to the store."

Joyce walks around to the front of the house. The lawn, she notices, is shaggy. She will ask Ed to run the mower when the guests have gone.

She rounds the corner just in time to see it happen: Vera clomping down the front steps, glancing over her shoulder at George and laughing her throaty laugh. There is a sharp crack like wood splintering, and Vera teeters backward. In a split second she is down.

"Oh, no," says Joyce, rushing toward her.

George hurries down the steps and kneels at Vera's side.

"My ankle," she moans. "I think I twisted it."

"It's broken," says George, who many years ago was a medic in the war. Gingerly he touches her foot. "See that? That's the bone coming through."

"Oh, Jesus. I can't look." Vera lies back against the stairs and hides her face with her hands. Her black dress is rucked up around her thighs. Joyce resists the urge to cover her.

"I'll call an ambulance," she says.

"No need," says George. "I can take her."

"Are you sure?" Ed calls from the porch, where a small crowd has gathered.

They watch as George lifts her into his arms.

. . . .

JOYCE NEVER SEES Vera Gold again. The emergency room doctor confirms that the ankle is broken and admits her overnight. The next morning, her foot in a cast, she flies back to Los Angeles. George Novak takes her to the airport, carrying first Vera, then her suitcase and crutches, up into the tiny plane.

Joyce spends that day as she does many others: first in the car with Teddy, then reading outdated magazines in a doctor's waiting room, then stopping to fill a new prescription. It is dusk by the time she leaves the pharmacy and begins the long drive home. By then Vera Gold seems no more real than a character in a movie, her visit fading like a dream.

A week later a large envelope arrives in the mail. The return address is Santa Monica, California. There is a note on perfumed stationery, in a sweeping, nervous hand:

> *Dear Joyce,*
>
> *Here are the papers Sandy left. There wasn't much else, just some clothes and household things. Let me know if you want them. He sold his car years ago and by the end he had nothing.*
>
> *I guess we will never know what happened. I saw him the day before he died and this will sound strange, but he seemed happy.*
>
> *I loved him and always will.*
>
> *—V.*

The envelope holds a tan leather wallet—worn and creased, its rawhide stitching coming loose—and a thin sheaf of papers: Sandy's birth certificate, unopened bills, and a pink carbon copy of a completed form, State of California Application for Unemployment Benefits. Between the papers are a few slippery photographs—

snapshots of Joyce's children, Rebecca and Teddy as infants, as toddlers. Each is marked in Joyce's neat cursive: *Teddy's first birthday.* *Rebecca Rose Hauser, 22 months.* A photo of her wedding, Joyce and Ed coming out of the church into a shower of rice. On the back, in her own handwriting: *We missed you.*

At the bottom of the pile is a typewritten transcript from Bakerton High, listing Sandy's quarterly marks: a string of A's in Algebra and Plane Geometry, D's in everything else.

Why would he have a copy of his transcript? Joyce wonders. Was he going to apply to college? For a moment, from lifelong habit, she hopes fervently for his future. For a single cruel moment she forgets that he is gone.

In the wallet she finds a dollar bill and a business card.

TERRY'S BAIL BONDS—FREE BAIL INFORMATION—
STRICTLY CONFIDENTIAL—24 HOUR SERVICE IN
HOLLYWOOD AND WEST L.A.

In an inner compartment is the stub of a raffle ticket, *To Benefit Van Nuys–Reseda Little League Grand Prize Color TV.* The drawing took place on October 3, 1974—Sandy's fortieth birthday, the day his body was found.

That's all? she thinks. A whole life, her brother's life, distilled down to this small sad pile. Not a whole life: half a life. The second half he discarded on purpose, the precious years cast to the wind.

The ticket stub is clearly marked: NOT NECESSARY TO BE PRESENT TO WIN.

She decides that this is good news.

THRIFT

Agnes has never spent a winter in a trailer. From the window she watches Luke leave for work, his truck roaring down the lane, gouging tracks in the muddy earth. It's a blustery morning in November, the ground slick with wet leaves. A storm overnight knocked the last color from the trees. Now the narrow kitchen feels drafty without him, and smaller, as though its aluminum sides have contracted in the cold.

The coffee is tepid, but she finishes it anyway, then picks at what's left on Luke's plate: a few bites of scrambled egg, a half-eaten slice of toast. She remembers a summer job—thirty years ago? is that possible?—busing tables in a restaurant. How the customers' leftovers disgusted her, contaminated by saliva from strangers' forks.

Once, when her niece was small, Agnes watched her sister share a lollipop with the child, the little girl squealing with delight as she passed the sticky thing from her own mouth to her mother's.

That's unsanitary, Agnes told her sister.

To which Terri merely shrugged. *She's mine.*

Is it odd that Agnes feels that way about Luke? That his body belongs to her and no part of it displeases her. That she can love his feet and armpits as she loves his eyes, his hands, his groin, his mouth.

She clears the dishes. From the window she sees a strange car make its way up the lane, tires sliding in the muck. The car is small and sporty, a new hatchback. The hunters and fishermen drive Jeeps and pickups. The nearest year-round house is a half mile up the hill.

Then the car stops and her sister steps out—as though, in thinking of the lollipop, Agnes has conjured her from the air. This has happened her whole life where Terri is concerned: simply thinking of her is enough to make the phone ring. Today she wears a long sweater-coat trimmed with fake fur. In stiletto-heeled boots, she picks her way through the mud. The white sweater-coat, a size too small, gapes open at her wide bosom. She is a woman whose clothes never fit properly; she is always dieting or gaining. She clutches the collar with one hand, close at her throat.

Agnes steps back from the window, her bare feet silent on the linoleum. She catches her reflection in the mirror above the sink: pale, shiny face; hair loose and needing a wash. It's her day off from the hospital, and she wears green scrub pants, no bra, an old flannel shirt of Luke's. The shirt is soft from many washings, gentle on her skin.

Terri's boots climb the stairs, sharp and adamant on the porch Luke built. The high, shallow windows have no curtains. Agnes has been meaning to make some. Oh, hell, she thinks, crouching low.

Terri knocks at the door. "Agnes? Are you there?"

Agnes holds her breath as the doorknob turns. Every morning Luke kisses her goodbye at the door. That morning, luckily, she remembered to lock it behind him.

"I know you live here. I saw your name on the mailbox."

Agnes nearly groans. Luke bought adhesive letters at the hardware store and spelled out both names, GARMAN and LUBICKI. She asked him to leave hers off, but it wasn't practical. Their bills—gas and electric, insurance for Luke's truck and motorcycle—come addressed to her.

"I can't believe you're living in a *trailer*."

Agnes waits.

"I've been trying to call you, but you don't answer. I'm starting to worry." There is a long pause. "We missed you at Thanksgiving. The kids miss their aunt Aggie."

This is a blatant lie. Agnes's niece is a sulky teenager, indifferent to relatives. The little twins might miss the candy she brought, the gifts on their birthday; but her company, itself, was never much of a draw.

"I just want to see you," Terri warbles. "To make sure you're okay." Her tone is one Agnes recognizes; it means she is about to cry.

A rustle then, a jangle of keys: Terri rooting around in her pocketbook.

"I found some old photos of you and Mum. Daddy, too. I thought you might want to have them."

It is just like Terri to entice her with these treasures, all that remains of their dead parents. Shameless. Yet in the silence Agnes feels a pang of longing, exactly as Terri intends her to.

"Fine," Terri huffs. "Be that way."

Agnes thinks, Please go away.

"He's using you. Don't say nobody warned you."

The screen door slams shut. Agnes exhales softly as Terri's boots clomp down the stairs.

Cautiously she approaches the window, just in time to see

Terri lose her footing on the path and land gracelessly on her wide behind. Agnes feels a flash of alarm, a wash of tenderness. *Baby fell down.* For a second she wants to burst through the front door and run down the porch stairs, to make sure her baby sister isn't hurt.

The moment, and the urge, pass swiftly. Terri gets to her feet. The sweater-coat is ruined, a blessing, really. She was doing her figure no favors in that coat.

TERRI, THERESA, HAS always been her baby—twelve years younger, a toddler when Agnes started high school. For the first year of her life, Agnes carried her around like a doll, and Theresa did, in fact resemble the dolls of that era: blond curls and a dimple, chubby hands that clapped and a tiny mouth always pursed for a kiss. She was born pretty and stayed pretty. Unlike Agnes, who was backward, Theresa was bubbly and sociable. *As different as they can be,* their mother often said. *Like apples and turnips.*

There was no doubt, ever, which sister was the turnip.

If they'd been closer in age, Agnes might have envied Theresa. Instead she felt nothing but pride that her baby sister did not stutter, did not blush, that she jumped rope with the other girls at noon recess. (Agnes had spent lunchtimes in the school library with a book.) On the playground, the school bus, Theresa was surrounded by girlfriends: a little chubby always, but still the prettiest, a girl everyone loved. Agnes and her mother took turns dressing her. At the dime store they studied the pattern books. They bought sprigged cotton and gingham, cherry pink and sunny yellow. They shared Theresa like well-behaved children. Each day after school, they kept her company at the kitchen table while she had her snack, a slice of homemade cake or pie. Theresa was an excellent mimic, adept at imitating her teachers and schoolmates. Agnes and her mother sat by patiently, waiting to be entertained.

They were two big, strong women, sturdy and plain as Russian peasants. Of the two, Agnes was slightly smaller and softer. She had the comfortable proportions of a woman who'd borne four children, without actually having done so; in fact, she had never been on a date. At that time she worked second shift at the hospital, four to midnight. The other nurses, married with children, groused about the hours, but Agnes didn't mind

They were happy years: her parents still living, the mines booming, her father sleeping all day, working the night shift—known locally as Hoot Owl—at Baker Eleven. Later, looking back, Agnes wished she had paid more attention, that she had noticed and savored every moment. Her mother would have liked more children, but Nature hadn't cooperated; and as she liked to tell her telephone friends, she wasn't one to complain. After all the miscarriages, she had been blessed with Theresa, a peppy girl with the energy of several, filling the house with life.

Then, in one bewildering year, several things happened. Theresa graduated high school and went on a diet and began calling herself Terri. She started and quit the nurses' training, married a town cop named Andy Carnicella, and moved into her own house behind Mount Carmel, the Italian church in town. And when the dust had settled, Agnes was thirty-one and living with two aging parents, and she understood for the first time that her family were isolated people. Her mother, an only child, had grown up on the

Hoeffer farm in the middle of nowhere. Her father's people, the Lubickis, had disapproved of his marriage to Mae: they were Poles, and clannish, and so Mae had never bothered with them. As a result, Agnes had a pile of Lubicki cousins she'd never met. These cousins lived a few miles away, in Fallentree or Moss Creek, but she'd be hard pressed to recognize them in the grocery store.

When Agnes was a girl, this had seemed unimportant. But her mother, as the years passed, was lonely. Before her marriage, during the war, Mae had worked three years in the dress factory; she'd retained a few friends from that time—a Mrs. Miller, a Mrs. Goss, women she kept up with by telephone. For most of her married life, Mae left the house only for church on Sundays. While Agnes or her father did the grocery shopping, Mae stayed home to work in the garden; to sew the family's clothes; to bake bread and pies; to put up quarts of vegetables and homemade preserves. Always she cooked enough for a crowd, even after Theresa left and she had only a single overfed daughter and a lean, fussy husband who ate like a bird. They lived in a newish house on the edge of town, a pleasant split-level with a large backyard, and yet Mae labored like a farm wife with a dozen children. Agnes was an adult before she understood that this was work that didn't need to be done, that her mother was simply desperate to fill the days.

Sometimes, her other chores finished, Mae would get down on her knees and scrub the garage floor with a brush.

She had never been a beauty—in the eyes of the town, an unlikely bride for John Lubicki, who as a young man had been handsome as a film star. He'd come back from the war determined to marry, a decision made while marching across Belgium sick with pneumonia. What, in that faraway place, made him think of Mae Hoeffer? In school she'd been two grades ahead; she had never been his sweetheart, or anyone else's. When the war ended, handsome John Lubicki had his pick of the Bakerton girls, and he chose her.

It had been pointed out—though not to Mae's face—that the Lubickis were dirt-poor, and Mae would inherit the Hoeffer farm. In marrying her, John had shown some initiative. The more charitable of the town gossips called it *a practical choice*.

IN THE AFTERNOON the rain stops. Agnes pulls on her boots and walks down the muddy lane to the road. Deer Run is high and winding, overlooking a deep valley. The abandoned coal mine looms in the distance, the rusted tipple of the old Baker Twelve. Years ago, PennDOT resurfaced Deer Run every year, for the hundreds of miners who drove it each day to work. Now the road is poorly maintained, the asphalt crumbling in places. Moving here was Luke's idea. On Deer Run they'd have no prying neighbors. Their trailer is invisible from the road.

Agnes climbs the hill to the mailbox, one of several mounted on an old railroad tie. The other mailboxes are unused, unlabeled— relics from an earlier time, when the property was covered with trailers. Five years ago a strip-mining company, Keystone Surface, descended on Saxon Mountain, peeling back the trees and vegetation and extracting what coal they could. They brought their own trailers and stayed just a year, but you can still see the imprints they left behind, rectangular depressions in the bare earth. Luke and Agnes's trailer is the only one left; they rent it from a man named

Jay Wenturine, whom Luke calls *my old buddy*. Luke speaks often of his *old buddies*, boyhood friends he's tracked down since returning to town. He was a teenager when his father was laid off and moved the family to Maryland. Luke reappeared in Bakerton ten months ago and met Agnes soon after. In that time she's met no *old buddies* except Jay Wenturine, who stops by the trailer on the first of each month.

In the mailbox she finds a phone bill addressed to her, a sale flyer from the grocery store. Behind them, wedged at the back of the box, is a slender packet of photographs.

I thought you might want to have them.

Greedily she shoves the envelope into her pocket. She walks fast and sticks close to the road. It's the first week of buck season, and the woods ring with gunshot. She should have worn Luke's orange jacket.

Back inside, she opens the packet. The first photo makes her throat ache. Agnes and her mother at the kitchen table, rolling dough for noodles. They sit shoulder to shoulder, Agnes in an old sweatshirt, Mae in one of her flowered housedresses. Their large hands are crusted with flour. They wear the same shy smile.

The next photos are from Terri's wedding, a day Agnes has no particular interest in reliving. It's disorienting to see her mother in the dress Terri chose for her, a pale blue sack covered with a tent of sheer lace. She is bigger than Agnes remembers, and Dad looks smaller. His tuxedo is a size too large. Terri stands between them in her frilly white dress and picture hat, which was the style at the time. Agnes herself lurks at the edge of the photo, in her nursing smock and slacks. That day, as always, she worked the second shift, though she could have swapped with someone if she'd wanted. She hadn't wanted. She was glad to skip the reception at the church hall, to which Terri had invited two hundred guests: Andy Car-nicella's large family, plus half her graduating class from Bakerton High. For bridesmaids, she'd chosen four friends from high school. *I didn't think you'd want to,* she'd explained to Agnes. *Getting dressed up and all. I know you don't like to make a fuss.*

Certainly this was true. She'd have been mortified to stand at the altar alongside the others, who, even young and slender, looked ridiculous in their shiny dresses, with puffed sleeves and a bow on each hip. Still, she'd have liked to be asked.

Agnes shuffles quickly through the photos. Each one sets a fire in her, sharp bright bursts like Fourth of July sparklers: a crackle, a smolder, a lingering trace.

The last photo is of her parents, younger than she has ever imagined them being: her father in uniform, his pompadour glis-tening with Brylcreem; her mother thinner then, a big raw-boned girl tightly corseted, her hair crimped into precise curls. They sit at a table littered with empty glasses; behind them, couples are danc-ing. On the back of the photo is a handwritten date: *June 1, 1946.* In six months they would be married. In two years he'd run the Hoeffer farm into the ground.

She studies the photo. Her father smiles easily for the camera, his arm around Mae's shoulders, a gesture Agnes finds startling. Her parents had never, in her lifetime, shared a bedroom. She can scarcely remember seeing them touch. In his final years, when John Lubicki was breathless and wheezing from black lung, it was Agnes who combed his hair and shaved his handsome face, who pounded his back to help him cough.

The years underground had ruined his lungs, though by local

standards he was considered lucky: to have a daughter who'd never married, a daughter who happened to be a nurse. Agnes, a strong girl, changed his oxygen tanks without fanfare; for many years a local company, Miners Medical, delivered them to the front door. She could strip his bedsheets almost without disturbing him, a magician's trick.

As miners did, he spent a long time dying. His wife, in those years, seemed sturdy as a tree. Then, ten years into his dying, Mae suffered a sudden stroke and went quietly in her sleep.

Two deaths in a single winter; two funeral Masses. After that Agnes lived alone, in the house her father had left her as payment for her devotion. Three days a week she worked double shifts at the hospital; the other days she slept endlessly. That spring she planted a large garden, as her mother had done. In September she canned sixty quarts of tomatoes.

The following year she planted nothing at all.

She lived on coffee and canned soup, sandwiches made with store-bought bread. Her uniform hung on her like a shroud. Taking in the smock seemed like too much bother, so she ordered new ones from a catalog. Clocks ticked in the quiet house.

This went on for years and would have continued forever if not for a thunderstorm the summer she turned fifty. A tall poplar in the backyard was struck by lightning. By God's design or His clumsiness, it tipped over onto the roof and brought Luke Garman to her door.

THE DAY IS vivid in her memory: the smells and weather, the trilling birdsong. She woke that morning in the narrow twin bed, hers since childhood, not imagining that everything was about to change.

For three days in a row, the roofers had appeared at dawn. When the noise of their hammering punctured her sleep, Agnes rose and dressed and closed the windows against their shouted conversations, their loud radio that played mostly commercials, the slap of shingles falling to the ground.

The roofers worked shirtless, and called each other by last name. Each hammered at his own pace. Wojick was scrawny and blond-haired. He worked fast but took frequent breaks; the lawn was studded with his cigarette butts. Garman had curly hair and a beard the color of caramel. He worked steadily and took his time.

The third morning, while Agnes was assembling her breakfast, Garman knocked at the kitchen door. He had put on a shirt but hadn't buttoned it. "Can I use your phone?" he asked softly, his voice surprisingly deep.

Up close he was baby-faced, younger than she'd imagined. The beard seemed like a disguise to make him look older, a prop attached with spirit gum, an actor's trick. And yet his grave voice did not belong to a boy. He had a man's voice.

"My partner fell off the ladder. He's all right, but he wants me to call his wife."

Automatically Agnes went to the sink. "Let me see him," she said as she scrubbed her hands. "I'm a nurse."

She followed Garman to the backyard. Wojick lay stretched out on the grass, gripping his shoulder. No blood or abrasions, but his face was white with pain.

"Jesus Christ," he said through gritted teeth. "I landed on my fucking shoulder."

Agnes blinked. His gaunt face surprised her. She had seen him only from behind, his worn blue jeans sliding down his hips, and thought him a teenager. She saw now that he was her age.

"Don't move," she said.

She knelt on the grass. Wojick's skinny chest was sunburned, the blond hair going gray at his throat. She slid her hands beneath his back. "Just relax. Let your body go limp."

Wojick did, aided probably by whatever he'd been drinking. Leaning over him, she could smell the alcohol fumes rising from his skin.

In a single smooth motion, Agnes lifted his lower back from the ground.

His eyes snapped open. "Whoa. What the hell?"

"You dislocated your shoulder. I moved it back into place."

She eased him into a seated position, remembering that one of her father's sisters—he'd had seven—had married a Wojick. This Wojick, if he was aware of the connection, seemed unlikely to care.

"Holy shit." Gingerly he felt his shoulder, as if making sure it was still there. "That's some trick."

Agnes helped him to his feet. "You should have an X-ray." She glanced at Garman, who stood watching. "Can you take him to the emergency room?"

"My wife can take me," said Wojick. "You called her, right?"

"Hold your horses," Garman said.

Agnes led him back into the house and showed him the telephone, an old rotary model on the kitchen wall.

"My grandmother had one of these," Garman said.

He dialed a number and spoke softly. Agnes closed her eyes and listened to his voice.

"Franny, it's Luke. Ken took a header. He's all right, but he wants you to come get him."

Luke, Agnes thought.

LATER, AFTER WOJICK'S wife had come and gone, Agnes went outside with a glass of cold water. The afternoon was muggy and still, no breeze blowing. Luke was kneeling on the grass, collecting shingles into a pile. His back was tanned and freckled, the skin peeling at the shoulders. His beard looked very soft.

"Here." She handed him the glass, struck by how easy it was. For three days he had labored in the hot sun. At any point she might have brought him a glass of water. Why had she waited so long?

He took it and drank deeply, half the glass in one gulp.

"What you did before," he said. "My buddy didn't thank you."

"That's all right," Agnes said.

"He's not usually like that." He stood. "Watch your step. There are nails everywhere."

They both looked down at her bare feet—bony and white, the second toe longer than it should be. She felt a sudden urge to apologize for her feet. "He'll need to rest his shoulder," she said instead. "For a few weeks, at least."

"That's okay. I can finish without him. One more day should do it."

Agnes shaded her eyes and looked up at the roof.

"Your gutters are shot," Luke told her. "I can replace them if you want. I can work up a price tomorrow."

"I thought you were a roofer."

"I do everything." He drained the glass and handed it back to her. His mouth looked moist and shiny. His fingers had left an imprint on the sweaty glass.

HOW THEY BECAME what they are is a question she's stopped asking. She accepts it as she accepts other miracles, the Resurrection and Ascension. A few she has witnessed firsthand—spontaneous remissions, children sick with leukemia who recovered without warning—but none involved her personally. Luke is the most remarkable thing that's ever happened to her, the only one, really. The great mystery of her life.

"I'm fifty years old," she told him only once. "Old enough to be your mother."

"My mother is dead," he said.

She'd died young, an aggressive cancer. At the end she'd cried tears of joy, ready to meet her personal Savior. After that her boys had run wild, looking for trouble. In Baltimore, where the family had settled, trouble was easily found.

"We never should have left Bakerton" was all Luke would say about it. "From that day on, everything went to hell."

It seemed unkind to point out that certain things would have happened anyway, that cancer didn't care where you lived.

In Agnes's room they pushed the twin beds together, the only possible solution. There were no double beds in the house.

Though she wanted to, she did not apologize for her feet, or any other part of her. She didn't tell him, *I've never done this before.* She imagined it was obvious enough.

The act itself was not quite what she'd pictured. The main difference was the presence of herself. Her fantasies, always, had involved other people: beautiful women desired, handsome men enraptured. They were late-night thoughts, unbidden and unwanted, secret movies playing in her head. She, Agnes Lubicki, never appeared in these films. Occasionally she wondered: did other women, normal women, have similar fantasies? Or did they dream only about themselves?

THE SUMMER UNROLLED like a satin ribbon. In the evening, after supper, they sat on the back porch until sunset. When the sky was dark, she followed him to the bedroom. Luke was an early riser: exhausted by nine o'clock, wide awake at dawn.

Was it strange that, lying in his arms, Agnes thought of her mother? Though hard to imagine, it was probably true: at one time, long ago, Mae had known a similar happiness. Agnes thought of her sister in the house across town, lying next to Andy Carnicella. They'd shared a bed for so many years that it must seem commonplace.

She thought of her own young womanhood, gone without her noticing: her twenties and thirties, her forties, even, each decade much like the last. It was pointless to wonder, now, how the years had escaped her. The hundreds of days—thousands—when she might have brought a man a glass of water, and changed the course of her life.

The house and the yard were their whole world. Luke had sug-

gested, once or twice, going out to eat, but Agnes found reasons
not to. Her mother had disdained restaurants. The prices offended
her—Mae called them *highway robbery*—but the truth, Agnes knew,
was more complex. Crowds, even small ones, had alarmed her. Each
Sunday she'd given herself a silent talking-to, to work up the nerve
to walk into church. I'm not like her, Agnes told herself often. All
day long, at work, she spoke to nurses and doctors and patients. Restaurants did not scare her. She simply preferred eating at home.

August was a dry month, good for house painting. Luke was
perched on a ladder when Terri's car pulled into the driveway. She
came in without knocking and found Agnes in the kitchen fixing
supper. She pointed out the window. "Who's he?"

"He's painting the house," Agnes said.

"I can see that." Terri's eyes narrowed. "I saw Mrs. Lipnic at the
market. She says his truck is parked here at all hours."

Agnes busied herself at the sink. "He's been doing some work
for me. He replaced the gutters and the fence."

Terri's eyes darted around the room, to Luke's boots lined up
at the door, his can of snuff on the table, his jacket hanging from a
hook on the wall.

"He's living here," she said in a low voice. "You're living here
together. In Mum and Daddy's house."

"Go home," Agnes said softly. Go home to your husband. Let
me have something.

"Do you really think he loves you?" Terri asked.

It was the look on her face as she asked the question, the scorn
and disbelief, that made Agnes say what she said next:

"I'm selling the house."

Terri looked stunned. "You *can't*. Daddy wanted you to live here. That's why he left it to you."

He's dead, Agnes thought. They're both dead. And I am still alive.

"Agnes, why?"

"I need the money." The lie rolled easily off her tongue. For twenty-eight years she'd worked double shifts. The large paychecks had gone into a savings account. She had never paid rent or taken a vacation. Her car, a frugal Ford Escort, was bought in cash ten years ago. "Don't worry. I'll give you half."

Terri stared at her, her face crumpling. She was near tears. "Agnes, what's happened to you?"

UNDERPRICED, THE HOUSE sold quickly. "What's your hurry?" the agent asked, disappointed by the small commission. "You're giving away the store."

Agnes knew it was true. Her mother's voice haunted her— *You're throwing away good money*—but she was learning to ignore it. Her time with Luke was beyond price. Their life together was a stolen thing—the months of happiness, years maybe, though she couldn't imagine being that lucky. She had the sensation, often, of living someone else's life. Sooner or later its rightful owner would steal it back.

Knowing this, she paid attention. She noticed everything: Luke shaving at her bathroom mirror, drinking coffee in her kitchen; his clean shirts spinning in her dryer in a dance of wild joy. From time to time the thought ambushed her: Someday I will be alone again. When the time came, she would manage. Solitude was an ache she knew, as familiar as her own body. She could bear to be alone again, but not in her parents' silent house.

IN THE AFTERNOON she vacuums the trailer, ignoring the telephone. She roasts a chicken for supper and takes Ore-Ida french fries from the freezer. They are her favorite food; she marvels at their uniform size and shape. Her mother grew potatoes by the bushel and stored them in the cellar. If she could see Agnes now, spending two dollars for a bag of frozen french fries! Made from scratch, they would cost twenty cents.

Again and again the phone rings. It strikes her as unusually shrill, an echo of her sister's voice. Certain telephones, she knows, can display the number of the person calling, but the phone company charges extra for this service. Her mother's thrift is an inherited disease, one she can't quite shake.

"Finally," Luke says when she answers. "I've been calling you all day." A large engine hums in the background. He shouts to be heard over the noise.

"I thought it was my sister," says Agnes. "She stopped by this morning."

"What did she want?"

To take me back, she thinks. To take me away from you.

"Where are you?" she asks. "I can barely hear you."

"At the site. We finished early." He's started working for an old buddy, Rick Marstellar, who gets state contracts to clean up contaminated lands. Unlike other businesses in Saxon County, Rick Marstellar's is thriving. There is a great deal here to clean up.

"Listen," says Luke. "I'm bringing someone home for supper. Someone I want you to meet."

THE DAYS ARE getting shorter. It is nearly dark when his truck comes down the lane. The passenger is a girl she's never seen before. Agnes meets them at the door.

"This is Renee," Luke says. "My daughter."

The girl is tall and slender and uncommonly pretty: little snub nose, velvet brown eyes like a puppy's or a deer's. Her eyes are ringed with dark liner, her hair bleached silver-blond. To Agnes, she looks older than fifteen.

"Welcome," says Agnes. She's known all along that Luke has children, that he was married and divorced years ago in Maryland. Then there were the girls he didn't marry. He'd told her on the phone that Renee came from one of those, when he was only sixteen.

They sit down to eat. Luke devours most of the chicken. He has the appetite of a teenager; watching, Agnes wonders if it will catch up with him. She tries to imagine him her own age, with thinning hair, a belly paunch. It is impossible to visualize.

Renee eats only a little. Her hands are delicate and birdlike, decorated with silver jewelry. She picks up a chicken wing and licks her fingertips when she is done.

In between bites Luke talks about his day. He started and finished a job in Kinport, pulling an underground tank from an abandoned gas station. The tank had been leaking for God knows how long, gasoline leaching into the soil. Luke's crew hoisted the tank, then dug out the tainted earth and loaded it into a dump truck. The driver—Luke calls him a *dirt merchant*—makes his living hauling contaminated soil to the incinerator.

The work is filthy and exhausting, but Rick Marstellar pays well. "He can afford to," Luke says, helping himself to more french fries. "He's making out like a bandit." He chews each mouthful three times, then swallows. He gobbles noisily, like a dog.

After supper, Agnes clears the dishes. Renee rises to help, her sharp hip bones visible through her jeans. I was that young once, Agnes thinks, but it isn't true. At fifteen she was middle-aged already. She is younger now than she was then.

Agnes washes and Renee dries, until Renee complains: "I don't know where anything goes." Agnes takes the dish towel and hands her the sponge.

"Thanks for letting me stay here." Renee takes four rings from each hand and sets them on the windowsill. "My mom kicked me out. I guess he told you."

"Why did she do that?" Agnes asks.

"She hates my boyfriend. She says he's too old for me. I don't think that matters." Renee squirts Palmolive into the greasy roasting pan. "Do you?"

Agnes thinks of herself at fifteen, a sophomore at Bakerton High. She recalls Spanish and history, chemistry and geometry. She has no recollection of even speaking to a boy. "I have no idea," she says.

Renee eyes her curiously. "You don't have kids, do you?"

"No," says Agnes.

"I can tell," Renee says.

. . . .

"I'LL TAKE HER with me in the morning," says Luke. "I can drop her off then."

They are lying in bed face-to-face, their feet touching.

"At school?" says Agnes.

"Yeah. It's on my way." He takes her hand. "Let's go out tomorrow. Celebrate my first paycheck. A day early, but so what." This is something local couples do, something Luke and Agnes have never done: drink beer and share a pizza at the Commercial Hotel.

"All right," Agnes says.

She wishes he would reach for her, but the walls are thin in the trailer. Unless she is dead asleep, Renee, on the foldout couch Agnes made up for her, will hear everything.

"How long is she going to stay?" Agnes whispers.

"Depends on her mother. They had a fight. About what, I don't know."

Her mother, Agnes thinks. Who is she? Did you love her? "She doesn't like Renee's boyfriend," she says.

"She told you that?" Luke looks surprised. "Did she say why?"

"He's too old for her."

Luke rolls onto his other side and stares up at the window. "How old is he?"

"I don't know," Agnes says.

IT IS STILL dark when the alarm rings. Rain beats at the roof of the trailer. Luke releases her with a little groan. In the living room Renee is asleep on the sofa bed. Agnes dresses in her uniform and decides against breakfast. It's only a dollar, she thinks, and buys a cup of coffee at a gas station on the way.

Her shift passes slowly. On and off she thinks of the Commercial Hotel, herself and Luke sitting at the bar, in full view of whoever might walk through the door. Anyone would say they make a strange couple. She recalls the photo of her parents, her plain, shy mother at a dance club—the Legion or the Vets—with handsome John Lubicki. By the time Agnes was born, Mae had retreated to the house; she had simply stopped trying. Was this the reason she'd withdrawn from the world? Was she so afraid of what people would say?

By the end of her shift, the rain stops. Wind chases her across the parking lot. The air smells wet and loamy, the rich perfume of decaying leaves. Agnes hears footsteps behind her, the sharp clop of high heels.

"Agnes!"

She turns. Her sister stands beneath a floodlight. She wears a wool coat several sizes too big, a scarf wrapped at her throat. She looks like a child dressed by a careful mother, bundled against the cold.

"Jo told me you were working," she says.

It is the curse of living in a small town. Jo, the charge nurse, was a high school classmate of Terri's.

"I didn't know what else to do. I haven't heard from you in months." In the strong light Terri looks tired. Her hair is shorter and parted in the middle. At the part Agnes notices a few strands of gray.

"I stopped by your house the other day. Your—trailer. I saw his motorcycle outside."

Agnes waits.

"You bought it for him," says Terri.

"No," Agnes lies.

They stand a long moment, staring at each other.

"Thanks for the photos," says Agnes. "I'm glad to have them."

A truck backs up to the delivery entrance, beeping loudly. The beeping waxes and wanes with the shifting wind.

"Why do you hate me?" says Terri. "What did I do?"

"I don't hate you," says Agnes, because she doesn't. The second question is harder to answer, and she doesn't try. "I have to go. Luke is waiting. We have plans." She digs for her car keys and turns away abruptly. She wants only to escape the beeping truck, her sister's stricken face.

"He was in prison down in Maryland," says Terri. "Did he tell you that? For armed robbery. Andy knows all about it."

Of course Agnes knows. The store was empty except for the clerk, who wasn't hurt. Luke was nineteen at the time. He served four years.

"You don't know anything about him," she says, opening the car door.

Terri grabs her arm. "I saw him in town yesterday. He had a girl with him."

"That's his daughter," says Agnes, not turning.

"How do you know?"

WHEN AGNES GETS home, the trailer is dark. Luke's truck is gone.

Inside, the sofa bed is closed, the sheets stripped and rolled into a ball. She changes out of her uniform and eyes the balled-up sheets—warily, as though some small animal, a squirrel or raccoon, has invaded her home.

How do you know?

The answer, of course, is that she doesn't. Luke's parents and grandparents came from Coalport, two towns over. Mae, if she were alive, would know the family's entire history, or would ask one of her telephone friends.

Of course, if her mother were alive, Agnes would have no need of this information. If her mother were alive, she wouldn't be living with Luke.

In the kitchen she puts away dishes, the clean Ziploc bags left on the counter to dry. She knows that thrift is not the disease; it is only a symptom. The underlying illness is more exotic—inherited from her mother, a familial loneliness and strangeness. It's a condition that can't be cured, only managed, like hypertension or diabetes.

Yet her sister somehow escaped it.

Why do you hate me? What did I do?

The Commercial Hotel would be lively at this hour, music pouring out the windows, a live band, maybe. Agnes has driven past often on Thursday nights, and knows that this is so.

IT IS NEARLY midnight when Luke's truck barrels down the lane. He smells smoky, a little beery. "We stopped out after work," he says. "Rick was buying, so I figured why not."

Because we had plans, Agnes thinks. Because I was waiting for you.

"Where's Renee?"

Luke shrugs. "Her mother's, I guess. She's pissed at me."

"Why?"

"Why do you think?" He struggles out of his jacket and tosses it on the couch. "She wants money, like everybody. She needs it for school. It's the only reason she tracked me down." He heads into the kitchen, his muddy boots leaving a trail on the carpet. "She says I never gave her anything."

"Did you?" Once a month he pays child support for the three boys in Maryland. Agnes has seen the check stubs. They're the only checks Luke ever writes.

He looks startled by the question. "I'm not even sure she's mine, you want to know the truth." He opens the refrigerator and studies its contents. "I wanted to take a paternity test, way back when. Her mother wouldn't let me." He nods once, as if vindicated. "That tells you something right there."

Agnes supposes it does. Though what exactly it tells her is not clear.

"Don't get me wrong. She's a good kid. I'd give it to her if I had it." He considers and rejects a bowl of leftover spaghetti. "Can't get blood from a stone."

THE NEXT MORNING, after Luke leaves for work, there is a knock at the door. Agnes remembers it's the first of the month and takes the checkbook from her purse.

A scrawny blond man stands on the porch. It takes her a moment to place him. When she does, she steps outside and closes the door. "How's your shoulder?" she asks.

Wojick looks at her without recognition. "Okay, I guess."

"I'm Agnes. You worked on my roof." She sees him eying the checkbook in her hand. "I thought you were the landlord."

"No, but I'll take his money." He grins, showing snaggleteeth. "Where's your man? He go hunting?"

"At work," says Agnes.

Wojick looks surprised. "He got a job?"

"At Penn Reclamation."

"Rick hired him? I never heard that." Wojick pats the chest pocket of his jacket, a worn Carhartt like Luke's. "I just cashed my settlement check. From that accident I had. It's a long story," he says, seeing her frown. "I need someone to help me celebrate."

"He's on a job in Fallentree. I'll tell him you stopped by."

"All right, then." Wojick ambles down the porch steps, hands in his pockets, his breath steaming in the cold. He stops to study Luke's motorcycle, parked at the bottom of the stairs. "That's some bike he's got. It's a twelve hundred, right?"

Agnes shrugs.

"Looks brand-new," says Wojick. "Where'd he get a bike like that?"

The idea comes to her all at once, with unusual clarity. It seems both correct and inevitable.

"It's for sale," she says.

THAT NIGHT SHE works second shift. She leaves a note for Luke: *Supper is in the oven.* When she comes home, his dirty plate is in the sink. He paces the trailer like a zoo animal, a large, healthy beast in a small, rickety cage.

"I saw Kenny Wojick today," he says. "He came by the job site."

Agnes does not respond to this.

"He was riding a motorcycle. My goddamned bike." Luke studies her intently, waiting for her to speak. Calmly she returns his gaze. "You could've told me you were going to sell it."

"That's true," she says. She squeezes past him and heads for the freezer, takes out pork chops for tomorrow's supper. "It wasn't practical. We have other expenses."

Luke stares at her, not comprehending.

"She's your daughter," she says, waiting for him to contradict her. When he doesn't, she adds, "Don't you owe her something?"

He looks dumbfounded. "Renee?"

Agnes turns to face him. She is nearly his height. He told her once that he liked tall women. He didn't mention her specifically, so it wasn't technically a compliment, but Agnes cherishes it as though it were.

"She'll be graduating in a couple years. She'll need money for school. We'll work it out with her mother." Whoever she is, Agnes could have added but doesn't. "We'll talk to her together."

She thinks: Leave me now, if you're going to. If you're going to go, just go.

THE COMMERCIAL HOTEL is lively on Friday night, already decorated for Christmas: an artificial tree with twinkling lights, tinsel hanging in loops from the pool table and the bar. On the walls are framed photographs, the owner with a series of sports heroes: a Pirate, a Penguin, a Steeler, men Agnes doesn't recognize until Luke explains who they are.

He finds an open booth, and Agnes slides in beside him. She glances around the room. They are bulky and anonymous in their jeans and parkas; they look like every other couple starting off the weekend with a pitcher of beer.

In the corner, beside the Christmas tree, the band is setting up. The Vipers are young boys—younger, even, than Luke; skinny and eager in their T-shirts and denim jackets, not knowing or not caring that they're underdressed for the cold. One makes adjustments to a drum kit. The others tune electric guitars. Agnes watches them, thinking how, in a few years, they will find jobs and wives, lose and then replace them. Children will be born, parents buried, paychecks cashed, time cards punched. Fatigue will set in, the weight of understanding, and the lean eagerness of these Vipers will dissipate. The years will grow on them like moss on a tree.

Luke orders a pepperoni pie and a pitcher. He eats six slices to Agnes's two.

"We should do this every week," he says between mouthfuls.

"I'd like that," Agnes says.

FAVORITE SON

For a certain kind of teenager, a small town is a prison. For another kind, it is a stage.

At sixteen I was one of the prisoners. Bakerton High was, to me, the world itself: an arena where great events were decided; a theater only in the sense that Vietnam had been, to American generals, a theater of war. The actors were boys and girls who'd grown up alongside me, the athletes and beauty queens who'd blossomed early and fierce. I worked evenings and weekends at Keener's Diner, and on Friday nights after football games, they filled every booth: the girls I envied and the boys I crushed on, coupling and recoupling like square dancers. Having none of my own, I marveled at their inexplicable self-confidence, these playmates who'd finger-painted with me in kindergarten, now inhabiting new adult bodies with effortless aplomb.

There was, in the school corridors, a protocol for making eye contact, for nodding and smiling and saying hello. Boys could get away with sullenness, or lose themselves in rowdy horseplay, but girls were bound by certain conventions. Ignore them and you'd be viewed as a misfit. If you happened to be the principal's daughter, you'd be branded as stuck-up or worse. My own face and body; other faces and bodies; all that compulsory nodding and smiling. These so absorbed my attention that I didn't see what was happening around me, outside the theater. Somehow I failed to notice that my hometown was starting to disappear.

Bakerton was a company town, always had been. In my grandparents' day, the Baker Brothers coal company built hundreds of company houses, and the mines employed nearly every man in town. Things continued this way, more or less, throughout my childhood. Then, the spring of my sophomore year, Baker Eleven closed—*mined out* was the expression used. It meant that no coal was left in the ground, at least none that could be gotten to easily. The Eleven was Baker's largest mine, and suddenly nine hundred men were cashing unemployment checks, confidently at first. They'd seen slowdowns before, and their union had looked after them. They owned houses and trucks, snowmobiles and motorboats. Certainly they were better off than my own family. It said something about our town that the high school principal earned less than a miner did.

But by autumn, the men had grown desperate. Their unemployment ran out, a sobering development. That fall was wet and windy. Leaves turned, leaves fell.

BUCK SEASON OPENED—STILL does—on the Monday after Thanksgiving. In Bakerton it is a holiday of sorts. School was closed for the day, and I reported to Keener's at four A.M. to serve eggs and sausages and countless cups of coffee to men in orange vests. Every table was full despite heavy competition, the annual pancake breakfasts at the Amvets, the Elks, and the Moose.

On opening day the woods rang with gunshot. Deer were hit, dragged, and hefted into pickup trucks. Taxidermy shops did a brisk business, and enterprising freelancers competed for the overflow, advertising with homemade yard signs: DEER PROCESSED FAST AND CHEAP. The biggest kills were photographed for the *Bakerton Herald*. The Monday after opening day, the front page ran a jubilant headline: *New Record for Opening Week*. No one said, but everyone knew, that it was a question of simple mathematics, the nine hundred men who now had plenty of free time to hunt deer.

At the center of the page, just above the fold, was a photo of Mitch Stanek in his backyard. Beside him a massive ten-pointer—a magnificent male specimen—hung upside down from a tree. Even in the grainy photo Mitch was handsome, his blond hair shaggy, his cheeks smudged with two-day beard. A woman named Charlene Dodd had been sent to take his picture, and she had flirted a little, asked him to take off his vest and cap. Mitch had a certain way of standing, head and shoulders back, left fist pressed to his upper thigh. He'd been photographed many times in this stance, for the *Herald* and for his high school yearbook, some fifteen years before.

Back in Mitch's heyday, my father had advised the yearbook staff. In our basement was a full set of the *Banner* dating to before I was born. As a teenager, I studied them like lost scriptures. I laughed at the outdated hairstyles, but really I was looking for wisdom, some secret to navigating a world where I felt misplaced, ridiculous, and shunned. Mitch Stanek was all over his yearbook, dressed usually in a numbered jersey. As a senior he'd captained teams in football, basketball, and baseball. For Bakerton it had been a winning season. Fifteen years later, the trophies were still on display, filling an entire glass case at school.

He was going to set the world on fire, my mother said, looking over my shoulder as I read. *Now he's out of work like everyone else.* Mitch Stanek had been her student in sophomore English, a job she'd abandoned, as female teachers used to, when she had her own children. Now she spent her days nursing my brother Teddy, who had cystic fibrosis and was in and out of hospitals. When she spoke of school sports or those who watched or played them, a sourness crept into her voice.

My father remembered Mitch differently. *That kid, now. He was something.* He spoke softly, though we were alone in his car and my mother couldn't possibly hear. On Saturday mornings Dad gave me driving lessons. The car's ashtray was always full, its radio set to the local AM station, which had broadcast Bakerton High football the night before. (Each Friday night he visited his mother in a nursing home two towns over. I imagined him kissing her goodbye at five minutes to eight, just before kickoff time.) He was the sort of father who'd have attended every game and most of the practices, if his own son were able to play.

We sat idling in the high school parking lot, Dad lost in memory, my driving lesson temporarily forgotten.

Mitch Stanek could have made it. He was the real deal. Best thing ever to come out of Bakerton.

My father was a gentle soul and meant nothing by it. I didn't point out that Bakerton had also produced me.

. . . .

WHEN MITCH WAS first laid off, he put in his name at Beth Steel for a job that would also prove expendable but at the time seemed as solid as the stuff the mills turned out. Beth Steel never called. This baffled him at first, when bad luck was new to him. "We'll wait it out," he told his wife. Unemployment would carry them through the summer. At the time he believed what everyone believed: that his old job would return, that Baker would break ground on a new mine, bigger and better than the Eleven.

His wife knew better, Deena who stretched the unemployment checks to cover the mortgage, the car and boat payments, everything their four boys ate and played with and wore. She worked for a time sweeping up hair at Ruth Rizzo Beauty, then got her own license and opened a salon in their basement. While Mitch waited for the phone to ring, she worked six days a week, shag cuts and highlights and permanent waves. (This was the eighties, remember.) But no hairdresser could earn what a miner had.

By August she'd had enough and sent him away. She got the idea from Cheryl Berks, whose husband had found a construction job in the Virginia suburbs. Lou Berks shared a cheap apartment with two other laid-off miners, and there was room for a fourth. Every weekend the men piled into somebody's car and drove the four hours back to Pennsylvania, where their kids, at least, seemed happy to see them again.

A temporary arrangement, Deena called it, but after a few months Mitch began to wonder. He suggested moving the whole family to Virginia, but Deena seemed not to hear him. He knew the reason. The goddamned house.

So every Friday night—exhausted, his back aching—he got behind the wheel and drove home to Bakerton, two hundred miles north and west. Though his truck burned gas at a sickening rate, he allowed himself this one extravagance. After a week in the crowded apartment, he couldn't face sharing a ride with the guys.

It was on one of these visits—the first Saturday in December—that Mitch snagged his ten-pointer. Afterward he stopped at the Vets for a few beers to celebrate.

"How many?" Deena demanded when he made his way home.

"Five," Mitch lied: he'd had twice that many, but beers were cheaper here than in Virginia, so he felt justified.

Deena frowned.

"Whatsa matter?" he demanded, smelling a fight and ready for it, but Deena didn't have time to argue. Mrs. Hauser—the principal's wife—was waiting in the basement, ten minutes early for her perm.

"Mitch was livid," my mother reported later, by phone, to her friend the school nurse. His move to Virginia had revived old gossip: that Deena was ready to divorce him, that he'd hit her with a closed hand. It wasn't hard to picture. Mitch was a big man, Deena so petite she wore shoes from the girls' department. Even after four babies, she was tiny as a doll. Though no fan of Mitch Stanek, my mother called the rumors baseless. True, Deena was once seen with a bruise on her shoulder, but no one *had* to wear a sundress. No one would, my mother maintained, if she had something shameful to hide.

My mother went to Deena's every Saturday for her wash and set. The beauty shop had its own entrance, so she never got a look at the rest of the house, a handsome split-level on the outskirts of town. My mother admired it, though she allowed that it was bigger than any family needed, with a three-car garage to hold Mitch's snowmobiles and as many bathrooms as children. She was not alone in this opinion. Most of Bakerton still lived in company houses, bought from the mines and disguised with porches and aluminum siding but easy to spot by the familiar floor plan, three rooms upstairs and three rooms down.

"Mitch thinks we should sell," Deena confessed as she rinsed my mother's hair at the sink. And sure enough, a few weeks later the house was listed in the *Herald,* at a price the town found insulting. No buyer could be found—which, according to my mother, was what Deena had intended. She wasn't about to lose that house

She came from poor people. We all did, I later learned, though at the time I thought we had rich and poor like any other place. Even by local standards, the Vances lived meanly, in a duplex behind the gas company, a dark street loud with fuel trucks. Deena's mother worked in the dress factory, and the United Mine Workers sent her a monthly check from the widows' fund. With half as many children, she might have lived in reasonable comfort.

Deena was the oldest of six, a little beauty. As a girl, she resembled the actress Kim Novak, except that Kim dyed her hair and Deena was a natural blonde. She met Mitch her freshman year in high school. Mitch was a junior then, busy with his various sports. In the summers he worked as a lifeguard. At the town swimming pool, in pairs or threes, girls in bikinis flocked around his chair, keeping him company during his shift. As they spoke, Mitch's eyes wandered, alert for swimmers in distress. He never showed the slightest interest in dating until Deena Vance.

My mother and the school nurse, who followed student

romances with an interest that now seems peculiar, shared in the general astonishment when Mitch took Deena to the winter ball. "For heaven's sake," my mother huffed. "Why *her*?" The Staneks were a solid family, Mitch's father a lector in our church. (Even now, when I read the letters of Saint Paul, I hear them in Herk Stanek's gruff voice.) Mitch was that rare thing in Bakerton, a boy with a future. When he played in the state basketball championships, scouts were spotted in the stands. In bars and barbershops, speculation was rampant: basketball or football? Penn State or Pitt? The question wasn't whether he'd go to college, but which one.

At Bakerton High the matter was debated in the faculty lounge, in a cloud of cigarette smoke. Like the crowd at a junior high dance, the teachers split along gender lines, women at the long tables near the window, men standing around the coffee machine. They spoke of many things—local affairs, movies, and politics—but were most animated when discussing their students. The men knew how far Mitch could throw a football. The women were more interested in Deena Vance.

"It won't last," my mother told the school nurse. "He's got bigger fish to fry."

My mother was wrong.

Mitch and Deena became inseparable. They walked hand in hand through the school corridors. In the summer she rode with him to work. Girls no longer approached the lifeguard chair, not with Deena stretched out on a towel a few yards away, eyes closed, working on her tan. Every hour Mitch took a break. To empty the pool, he blew two long blasts on his whistle. He approached Deena's towel and knelt at her feet. She was fifteen years old, beautiful and naked but for two bright strips of nylon. Mitch Stanek was a giant fallen to his knees.

"You wait," my mother told the school nurse. "Wait until school starts."

By *school* she meant football. The first home game was the last weekend in August, a sultry night; the spectators wore shorts and tank tops. A few bare chests were painted in the team's colors, black and gold like the Steelers'. In that crowd, the two men in suits were as conspicuous as drag queens. More scouts were spotted a week later, and again in October. In November Mitch made his decision: not Pitt or Penn State but *Florida* State, a choice that blinded the town with its sheer exoticism.

Could Mitch play in hot weather?

And what about poor Deena?

I imagine her grim face as they walked the halls of Bakerton High, Mitch stopping to receive hearty handshakes, the squeals of disbelief and delight. The cattier girls congratulating Deena—*You'll be down there every month to visit!*—knowing she couldn't afford bus fare to Altoona, never mind a plane ticket.

Florida State gave Mitch the hero treatment, flying his parents down to have a look at the campus, paying for their meals and airfare and Mitch's new clothes. The *Herald* ran a story on page one with a picture of Mitch in a jacket and tie. It was the first time he'd been photographed out of uniform.

He left Bakerton just after graduation, in time for summer training camp. Herk drove him to the airport in Pittsburgh, with Deena riding along. Mitch's sister took a photo of his plane taking off. It was printed in the next week's *Herald* beneath a bold headline:

Town's favorite son marches on.

STANEK HEADS SOUTH!

Fall came. For three months of Saturdays, the town was glued to the television. Mitch sat out two games but—my father would remember it always—threw a touchdown in the third. The elementary school classes wrote him letters of congratulation. Then Mitch came home at Thanksgiving and announced he was quitting school.

Soon all of Bakerton had heard about the drugs *down there,* how his roommate smoked marijuana at night while Mitch was sleeping, how just breathing that smoke made him feel sick and crazy. In bars and barbershops, men debated Mitch's decision. The young ones called him foolish. Their fathers argued that you didn't mess with drugs.

"She's pregnant," my mother told the school nurse. "Mark my words."

Mitch got his union card by Christmas, but a full year passed before he and Deena married. Once again my mother was wrong.

I GREW UP and forgot these stories. I went away to college, and Bakerton receded from my imagination. Like Mitch Stanek, I was a scholarship case, but I had no intention of wasting my chance.

At holidays, at school breaks, I came back to visit. Driving down Main Street was like visiting a beloved aunt in hospice, a breath away from the grave. Baker Nine had closed, and the Fourteen would soon follow. At Baker Six the men worked three days a week. FOR SALE signs appeared on lawns, in windows, but no one was buying. Families divided, as the Staneks had done. At Bakerton High the classes were shrinking. My father took the early retirement that the state offered, thankful for his pension, glad to get out while he could.

At college I worked and studied. I came back jaded and worldly from a junior year abroad. After graduation I visited less frequently. My parents aged before my eyes, gradually and then rapidly. One year at Christmas my father was shockingly gaunt. His dry cough had grown into something more ominous. He had suffered through a hard month of treatment, but the prognosis was clear.

For his benefit, we walked through the old rituals: Bing Crosby on the stereo, the tree hung with familiar ornaments, a Popsicle-stick angel my brother had made before he died. By Christmas Eve my father was exhausted, his cough nearly constant. "The Lord will forgive me," he said. "You two go ahead." With a creeping dread, I dressed for midnight Mass. I had been a college atheist; now I lacked even that conviction. I hadn't been inside a church since Teddy's funeral. Under other circumstances, I would have declined politely, but that year I didn't have the heart.

The church was crowded, families reunited for the holiday. We squeezed into a pew near the front. I recognized Mitch and Deena Stanek with their four sons, arranged in order of height, smallest to tallest, like a set of Russian dolls. From behind, Mitch still resembled a college athlete, his thick neck and broad shoulders, his blond hair untouched by gray. I'd seen his truck parked behind the church, one of many with Virginia plates. Watching him, I was filled with an old longing I'd nearly forgotten: to be Mitch and Deena both, not now but a lifetime ago, when they were beguiling and rare.

I was thinking such thoughts when Father Veltri swept down the aisle, a portly man in white holiday vestments. He stopped just ahead of me and leaned in to touch Mitch's shoulder, so close that I could smell his aftershave.

"Merry Christmas, Mitchell," he whispered as they shook hands. "I have a favor to ask." He handed over a leather-bound book, the page marked with a red ribbon: Paul's epistle to Titus. I knew it almost by heart.

"I'd be grateful if you could read this," said the priest. "In memory of your father. Herk would be proud."

Mitch's face reddened. "I'm sorry, Father. I'm not much of a public speaker."

"Come on," said Deena. "Pop would want you to."

"I said no." Mitch's whisper was harsher somehow than if he'd shouted. Deena looked as stricken as I felt. Even then, in my secular phase, I couldn't imagine saying no to a priest.

Father Veltri, apparently, couldn't imagine hearing it. "It isn't long," he told Mitch. "Just come to the lectern after I say the blessing. I appreciate it, Mitchell." He left the book in Mitch's hand and swept away in a rustle of satin, a plump little swan.

A moment later the Mass started. The aging choir warbled the opening hymn. Without a word to Deena, Mitch turned his back to the altar. Stone-faced, in front of God and everybody, he marched out of the church.

. . . .

I NEVER SAW Mitch Stanek again. That spring my father lost his battle with lung cancer, and I went back to Bakerton for the funeral. The day was warm and springlike, the snow nearly melted. I borrowed my mother's car and spent an afternoon on the country roads where Dad had taught me to drive. I saw then that the Staneks' house stood empty. They had finally moved to Virginia, enrolled their boys in school there. A Century 21 sign was spiked into the front yard.

That Christmas Eve, after church, my mother and I had ridden home in silence. The Mass had droned on for over an hour, but Mitch did not reappear. Deena had gone to the lectern in his place, her voice shaking a little on the first words: *Dearly beloved, the grace of God our Savior has appeared to all men.*

"He can't read," I said.

My mother kept her eyes on the road. A light snow was falling, and her reflexes aren't what they once were. Driving now requires her full attention, especially after dark.

"That's why he dropped out of college," I said. "Drugs had nothing to do with it."

Still she didn't respond.

"You were his teacher." Sophomore English: *The Red Badge of Courage, The Scarlet Letter, Billy Budd,* books Mitch Stanek had been tested on. His comprehension had been judged adequate. He'd been given a passing grade.

Finally my mother spoke. "He had a problem. A form of dyslexia, I believe. It was never diagnosed." With great care, she braked and signaled. "Times were different then, Rebecca. We didn't know about that sort of thing."

"But he graduated." You let him, I thought.

"It seemed best. I agonized over it at the time. Now I'm not sure it made any difference."

I saw her point. Without a diploma, Mitch would have mined coal anyway, been laid off anyway. He'd have lost only those few months in Florida, his picture in the paper, the enduring legend the town still cherished. For Bakerton, it had been a net gain. For Mitch Stanek, the outcome would have been roughly the same.

She pulled the car into the driveway and cut the headlights. "Ed doesn't know," she said, and I thought of the radio in his old Buick: my father listening to the games in secret, away from my mother's disdain, her caustic and sometimes merciless tongue. The local heroes—the Mitch Staneks—had been her favorite targets, but in the end she was not merciless. She left my father his idols. Maybe she wanted Mitch to win, just like everyone else did.

We sat a long moment in the dark car. The white flakes landed like news from heaven: notes from elsewhere, fallen from the stars.

THE BOTTOM OF THINGS

Ray and his second wife drove into Bakerton on a clear winter morning, in a Ford they'd rented at the Pittsburgh airport. The road snaked through mountains, alongside streams and frozen fields. Their flight had left Houston at dawn. They'd traveled a thousand miles to attend a small party at the Bakerton fire hall, to celebrate his parents' fiftieth wedding anniversary.

The invitation had arrived one morning in the mail. When Ray came home from work that night, Evie was already on the phone with his mother: *Of course we'll come. We're overdue for a visit.* In fact, the women had met just twice, though they spoke every month on the phone. Each year Evie suggested spending Christmas in Pennsylvania, but always there was a reason not to: work; a ruptured disc in Ray's back; the weekend ranch they'd bought and were moving into bit by bit, where they'd eventually retire. Ten years before, Ray and a buddy had quit their jobs at Exxon and started their own company, Pueblo Energy. The venture was as consuming as a new baby; time had passed without him noticing. In that time his parents had grown older; Bakerton, even farther away.

"Are we almost there? These roads make me queasy." Evie slipped on a pair of sunglasses, red tortoiseshell. She was an optometrist and fond of jazzy frames.

"It's just over this hill." He hit the gas; the Ford's motor roared. They passed the Baptist church and cemetery and climbed what, as kids, Ray and his brother, Kenny, had called Holy Roller Hill. At the top he slowed. The town lay before them in a deep valley, settled there like sediment: the main street with its one traffic light, the rows of company houses, narrow and square—some brick-cased now, or disguised with porches and aluminum siding, but at this distance you could see how alike they all were. From a few chimneys came streams of dark smoke; most had coal furnaces still. The snow had an established look—dirty at the edges, crusted over with ice. Ray accelerated, racing down the hill.

"Ooh," said Evie, clutching her stomach.

He felt it, too, the sudden sinking in his belly. As a boy he'd loved the feeling, urged Pop to take the hill faster, waiting for the drop with dread and glee. At the bottom of the hill, he braked. The Ford handled well, a surprise: he hadn't driven an American car in years, though he'd once worked on an assembly line building chassis for Pontiacs and Chevys. Back then, living in the Cleveland suburbs with his first wife, he'd owned a red Corvette—a car he still drove occasionally, in dreams.

The town was quiet that morning, sidewalks deserted. A single car idled at the traffic light.

"I don't remember this," said Evie. "Nothing looks familiar." She'd been to Bakerton once—three years before, for his brother's funeral. A quick trip in the middle of summer, in and out in two days.

"It looks different in the winter." Worse, he thought, sadder and more dilapidated. Empty storefronts lined the main street. Above the abandoned train station, a punk with a spray can had defaced the old sign: BAKERTON COAL **B**LIGHTS THE WORLD. He avoided looking at the vacant lot where the Commercial Hotel had once stood. The place had burned down years ago, and no one had bothered to rebuild it. More and more, Bakerton looked like what it had always been, a town of churches and bars. As a young man, Ray had lied about where he came from, said Pittsburgh when anyone asked. Over the years he'd stopped lying, or maybe people had stopped asking. He'd be fifty-three in June.

His parents lived on a dead-end street at the edge of town, a narrow stretch of gravel lined with neighbors' cars. Ray idled while a pickup truck made a three-point turn in the middle of the road. On Dixon Road this maneuver was performed many times each day. There was no other way to turn around.

The house was unlocked. Ray knocked lightly, then opened the door. He was a big man, six-four, and his head barely cleared the door frame. The living room was narrow and dark, crowded with furniture. Framed photographs covered the paneled walls. The front-facing window was heavily decorated—velvet drapes, ruffles, sheer curtains underneath—as if, having only one window, his mother had lavished all her attention on it.

"Anybody home?" Ray called.

"Coming," Pop answered from the kitchen.

Ray glanced at the photos on the wall. Himself and Kenny in parochial school uniforms; Kenny in army greens and later, near the end of his life, smoking a cigarette on the back porch, in the ratty plaid hunting jacket he'd worn nine months of the year. His graying hair was long and straggly. He had the raw, windburned look of an old sea captain.

Pop emerged from the kitchen, slightly breathless. He kissed Evie and clapped Ray's shoulder. "Hey, buddy," he said, offering his hand. The hand was hard and wiry, half the size of Ray's and twice as strong. "Fran took your mother to the bake sale. You got here quicker than we thought."

"You remember Fran," Ray told Evie. "Kenny's wife."

"Of course." Evie looked pale and slightly clammy, still carsick, he supposed, from the ride. Ray sent her upstairs to take a nap, and in the kitchen he drank coffee that Pop had reheated on the stove. They talked about road conditions, the highway under construction, the Pennsylvania primaries a week away. They would never agree on politics. Pop was a lifelong Democrat, though once—after the war, out of loyalty—he'd voted for Eisenhower. *I learned my lesson right there,* he liked to say. The day of the inauguration, he'd lost his job driving a bread truck. No one could persuade him the events were unrelated.

"Evie's a nice girl," said Pop. All women were girls to him: matrons, elderly nuns; his own sisters, now in their seventies. Evie was only forty. To him she must look like a kid.

"Yeah," said Ray. "She's great."

"Ever hear from Georgette? If you don't mind my asking." He was fond of Ray's first wife, had worked in the mines with her father. For thirty years they'd been pinners, the first men to set foot in a newly blasted seam of coal. Pop and Red had worked as a team, spacing thick wooden posts at intervals to hold up the ceiling, then hammering the posts into place.

"No," said Ray. "Not in a long time."

"She calls your mother once in a while. Sends pictures of the boys."

Ray nodded. "How are they doing?"

"Ray Junior's got his own shop now. I guess you knew."

"Sure," Ray lied.

"He does all foreign cars. Hondas, Toyotas. I guess they're better than they used to be."

"How's Bryan?"

"Still living at home."

"You look flushed," Ray said. "How's your blood pressure?"

"Up a little, I guess. Too much excitement. The party and all."

Outside, a dog was barking, a beagle the neighbors kept for hunting.

"It's going to be quite a shindig. Fran invited half the town, from the sounds of it." Pop looked down into his coffee. "It was her idea, you know. The party."

"Nice of her," Ray said.

"She means well. Of course, if it were up to Mom and me—" He broke off. "You know we don't like a fuss."

"I know." Ray finished his coffee and stood. "I'm going to check on Evie."

. . . .

HIS MOTHER HAD married Pop just after the war, a month after he returned from the South Pacific. At that time Ray was three years old. He had no memory of the wedding, wasn't sure he'd even attended. Perhaps, in those days, young children were kept away from weddings (a fine idea, in his opinion). The bride's young child, in particular, might have been kept away.

His mother was young then, barely twenty, the fifth of nine children. She hadn't finished school, had instead gone away to New York City to work as a live-in maid, as her older sisters had done. Like most of their neighbors, Ray's grandparents were Polish; during the Depression their daughters found work with the wealthy Jews of the Upper West Side, who preferred Polish-speaking help to keep their kosher kitchens. Ray's mother was sixteen when she left Bakerton—terrified, probably; a small-town girl, an innocent. She traveled by train to Penn Station, her passage paid by her new employers. A year later she came back to Bakerton at her own expense—alone still, and pregnant. She had suffered; of that Ray was sure. He remembered his grandfather, silent and stern; his devout grandmother, who'd spent her final years saying rosaries, being blessed by priests.

He was born in his grandparents' house; his grandmother, a midwife, had delivered every child in the neighborhood. His mother went to work at the dress factory in town, and Ray spent the days in his grandmother's kitchen. He remembered a warm corner near the coal stove where he'd played, the apples she'd baked each morning for breakfast. He could recall playing in the woods with his aunts and uncles—the youngest aunt was his own age, the youngest uncle a year younger. The aunts

had cried the day he and his mother drove away, their belong-
ings in the back of a pickup truck. Looking back, he imagined
it was the morning after the wedding—his mother's wedding
to Pop.

No one had told him this; he'd pieced the story together himself. In her old age, his grandmother had been confused, voluble.
She cried, ranted, told stories in English and in Polish. *It was my
fault,* she'd once told his mother, *for sending you away.* Ray was
twelve when he found his birth certificate in a strongbox in his
grandmother's attic, the paper marked *Father Unknown.* (Years
later, when he needed a birth certificate to register for the draft, his
mother claimed it was lost. Selective Service accepted a baptismal
certificate instead.) In the same box he found his parents' marriage certificate, written in Polish by the parish priest. He noted the
names and dates, and after that the world looked different to him.
He himself looked different. He was a dark-haired boy, tall for his
age. His brother, Kenny, was fair and blue-eyed, slightly under-
sized, the very image of Pop.

THERE WERE TWIN beds in his childhood room, each covered with
a crocheted afghan. Evie lay on Kenny's old one near the window.
Six years older, Ray could remember his brother sleeping in a crib
and, later, wetting the bed, waking from nightmares. "Go back to
sleep," he'd grumble when Kenny woke up crying and wanted to
climb in bed with him. Ray was nine or ten, then. It had seemed
to him a tremendous burden, sharing a room with a big baby.

He stretched out on his old bed, breathing deeply. He'd had

asthma as a child; the attacks had stopped in his teens, but every once in a while he felt tightness in his chest. This happened mainly when he visited Bakerton—the coal heat, he supposed.

The party wouldn't start until evening. Ray imagined his mother shy and awkward, Pop stiff and uncomfortable in a new button-down shirt. *You know we don't like a fuss.* In all their years of marriage, he'd never known them to celebrate an anniversary.

Ray glanced around the room, unchanged since his last visit, the bookcase packed with his science fair trophies, his old Boy Scout manuals—Wolf, Bear, Eagle. Kenny's posters of rock bands and fast cars had disappeared long ago. Ray didn't blame his parents for that. They'd done all they could for Kenny. He had simply worn them down.

In the other bed Evie stirred. "Ray? How long have you been sitting there?"

"Not long." He adjusted the pillows behind his back. "The party was Fran's idea. So that's one mystery solved."

"Fran doesn't know?"

"I doubt it. Kenny never knew."

"How strange." She rolled onto her side, facing him. "The secrecy, I mean. Today nobody gives it a second thought. Single mothers, kids who"—she hesitated—"kids with stepfathers." Ray noticed she avoided using the word *illegitimate*. "It's nothing to be ashamed of."

"I don't know if they're ashamed, exactly," said Ray. "We just never talked about it."

Evie rubbed her belly. "My stomach's in a knot. I think I'll take a bath." She'd been queasy for weeks; she blamed the prenatal vitamins. In two weeks she'd be in the second trimester; then, supposedly, the sickness would pass.

They had never planned on children. *I'm not the Mommy type,* she'd said on their first date. She was thirty then, with her own practice, nieces and nephews she adored. He had taken her to Italy, to Greece; they had learned to scuba dive. To Ray their life seemed full. He'd been stunned when she changed her mind. She didn't want to miss it, she said. To go through her whole life not knowing what it was like.

It's different for you, she said. *You had your boys. You've already had that experience.*

Yeah, he said. *Look how that turned out.*

UPSTAIRS, WATER CLATTERED into the tub; downstairs, Ray waited in the living room for his mother to return. He took a photo from the wall and held it in his lap. Himself and Georgette, dressed for the high school prom, Georgette's arms bare, her red hair teased into a beehive, a corsage of carnations pinned at her waist. At seventeen she was somehow womanly; he, a year older, looked like a kid: slouching, his shoulders thin as a coat hanger in the rented tux. They'd driven to the dance in Pop's truck. Ray wanted to park by the reservoir first, but Georgette refused to mess up her hair. He hadn't yet told her he was leaving. She wouldn't understand it. Coal was booming then, Baker Brothers mining literally day and night, the company so rich it provided a free bus service to transport the men to work. He couldn't tell her that he feared the life unfolding before him: married to the only girl he'd ever laid, living in a company house just like his parents', never seeing any more of the world than the town he was born in. His buddy Steve Marstellar could get him in at Fisher Body, a division of General Motors. Cleveland and its city pleasures, its exotic women, lay before him.

Georgette cried when he told her, begged him to wait until she graduated high school. "It's only a year," she said, but Ray knew what that meant. He'd seen it enough times: guys just ahead of him in school, stuck with a wife and kid before they were twenty. Only Steve Marstellar had escaped.

"I'll come and visit," he promised, and for a while he rode the Greyhound bus to Bakerton every other weekend. (He was saving for a car.) When he returned to Cleveland, Marstellar filled him in on what he'd missed: the ball games (Marstellar, an Indians fan, rarely missed a homer), the girls. Finally Ray grew tired of the bus rides and tired of Georgette, who still dragged him to school dances; who wouldn't drink or smoke; whose idea of a good time was hanging out at Keener's Diner on a Saturday night. Months passed while he worked up the nerve to tell her, and by then it was too late. She was already pregnant.

"Does her dad know?" Pop had asked when Ray told him. They were sitting on the back porch, smoking cigarettes. Pop didn't mind Ray's new habit but advised him to keep it from his mother.

"Not yet. He's going to have a fit."

Pop shrugged. "He'll get over it. Red always liked you. He'll be glad to have you in the family." He leaned forward in his chair. "Talk to the priest before you go. No sense waiting until the last minute."

Ray's face heated; his chest felt tight. "I don't want to talk to the priest."

For a long time Pop said nothing. When he did, it was as if Ray hadn't spoken. "She's a good girl. Everything will work out. But first you have to make it right."

Ray stared at him. For a moment he forgot all about Georgette, the baby she was carrying. It seemed that everything in his life had led to this moment. "Is that what you did? Made it right?"

Pop looked away. At the bottom of the hill, men were waiting for the company bus.

"You were overseas when she got pregnant," Ray said, his heart hammering. "It wasn't even your mistake."

Pop was silent. "I should have told you myself," he said finally. "I guess you figured it out."

Ray said nothing. Inside him, something was bursting. Until that moment he'd still hoped he was wrong.

"Don't say anything to your mother," said Pop. "She's sensitive about it. In those days they blamed it all on the girl. That isn't right."

Ray nodded, his cheeks burning.

"She was just a kid, alone in a big city. She didn't know what she was doing. The fellow took advantage of her."

Who? Ray thought. Who took advantage of her?

"He was nobody," Pop said, as if he'd heard. "Sorry, buddy, but it's the truth. He let her face it all by herself. That's not a man. Not in my book." He looked away, red-faced. "I knew her my whole life, since we were kids. I didn't care what people said. I knew what kind of a person she was." It was, for him, a tremendous speech. He sat back in his chair, as if exhausted by the effort.

"You didn't mind?" said Ray. "All those years, raising someone else's kid?"

"I didn't see it that way. You were my boy, same as Kenny. It was no trouble." Pop rose to go, gathering his things: snuff, dinner bucket, a clean set of miners slung over one arm. That spring he worked Hoot Owl, midnight to eight. "You were a good boy. I didn't mind at all."

They were married at St. Casimir's the first week in June, two days after Georgette's high school graduation. That night they piled her things into the secondhand Ford he'd borrowed from Steve Marstellar, and Ray spent his twentieth birthday driving back to Cleveland.

They rented a tiny apartment in a building downtown, half a mile from the river. That summer, the hottest on record, the Cuyahoga reeked of sewage. Their fourth-floor apartment held the heat like a greenhouse. At night they slept on the fire escape, waiting for a breeze. One Sunday afternoon they filled the bathtub with ice and spent the day there, wrapped around each other like pretzels. Most nights and some mornings, they made love in the narrow Murphy bed; he was crazy for her little belly, her heavy breasts. When he looked back, it amazed him, the constriction of that life; yet at the time he'd been able to breathe. Only later, after they bought the house in Parma, did he begin to suffocate. The split-levels in their subdivision were as alike as Bakerton company houses. His neighbors wanted nothing more from life than they already had: steady work, a new Chevy each year, weekends in front of the television drinking beer and watching ball. It wasn't a bad life, if you considered the alternative. Kenny had been drafted,

Steve Marstellar killed in the battle of Khe Sanh. Ray owed his life to Georgette and the baby, yet he was not grateful. He saw only that the life he'd feared had caught him, that he might as well have stayed in Bakerton after all.

He wondered—his whole life, but in those years especially—about the man who'd fathered him. A city man, he imagined, bred for a different kind of life: fast, complex, constantly changing. He decided that restlessness was in his blood—not a character flaw, as Georgette saw it, but a biological fact like his height, his dark hair; a trait beyond his control. A trait some (not Georgette, but *some*) might call admirable. His restlessness got him off the assembly line and through six years of night school, difficult courses in geochemistry, mineralogy, petrology. By his thirtieth birthday he had a new job, the first college degree in his family, and something even more valuable: an understanding of time. Geologic time, large and long; the patient earth incubating its treasures—diamonds, petroleum, coal. By comparison, his life no longer seemed so static.

Slowly, slowly, things were changing. With the boys in school, Georgette got a beauty operator's license and opened a shop above their garage. In a few years she'd be able to take care of herself; the boys would leave for college, and Ray would go and find his life. He hadn't planned on being laid off or on finding the right job, the Exxon job, just as his unemployment ran out. "I have to take it," he told Georgette, and for once she couldn't argue. They'd pretended at first that she'd join him once the school year ended; or maybe only Ray was pretending.

Until then he'd be on his own in Houston.

At first he'd behaved himself: flew back to Ohio every month to visit, spent evenings in front of the television in his studio apartment. Finally the possibilities overwhelmed him. Women were everywhere. He had money, time, and freedom—at least, the illusion of it. Never before in his life had he possessed all three things at once.

Guilty, he called Georgette daily. Every two weeks he sent money, each paycheck more than he used to earn in a month. For his younger son's birthday, he flew both boys down to Houston and took them to a game at the Astrodome, where Ray Junior had rooted for the visiting team and Bryan spent two hours reading a magazine. At twelve, Ray Junior could still be distracted; Bryan, four years older, could not. "How come you never answer the phone?" he'd asked as they ate breakfast in Ray's apartment. It rang constantly that weekend. Ray had met Evie that spring when she fitted him for reading glasses. They'd been dating on and off for months.

It was Georgette who asked for the divorce. She demanded the house, alimony, child support. Guilty of everything, Ray conceded. She kept the money they'd set aside for the boys' education; what she did with it, he never knew. Neither of his sons was interested in college. Ray Junior studied automotive repair at Lincoln Tech. Bryan went to the same cosmetology school Georgette had attended. For years he'd worked above his parents' garage in Parma, cutting hair alongside his mother.

Neither of his sons had come to the wedding. "No way in hell," Bryan said when Evie invited him. Ray Junior had been more casual: he'd used up his vacation days in hunting season. He and Ray rarely spoke, though Evie sent the boy a card each Christmas and received one in return: *Happy Holidays from Raymond and*

Sherri. The neat handwriting belonged to Ray Junior's girlfriend, a woman Ray had never met.

He replaced the photo on the wall. Below it hung a more recent shot, his grown sons standing before a Christmas tree. Bryan, he noticed with a kind of shock, was balding; a diamond stud twinkled in his right earlobe. Ray Junior wore sideburns and a goatee. The last time Ray had seen him, the kid was barely old enough to shave.

His whole life, he'd believed there were two kinds of men: the kind who'd fathered him and the kind who'd raised him; men who took advantage of their freedom and men who threw it away; men who lived big lives and men who were content being small. For years, living in Parma with his family, he'd believed himself the latter kind, a small man who would never be free. Later—too late—he saw that he had it backward. He wasn't, could never be, like Pop. He was his father's son after all.

HIS MOTHER CAME home from the bake sale loaded down with packages: raisin bread, poppy-seed roll, strawberry-rhubarb pie. "You're looking good," said Ray, watching her bustle around the kitchen, wiping down clean countertops, reheating leftovers for lunch. His mother, sturdy and compact, her white hair freshly set. Except for a few wrinkles at the corners of her eyes, her skin looked tight as a girl's.

"When you're young, they say you're good-looking. At my age, they say you're looking good." She set the table with familiar dishes: dark bread, beet soup, cucumber slices in sour cream. "I can't complain. My sugar's good. Fran took me to get it checked.

Some of those ladies up the church take a dozen pills a day. Me, nothing. I'll live to be a hundred." She set down a steaming platter mounded with pierogies.

"This looks delicious, Florence," Evie said.

The name hung awkwardly in the air. Ray's first wife had called his mother "Mom"; Kenny's wife did the same.

The dishes circulated. Evie talked about the Ovo Café, an elegant bistro in Houston. Recently pierogies had been added to the menu at the astounding price of twenty dollars a plate.

"Twenty *dollars*?" Ray's mother looked down at her plate. "They're nothing but potatoes and flour. You can make a dozen for a quarter." She watched as Evie finished her soup. "You're eating good. Last time I remember you ate like a bird."

"I've gained a few pounds." Evie's eyes met Ray's; for a moment he saw the question in them: Can I tell her?

"Where's Pop?" Ray asked his mother, avoiding Evie's gaze. She'd be disappointed, angry with him for changing the subject, but he couldn't help himself. He wasn't ready for anyone to know.

There was no sensing waiting for Pop, Ray's mother explained. His appetite wasn't what it used to be. "If I don't feed him, he forgets to eat. He's as bad as your brother was."

Ray thought of Kenny as he'd last seen him: gaunt and wizened, his face lined as an old man's. In his final years he weighed less than he had in high school. In Vietnam he'd contracted a parasite from drinking untreated water. The army doctor gave him pills and pronounced him cured, but he couldn't shake the feeling that something was eating him from the inside.

. . . .

HE CAME HOME on furlough in '69, a week of freedom before his second tour of duty. *I re-upped,* he'd written to Ray in a rare letter. *Don't tell Mom.* Ray drove in from Ohio to see him and was surprised by how well he looked: strong, suntanned, somehow feral with his white teeth. By comparison, Ray felt middle-aged, weak, and indoorsy. He was prone to backaches. His hands looked girlishly soft.

For three nights they sat on the back porch, smoking and drinking. Kenny had nothing to say about the war, his life as a soldier. Instead they talked about the past, the childhood that, with their age difference, they hadn't quite shared. Still: there were nuns who'd taught them both in grade school, neighborhood boys they both remembered, pretty girls they'd watched from afar. They talked late into the night. Kenny never seemed to get tired. "Where do you think you're going?" he asked when Ray, bleary-eyed, rose to go to bed.

A year later Kenny came back for good. "He's changed," Ray's mother warned him over the phone. When Ray visited at Christmas, he was stunned at his brother's appearance: hollow-eyed, skeletally thin. He was missing a front tooth—he had a fake one, he said, but couldn't be bothered to wear it. There was no reminiscing during that visit, no late-night drinking. Ray and his family were staying with Georgette's parents, and Kenny spent most of the time in his old bedroom with the door closed. He slept all the time now, Ray's mother whispered. He slept as though he hadn't slept in years.

He was hired in the machine shop at Baker Eleven, a greaser. All night long he lubed the moving parts of shuttle cars. "It's a start," Pop said, though Ray knew he was disappointed. Shop positions were dead-end jobs; the real money was underground. For Kenny, that was precisely the problem. "I can't do that," he told Ray. "Crawling around in caves like a rat. I done enough of that over there." He phoned late on his nights off, drunk usually, and reminisced about his crazy army buddies, the drugs they'd taken, the girls they'd balled, the hell they'd raised. These monologues could last an hour or more. "One more thing," he said again and again, before launching into another tale. He talked so fast that Ray could barely understand him, as though he were running out of time.

He worked Hoot Owl, which suited him; all day he slept in his and Ray's old room. Weekends he dated Fran Wenturine, a girl he'd known in high school. Fran lived with her widowed father, who tended bar at the Legion. The old man was fond of Kenny, would often slip him a free shot of whiskey when Kenny stopped in before work. When the mines slowed, Kenny was switched to day shift; he worked three days a week and closed the Legion the other four. Broke, he sold reefer on the side. Every couple months he drove Fran's car down to Kentucky and came back with a bagful of dense, flavorful skunk, grown by an army buddy on his family's tobacco farm.

By then he'd stopped calling Ray. Married to Fran, he had someone else to listen on those drunken nights when his words ran together in his eagerness to get them out. Ray learned the details of his life thirdhand, from Georgette. Fran called her in a panic a few times a month, when Kenny drank more than usual and scared her with talk of suicide. For years he'd suffered from nightmares; often he walked in his sleep. One night she'd found him on the front porch dead asleep, her father's hunting rifle across his knees. "I have to go," he said when she called his name. "Time for me to go."

Each morning Fran made him breakfast, then left for her job at the A&P. If he was working, she'd drop him off at the mine; if not, she'd leave him sitting at the kitchen table with her father. They'd spend the day there, playing cards and drinking into the afternoon, until the old man left for work at the Legion. Life went on that way for years, until Fran's father found a bag of marijuana stashed in the basement. When she came home from work that night, she found Kenny alone at the table, his left eye bruised where the old man had hit him.

After the Eleven closed, he worked as a roofer, a trash collector, jobs that slipped mysteriously through his fingers. Finally he became a volunteer fireman. The work was good for him, according to Ray's mother; at least it was better than sitting home all day. Fran got pregnant—intentionally or not, Ray never knew. Probably she'd talked to Georgette about it, but by then Ray and his wife were no longer speaking. She had already filed for divorce.

THE BAKERTON VOLUNTEER Fire Company sat at the corner of Baker and Susquehanna, what used to be the busiest streets in town. Years ago, Keener's Diner had been located across the street, flanked by a bowling alley and a pool hall. Weekend evenings, after dances or football games, these places had been crowded with young people. On warm nights the firemen set up folding chairs on the sidewalk and called to the girls walking in pairs or threes down Baker Avenue. In August came the Firemen's Festival, the town overrun by volunteer firemen from neighboring towns, drinking and gaming at the booths set up along Susquehanna. The festival closed with a parade and an open-air dance, musicians crowded onto a platform outside the fire hall: shrieking saxophones, the silvery hiss of a cymbal. Since then the bowling alley had been torn down, the pool hall converted into a Goodwill store. Keener's Diner had become the public library. All along Baker Street, the windows were dark.

That night a light snow was falling. Wind tugged at Ray's coat as he helped Evie out of the car. They went in through the side entrance. The first floor of the hall was for firemen only: garage, equipment room, and in one corner, a dark, smoky barroom known as the Firemen's Club. Once, years ago, Ray had gotten drunk there with his brother. After the mines shut down, Kenny had spent all his time at the hall, smoking and throwing darts while he was on duty, drinking himself unconscious when he was off.

They lingered in the lobby, brushing snow from their shoulders. Evie stood before the glass case in the corner, examining the trophies inside, won in games—tug-of-war, battle of the barrel—at firemen's festivals across Saxon County. Hanging inside the case was a heavy wooden plaque carved with ornate letters: REMEMBER OUR FALLEN HEROES. The plaque was decorated with gold nameplates.

"Did you see this?" Evie asked, pointing.

Ray leaned close, his breath steaming the glass. His brother's name was at the bottom: *Ken Wojick*. No other fireman had died since.

"Come on," he said, taking her hand. "Let's go upstairs."

They climbed the steps to the social floor. The room was decorated all in white: crepe-paper streamers, Kleenex flowers, cardboard cutouts in the shape of wedding bells. A polka band was setting up in a corner; the drummer was a cousin of Pop's. On the back wall, a hand-lettered sign: CONGRATULATIONS FLORKA AND PAUL.

"Go sit down," Ray told Evie. "I'll join you in a minute."

A card table had been set up near the door. Fran stood behind it, filling out name tags with a Magic Marker. Ray studied her a moment: stout, broad-bosomed, dark hair hanging in a braid down her back.

"Hey there," he said, approaching the table.

She looked up and broke into a smile. "J.R."

His stomach dropped. It had been Kenny's nickname for him, a character from an old TV show Ray had never seen, about the crooked dealings of a wealthy oil baron.

"Hi, Franny," he said, embracing her. She was heavier than he remembered, twice as big around as Evie or his mother. Her braid was shot through with gray.

"I'm glad you made it," she said. "Mom and Pop are thrilled."

Ray took the name tag she handed him and stuck it to the lapel of his jacket. "Are you sure it isn't too much for them? All the"—he remembered Pop's word—"excitement."

"Fifty years of marriage, I'd say they could use some excitement. Come on," she said, taking his hand. "You've got to see this."

She led him across the room to a table. At one end sat a pile of gifts; at the other, an elaborate tiered wedding cake. Beside it was a black-and-white photo, slightly out of focus. Ray leaned in to examine it. Pop in uniform, his skinny shoulders squared, a boy trying to look bigger than he was. Balding already, with a wispy blond mustache, the kind teenagers grow to prove themselves. Ray's mother in a simple dress, not white but pale; her face serious, her eyes sad. She was a tiny thing, narrow-waisted. It was hard to believe she'd carried a child.

"It was the only picture I could find," said Fran. "Can you imagine? Married for fifty years and no wedding album."

"Where'd it come from?" Ray had never seen a photo of the wedding; he'd believed none existed.

"Pop's sister gave it to me." She gave his hand a squeeze. "They didn't have a wedding reception. No honeymoon. They just got married, and nobody paid any attention."

Ray looked around the room. There seemed to be hundreds of Kleenex flowers. Fran must have been making them for weeks.

"The place looks great," he said. "You did a hell of a job."

"Thanks, J.R. I wish Kenny was here to see it."

A tickle in his chest, his lungs tightening. He disengaged his hand. "Be right back, Franny. I need to take a breath."

DOWNSTAIRS AT THE Firemen's Club, he ordered a drink. "I'm not a member," he told the bartender, a bearded man with a familiar face.

"That's okay," said the bartender. "I knew your brother."

Ray colored. It was, he realized, the same bartender as last time. A few years ago, when Ray came to town for a high school reunion, Kenny had insisted on taking him for a drink at the club. He'd ordered them each a shot and a beer, and for a moment the bartender had hesitated. He'd asked if Kenny was on duty that night.

"No, I ain't on duty. Are you?" Kenny's voice rising. "If you are, maybe act like a bartender and pour me a shot." He turned to Ray. "It's good to see you, buddy. Don't see much of you anymore."

"I've been busy." It was the wrong thing to say, but Ray had no other answer. "I hired two new pups last week. I spend more time telling them what to do than it would take me to do it myself." He was working for Exxon then, heading a crew of geologists. He told Kenny he was thinking about striking out on his own.

"Good for you, J.R." Kenny downed his shot. Red capillaries bloomed at his cheeks and nostrils. He looks like an old man, Ray thought. An old drunk.

"You did the right thing, getting the hell out. Could be time for me to do the same." The mines weren't coming back, he said. Fran couldn't sell a house with a coal furnace. She had gotten a real estate license, though who'd buy property in Bakerton, Ray couldn't imagine.

Ray chugged his beer. He remembered a time—years ago, during a slowdown—when a group of miners picketed Friedman's Furniture. The store had replaced its coal stove with an oil furnace. It seemed comical now: the miners' sense of injury, their belief that picketing one store would make a difference.

"Where would you go?" Ray asked. "If you left town. Any ideas?"

Years later he would remember his brother's odd smile, close-mouthed to hide his missing tooth. "I hear Texas is nice."

Ray drained his glass. "Times are tough everywhere, Ken. The drilling crews aren't hiring. They're talking about layoffs."

Kenny frowned. "I thought you just hired a couple of guys. A couple of pups."

"Geologists," Ray said, red-faced. "College boys."

The bartender came with two more beers—Iron Cities, what every bar in town poured automatically unless you asked for something different. Ray took out his wallet.

"I got it." Kenny scrabbled in his pocket and laid a crumpled bill on the counter. "I may not be good for much, but goddamn if I can't still get my big brother drunk."

Later—climbing the hill to his brother's house, with Kenny leaning on him like deadweight—Ray would regret that moment, the way he'd reached for his wallet. "I'm sorry, Ken," he said, but by then his brother was barely conscious. Only later, when Ray laid him out on the couch, did he speak.

"That's okay, J.R. Ain't your fault."

AFTER DINNER FRAN pulled up a chair next to Ray. "Hi, stranger. You used to come around a lot more before you struck it rich."

He glanced uncomfortably across the room. Evie was making the rounds with a coffeepot, an apron wrapped twice around her small waist.

"I don't blame you," Fran continued. "It must be boring for Evie. God knows there isn't much to do in this town. But maybe you could come by yourself once in a while. Mom could use the company."

"It's not Evie. She loves coming here. It's me." The words came out too fast. "I can't look anybody in the eye. Mom. Pop. You."

"Me?"

"I could have done something for Kenny after he got laid off."

His heart hammered. Across the room the band was tuning up. The sound seemed very far away.

"That's crazy. There's nothing you could have done."

"I could have found him a job." Tightness in his chest. "Then he wouldn't have been fighting fires. He'd still be alive."

"A job?" said Fran. "Around here?"

"In Houston."

Fran snorted. "Are you kidding? Kenny never would have gone to Houston. Where would you get an idea like that?"

"He asked me about it," said Ray. "The last time I was home. I made excuses, but really, I didn't want him down there. His troubles." He met her eyes. "If I gave him a job, he would've come. He said so."

"Kenny said a lot of things. Believe me, I heard it all. But nobody made him stay here. He stayed because he wanted to."

Ray thought of Kenny as he'd last seen him, shoveling the sidewalk on Dixon Road in his old hunting jacket, a lit cigarette dangling from his mouth. *Don't be a stranger,* he'd called as Ray pulled away from the curb.

"He loved being a fireman," said Fran. "It made him feel alive. He said it was like being a soldier again."

Ray nodded, remembering how Kenny had shown him around the equipment room. How proud he'd been. Ray imagined him suited up in the asbestos pants, the yellow jacket, climbing the stairs of the Commercial Hotel. The fire had started in the kitchen but appeared contained. When Kenny charged into a second-floor bedroom, the floor had crumbled beneath him.

"The night of the fire," Ray said. "Was he drinking?"

"He was always drinking." Fran took his hand in both of hers.

"J.R., sooner or later you have to let go of things. Stop feeling bad about what you can't undo."

Her hands felt cool; for a moment Ray wished he could put them on his face, his cheeks burning with shame.

"I'm not just talking about Kenny. When's the last time you saw your boys?"

"I was hoping they'd be here tonight, but I guess they heard I was coming. Years, Franny. It's been years." He met her eyes. "Do you ever see them?"

"Well, sure. Ray Junior came with Georgette at Christmas. And Bryan comes every few months to give Mom her permanent."

"You're kidding." Ray thought of the boy in the photo—a man now, with his diamond earring, his thinning hair. "He drives all the way out here—two hundred goddamn miles—to do Mom's hair?"

"He's done it for years. He's a sweet kid, Ray. He turned out fine."

"Jesus." Ray lowered his voice. "You know, I still can't believe it. My son, a beautician. For Christ's sake."

"You sound just like Pop. 'What's a big boy like that doing in a beauty shop?'" She laughed. "He makes a good living. And there're worse jobs. He's not going to get himself killed giving permanents."

Ray laughed, too. Air filled his lungs; for the first time in hours, his chest relaxed. "I failed them," he said. "Just like I failed Kenny. And Mom and Pop. I'm not much of a son."

"You're not dead yet."

"I have news," he said. "Evie's pregnant."

Her eyes widened. "Oh, J.R. That's wonderful."

Yes, he thought, it is a wonder. His life, he knew, had been unfairly blessed. Over and over he'd been saved from what he was born to: fatherlessness in a time when that meant something. The mines. Vietnam and whatever horrors had followed Kenny back from that place. He was saved first by Pop, then by Georgette; deliverance he'd neither asked for nor deserved nor recognized when it came. Now, again, he was being saved.

"I thought I was done with all that," he said. "After I flunked the first time."

Fran shrugged. "That's what flunked means. You do it over, whether you like it or not."

"You don't think I'm too old, do you?"

She considered this. "No," she said slowly. "I'd say you're finally old enough."

CAKE WAS SERVED; the music started. "Here we go," Ray told Evie. He'd been exposed to polkas periodically throughout his childhood— at church festivals, at family weddings—and had built up a tolerance for the bad singing and dimwitted lyrics, the relentless accordions and shrill clarinets. Evie had no idea what she was in for. A couple hours of this, he thought, and she's going to lose her mind.

The singer stepped up to the mike and said something in Polish. Then in English—in the same flat, tuneless tenor as every polka singer Ray had ever heard—he sang.

Enjoy yourself, enjoy yourself.
It's later than you think.

Two by two the guests got up to dance: relatives and neighbors, Pop's union buddies, elderly couples Ray recognized from St. Casimir's. He hadn't seen these people in years. Their broad Slavic faces had aged little; only their bodies had changed. The women were stout or stooped and frail; the men moved stiffly, leaning on their wives. They suffered from miner's knee, miner's hip, miner's back; in everyday life they walked with canes; but somehow—only God knew how—they were getting up to dance.

Enjoy yourself, enjoy yourself.
It's later than you think.

The floor filled with couples. The singer whooped into the microphone. Pop's cousin Joe, eighty that spring, tapped gamely at the drums.

"Look," Evie said, pointing.

Ray watched his mother and father join the dancers. Pop quick despite his bad knee, arthritis in his hips; Mom almost girlish in her flowered dress. The other couples stepped back to clear their path, and in a moment they were the only dancers on the floor. The singer said something in Polish, and the crowd responded, clapping in time with the music. Mom and Pop whirled around the floor. Her white curls bounced; her round face was flushed with pleasure.

"She looks beautiful," said Evie, and it was true. His mother who'd lost her first love and married her second, surrendered her good name in a town where nothing was forgotten. She had been hurt; undoubtedly she had regrets. Still she got up to dance.

RAY AND EVIE rose early Sunday morning. Bells rang in the distance, the eight o'clock Mass at St. Casimir's. The air smelled of wet earth, an early spring. Ray hoisted their suitcases to his shoulder. Arm in arm, Evie and his mother followed him outside.

"Thanks for everything," said Ray, kissing his mother's cheek. He touched her white curls and thought of Bryan driving in from Cleveland with his hairpins and rollers. His good son.

Ray loaded the luggage into the rental car.

"Need a hand there?" Pop leaned against the porch railing, wearing Kenny's old hunting jacket.

"Nah, I got it."

"Safe trip," Pop said, offering his hand. "Don't be a stranger."

Ray turned the Ford in the narrow road, scattering gravel; he honked and waved. The town disappeared behind them in the rear-view mirror: Dixon Road; the fire hall; the dirt lane behind the high school, where Pop had taught him to drive; Holy Roller Hill, where he and Kenny had raced their sleds. He passed the turnoff to the deserted road behind the reservoir, where he and Georgette had parked late at night, where his son Bryan had been conceived. At the edge of town he passed McNulty's service station, its concrete wall painted with bold letters: TOUGH TIMES NEVER LAST. TOUGH PEOPLE DO. He reached for Evie's hand, and she placed his on her belly. I'll do better this time, he thought. I'm not dead yet. They would land in Houston at dusk and drive into the city for dinner, to a new Thai place that had opened downtown. The streets would be quiet on a Sunday night, resting for the week ahead. But Monday morning they would come alive, and Ray with them; himself still new, and still becoming.

WHAT REMAINS

At the northern tip of Bakerton, along the winding country
road called Deer Run, lies a sloping parcel of land once cleared
for farming. A century ago, a family named Hoeffer owned it, got
rich on corn and soybeans and—briefly, during war rationing—
even coal, after Quentin Hoeffer found a shallow bed in his back
forty and took a pick and shovel to it. Then Hoeffer's son-in-law,
no farmer, tried his hand at raising sheep, with disastrous consequences. Saxon Savings repossessed the property and let the place
go to seed.

By the time Sunny Baker bought it in the 1970s, the Hoeffer
farm had lain dormant for a full generation, and a young forest
had taken root: fast-growing paper birches and Norway spruce; a
spongy ground cover of aggressive kudzu; in the deep shade, soft
pockets of fern. She lived in the old farmhouse barely visible from
the road, surrounded by what resembled, from a distance, a dense
jungle of metal and plastic. Passersby on Deer Run could pick out
two junk cars, several old refrigerators, a decrepit lawn tractor, a
busted generator, a ramshackle aluminum shed. A child's swing set,

an old Victrola, a toilet, a motorcycle, a snowmobile, and a rusted dinghy filled with dirt. At the edge of the property, with weeds growing up between them, lay piles of building supplies: ten-foot lengths of PVC piping, a heap of warped two-by-fours. Water-logged parlor furniture—armchairs, a sofa—clustered at the center in a conversational grouping, as though a family might sit there watching television.

Sunny's junk was an eyesore, but for a long time no one was looking. Her nearest neighbor was a dairy farmer a mile down the road. The farmer's wife noted Sunny's comings and goings. Her car, a twelve-year-old Thunderbird, looked much like the others propped up on blocks in the front yard, yet it ran well enough to get her into town a few times a month. In the A&P and the state liquor store, she was instantly recognized by her general dishevel-ment and the jacket she wore regardless of the weather—a plaid hunting coat, red-and-black-checked, left behind years ago by one of her men.

The town, Bakerton, wasn't named for Sunny or even her great-grandfather; but for the coal mines he'd dug in that valley. Mines brought miners, miners built camps. Mining camps multi-plied until someone called them a town.

Bakerton.

Did Sunny hear her own name when the town was mentioned? Or was Bakerton no more than an address, like any other place in the world?

Over the years her junk multiplied, covering a full acre. A horse trailer appeared; rolls of chicken wire; a doghouse. Certain objects were discernibly Sunny's own: a ten-speed bicycle she'd been seen riding, a beautician's sink she'd acquired from her aunt Rosalie, the actress, who'd hired a local hairdresser to keep her in pin curls. Other items—a crib and high chair, a green plastic Inchworm—were presumably connected to Sunny's children, back when she still had them, back before someone—their father or her aunt or the Commonwealth of Pennsylvania—intervened to save them, since they weren't grown enough to run away themselves. But most of the junk was plainly masculine, a rusty scat trail: the unsightly droppings of Sunny's men, who'd met her in one bar or another and figured out who she was, or had been.

The first was a man she'd brought back from Oregon, a hippie type who might have loved her when she was young and less obviously crazy, before she'd drunk away her looks and her health and what Baker money she could wheedle out of her aunt, Virgie Baker having clutched the purse strings even on her deathbed. The hippie had tooled around Bakerton in a dilapidated van, amber-colored, with an iridescent starburst airbrushed on one side. Sunny was pregnant then, her second: the hippie's, probably, though there had been no wedding as far as anyone knew. The new baby, a girl, was seen eventually in town, strapped to the hippie's back like an Indian papoose. After a year or two the hippie disappeared, taking (it was thought) the two babies but leaving behind the beginnings of Sunny's own private salvage yard: the starburst van, a nonfunctioning rototiller. He'd been an enthusiastic gardener, as hippies were.

There had been, locally, some goodwill toward this hippie, seen picnicking at Garman Lake when Sunny was immensely pregnant, helping her up tenderly from the grass. That meant something, the women agreed: if a man loved you at eight months, tired and bitching and big as a bus, he loved you to the very end. Later, though—in the revisionist history of Sunny Baker, the story as it was told after the ending was known—the hippie would be judged more harshly. It was the hippie who'd left the first junk on Sunny's lawn, who'd *pioneered* the leaving of junk, and paved the way for the rest.

SHE WAS THE last of the Bakers: a spoiled lonely girl without siblings, without cousins, raised by two maiden aunts who'd lost everything—one histrionically, the other in silent bitterness—and invested all their hopes in her.

Sunny's great-grandfather Chester Baker had thrown the first shovel; but it was Chester Junior, known as Chessie, who grew the two Baker mines—in a few decades, with the help of two wars—into twelve. Chessie was a mine operator, and only that; the planet, to him, the scene of a cosmic shell game. Its land masses existed for one purpose only, the hiding of bituminous coal. He kept the company name, Baker Brothers, though he'd long been brotherless. (Edgar Baker had been killed at the Somme.) From his youth, Chessie lived only for his mines, a man so single-minded that he'd never once gone to the pictures, never watched a single game played by the Baker Bombers, his company's baseball team.

Yet he found time to marry and raise three children, or at least get them started. There was a clever girl named Virginia, a pretty one named Rosalie. The boy, Chester III, was known in the family as *Third* or simply *The Youngest,* a title shortened in childhood to the tender moniker *Ty.* These names were part of Sunny's childhood, each matched to a framed portrait on the parlor wall of the Baker house on Indian Hill. The house referred to, in town, as *The Mansion,* with audible capitals, and by the Bakers as *the big house* or simply *home.*

For all of Sunny's girlhood, the wall was laden with photographs. Chester and Elias (known as *the Brothers*) posed before Baker One in string ties and muttonchops, the coalman's uniform of the day. There was a stern portrait of her grandfather Chessie, in his vest and round spectacles, and a lovely one of Chessie's lost brother, a slender blond boy in tennis whites. There were the aunts who'd raised her, each captured at the time of her greatest happiness: Virgie in tweed and cashmere, crossing the quadrangle at Wellesley College with her great friend Tess Drew; Rosalie under a velvety layer of Max Factor in a publicity still for *The Edge of the Universe*—the David O. Selznick extravaganza, never released, that was to have made her a star.

At the center of the display—the place of honor, the fulcrum around which the others were balanced—hung a wedding portrait of Sunny's parents. Its mahogany frame had cost a hundred dollars, back when a dollar bought dinner and a hundred could get you a car. The photo was taken in a church in England where the couple had been married. Ty Baker wore his dress uniform, decked with medals; his blond hair waved back from his forehead like the actor Leslie Howard's. Nola, his English bride, was draped in white.

Of these parents—dead before her fifth birthday—Sunny had two memories. The first: sitting at the dressing table in her mother's bedroom, Nola painting her mouth with lipstick (*Hold still, darling*) while demonstrating the proper position, lips puckered for a kiss. The second: Ty and Nola in the foyer of the big house wearing hats and long wool coats, dressed for one of their trips. Sunny had been distraught, overcome with the exhaustion that came when you'd cried so long that you couldn't remember the feeling of not crying. She'd crouched on the staircase, peering through the banister, and shrunk away when her mother bent to kiss her. Nola had protested wearily—*Beatrice Emma, don't be tiresome*—but Sunny wouldn't give in, wouldn't let herself be touched.

Let her sulk, then. Ty Baker nodded curtly and led Nola to the door.

Had it been their final departure, Sunny's last glimpse of her parents? Her whole life, the possibility would haunt her: that she'd been so sulky and unpleasant, they'd been glad to be rid of her; that she'd refused her mother's final embrace on the day their plane went down. The question tore at her. It also made her angry. She felt wrongly judged, the victim of a gross injustice: branded a tantrumming brat when in fact she'd been a jolly child, earning her nickname.

Only Sunny's mother, in an irritable mood, had ever called her Beatrice.

After her parents were gone, she became Poor Sunny. There was no way to make up for all the child had lost, but her aunts did their best. Her girlhood was filled with hugs and kisses, bedtime stories and unexpected treats. There were darling dresses, music lessons, a pony. One Christmas brought dolls from all over the world, dressed in exotic costumes—Balinese princess, geisha, Eskimo. The everyday gifts were, in a way, even more extravagant: the full attention of two grown women with nothing else to live for, who spent their days dreaming up entertainments for her. Like three little girls, they hunched over dolls and jacks, Parcheesi and checkers and Saturday-morning cartoons. Summer brought picnics and croquet and rides on horseback—with both aunts, when Rosalie was still able, and later with Virgie alone.

At fourteen Sunny was sent, as her aunts had been, to Miss Porter's in Connecticut, an endless train ride. She was an excellent student, well rounded and popular; a thoroughly well-adjusted girl, until she wasn't. Halfway through her final year at Miss Porter's, a nurse was sent by train to bring her back to Bakerton, the first of many such rescues. In later years nurses would be dispatched to New York; to Atlantic City; to Berkeley, California. Each time the mission was the same, to calm and cajole and, if necessary, sedate her; whatever was necessary to bring the last Baker home.

THE MEN TOOK the long way out of town, with Dick Devlin— president of the Bakerton Borough Council, owner of the reopened Commercial Hotel—at the wheel. Beside him sat Chuck Helsel, a bigwig with the Pennsylvania Department of Corrections; in the backseat, Dominic Nudo of Nudo Construction, the state's contractor. They looked uncertainly out the window as the Jeep roared up the hill, its old engine straining.

"Man, these Jeeps are something," Nudo said.

"I'll say." Helsel shifted in his seat. "I drove one in the army. I swore never again."

Dick kept quiet. His new son-in-law drove a Land Rover made by Mitsubishi. Matt claimed they were all over the roads in Maryland, where he and Katie lived. Dick had driven it once and was impressed by the smooth ride but couldn't bring himself to buy one. A lifetime ago, after high school, he'd spent three years on an assembly line for Fisher Body, making chassis for Chevys. He bought American. He was, he knew, a dying breed.

"Wears like a tank, though," he pointed out.

"Rides like one, too," Helsel said.

It was a false spring day in March. Garman Road—a rocky trail marked out with red dog—was sloppy with snowmelt. Rust-colored mud spattered the Jeep's winter tires.

"Not much of a road, is it? Hard on the vehicle." Helsel was big and blond, a former police officer or maybe a prison guard. Dick could spot the type a mile away—the sort of man who drove his *vehicle* to his *residence;* who lived his whole life in the language of cops.

Dick gave his politician's smile. "Won't be bad in summer. If it ever comes." The weather, a safe topic. "I guess the little bastard saw his shadow."

Helsel frowned. "Does that mean spring or more winter? I can never remember."

"More winter," Dick said. Punxsutawney was just fifty miles away; as a boy of ten, he'd been taken to see the groundhog come out of its hole. He'd expected a silent snowy forest, the creature, driven by some ancient instinct, popping furtively from the ground. The reality—the noisy crowd, the stunned rodent tossed out in front of a throng of cameras—depressed and perplexed him. Why go through the motions if everyone knew it was a sham?

As an adult, he understood the reasons. Punxsutawney—like

Bakerton, like the entire western half of Pennsylvania—was down on its luck, its population dwindling, its mines and mills closed. All of Punxsy's businesses, in fact, were struggling. (Dick's own restaurant was outfitted with secondhand ductwork from a failed Punxsy diner. He'd saved himself a bundle there.) But for a few days each February, every motel in Punxsutawney was booked; at the Mobil station, a dozen rental cars idled in line. The TV crews bought breakfasts and newspapers, coffee and cigarettes. When Groundhog Day coincided with a lake-effect snowstorm, the local True Value sold out of ice scrapers and rock salt. It was no replacement for real industry, the union jobs that once supported local families. But a few days each year, the groundhog nonsense attracted national attention, a chance for Punxsy to trumpet its other virtues: low cost of living, tax breaks for new business, a heartbreakingly eager workforce. For Bakerton there was no TV coverage, no famous rodent, but Dick trusted in the resiliency of the American economy. He believed—he had to—that deliverance would come.

At the top of the hill, he parked. The proposed site was fifty acres, half covered with forest. The land was bordered to the north and east by pastures belonging to Dickey's Dairy. The owners—the former Marcia Dickey and her husband—had promised their support.

"And to the west?" Helsel asked.

"A private landowner," Dick said. He charged ahead, preempting further questions. Water and sewage would be handled by the borough, the roads serviced in winter by Carbon Township. The township owned just three plows but would gladly buy another, to be used solely on the roads around the new prison.

"We'd need to get that in writing," said Helsel.

"No problem," Dick said.

They piled back into the Jeep. "I'm not thrilled about this road," said Helsel.

"We could have it paved inside a week."

"Still, it's pretty narrow. All these sharp curves."

Nudo looked up from the topo map in his lap. "Looks like there's a more direct way back to town. What's Deer Run?"

"An old mining road," said Dick. "Needs some patching."

"Is it paved?"

Dick nodded.

"Let's take it," Helsel said.

LATER, BACK AT the Commercial, Dick's wife brought out their lunches: burgers for Dick and Nudo; a chef's salad for Helsel, who'd had one coronary and was watching his weight.

"Geez Louise," said Nudo. "That was some spread. I've never seen anything like it."

"It's a mess," Dick agreed.

"You never tried to make her clean it up? Send an officer out to the residence?" Helsel salted his salad. "I'm surprised the neighbors haven't complained."

"There aren't any neighbors. I think that's why she bought the place."

"What's the matter with her? A woman, especially. She must be crazy to live that way."

"She's had her troubles." It was known in town that Sunny Baker had spent time in Torrance and, later, a private mental hospital. Though what had precipitated these stays, the exact nature of her affliction, no one could say.

"How long has she lived out there?" Nudo asked.

"Twenty years. Maybe longer."

Helsel clicked his tongue disapprovingly. "I'm surprised you let it go on that long."

For Pete's sake, Dick thought, who's she hurting? It's her own business if she wants to live like a pig.

"We can't be running a state facility next door to *that*."

It's a prison, Dick thought.

"I don't think the inmates are going to complain," he joked.

Helsel did not smile. "Well, we can't have the COs driving past that every day to work."

"Of course not. She'll clean it up, of course."

"She'll have to," Helsel said.

THE BAKERTON BOROUGH Council met the first Monday of each month. A century ago they'd been called the Town Bosses, eight men handpicked by the Brothers themselves. (All of Bakerton, in those days, spoke the language of mining, in which every sort of authority was conveyed by the title *Boss*.) Under Chessie Baker, the system was codified, the Bosses duly elected. But by then the town was full of immigrants who viewed voting with suspicion. The voting minority—English-speaking males—chose people like themselves, the same Bosses Chessie himself might have picked.

In the spring of 2000 the council included two women, a fact that would have shocked Chessie. Neither would he have chosen Leonard Stusick, the town doctor, with his foreign-sounding name. Davis Eickmeier, who'd taken over Dickey's Dairy after marrying Marcia Dickey, was at least a businessman, though his surname, too, was troublesome. (Chessie's brother had been killed by Germans.) The other councilmen were even more objectionable. Leo Quinn was a barman, naturally. (In Chessie's view, the Irish were constitutionally alcoholic.) Eleanor Rouse wore trousers. The undertaker, cop, and beautician were all Italian. To Chessie, it was nearly the same as being black.

The council met in a conference room at Saxon Savings and Loan, by long tradition: in Chessie's day, the Bosses also meted out the mine's payroll, and it was deemed safest simply to meet at the bank. Ruth Rizzo, the beautician, read the minutes. So little had happened at the last meeting that her report lasted, in fact, just a minute.

"That's it?" Dick asked when she'd finished.

Ruth nodded.

"Well, then. On to new business. I've been in touch with the Department of Corrections." He paused, savoring the moment. Like his father—a long-standing president of the Mine Workers' local—he was a natural public speaker, happiest in front of an audience. "We took a walk of the proposed site. They had some questions about snow removal, which I answered. Also, they want Garman Road paved."

"Hang on there," said Davis Eickmeier, the dairy farmer. A famously slow talker, he needed a moment to formulate his question. "How come you took them up Garman? Deer Run goes right to the highway."

It was the first night of baseball season, Cleveland at Baltimore. Jerry Bernardi, the undertaker, looked at his watch.

"They figured that out eventually." Dick hesitated. "They got a good look at Sunny Baker's."

"Oh, dear," said Eleanor Rouse, the school nurse.

"I tried taking them the back way, but they smelled a rat."

"Well," said Eleanor, "it was worth a try."

"For the love of Mike," said Leo Quinn. "They're *prisoners*. What are they going to do, stage a walkout?"

A few titters around the table, a shudder of mirth. Leo Quinn was a comedian the way Dick Devlin was a politician, by temperament and by blood. His physiology, even, seemed engineered for it: the broad pliable face, the twinkling blue eyes.

Dick shrugged. "It's the guards, I guess. The DOC doesn't want them to drive past a dump on their way to work."

"They have a point," said Ruth Rizzo.

"They don't, either, Ruth, and you know it." Eickmeier sat back, arms crossed. He was known to be country-stubborn. "I drive past it every day, and it hasn't hurt me any. Hell, I don't give a care."

"How did you leave it with them?" asked Dr. Stusick, who could summarize a half hour's worth of blather in a single terse sentence. This habit irked Dick Devlin, with his love of oratory, though no one else seemed to mind.

"I said we'd make her clean it up."

A silence fell. Leo Quinn chuckled in disbelief. Ruth Rizzo put down her pen.

"*We* will, will we?" said Leo, grinning broadly.

Dick ignored the satiric tone. "Someone will have to talk to Miss Baker."

"Well, good luck with that." Davis Eickmeier reached into his pocket for a tin of Skoal. Eleanor Rouse grimaced with distaste. "She's been my neighbor twenty-five years," he said slowly, his lip packed with snuff. "And I can count on one hand the times I've seen her come out of that house."

Another silence.

"Anyone?" Dick glanced around the room, appealing for help. "Jerry?"

"I got nothing to offer here," said Jerry, who was missing the game.

"The Bakers have always kept to themselves," Ruth observed.

The council remembered, all at once, Ruth's special connection to the Baker family. Even in her old age, Rosalie Baker had kept up appearances. For many years she'd had a standing appointment on Monday morning, Ruth reporting to The Mansion by a back door to do Miss Baker's wash and set.

"I was hoping *you* could talk to her, Ruth," Dick said.

"Oh, I couldn't. What on earth would I say?"

There were nods of agreement. It wasn't just a question of approaching a Baker, any Baker (let alone Sunny, who was known to be cursed). It would have made for awkward conversation between *any* neighbors: *Your yard is a pigsty. Even rapists and murderers refuse to live beside it.*

"It's private property!" Davis Eickmeier nearly shouted.

The council started. Davis never raised his voice.

He spat deliberately into a coffee mug he'd brought for the purpose. "Now, I don't like looking at all that junk. I don't guess

Miss Baker likes smelling my cows, either, but in twenty-five years I haven't heard a peep out of her. To me, that's a good neighbor."

There was a murmur of agreement.

"You've got to be joking," Andy Carnicella said.

Seven heads turned in his direction. He was the town cop, known all over Saxon County as Chief Carnicella, despite having no Indians. (The borough's budget provided for a police force of one.) The youngest council member by twenty years, he'd been silent for the entire meeting. Dick had forgotten he was there.

The chief leaned back from the conference table. He had a habit of rocking in his chair, like a restless schoolboy. "I can take the cruiser out there tomorrow. Write her a citation, if I have to. Should of done it years ago, if you ask me."

Ruth Rizzo looked aghast.

"I'm not sure that's a good idea," said Dick.

"Come off it, Dick. I don't know what you're all afraid of. To me, she's just an old crazy lady. A crazy old drunk."

"Andy, that's enough," Dick said.

There was silence.

"Miss Baker has had her problems. We all know it." Dick took his time, pleased to have regained the floor. "And it might not be so good for her to have a police car show up in her front yard with the lights flashing. I'm no expert, though." He nodded toward Dr. Stusick. "Len, what do you think?"

LATER, THE MEETING adjourned, Dick led Dr. Stusick across the street to the Commercial. The dining room was closed, Dick's wife vacuuming the carpet. He ducked behind the bar for a bottle and glasses, as nervous as a schoolboy on a date.

The two men had never raised a glass together. They had nothing against each other personally, but their fathers had been mortal enemies. For nearly twenty years, Regis Devlin had been president of the Mine Workers' local—a position he'd expected to die in and likely would have, if Eugene Stusick hadn't run a dirty campaign against him. Stusick's platform had been simple and vicious: Devlin was in bed with management, making backdoor deals with Baker and leaving his men out in the cold. It was an easy charge to make and a hard one to refute. Stusick appealed to the men's greed and paranoia and won by a healthy margin. Regis Devlin—for thirty years a celebrity in town, more powerful than ten mayors—never recovered from the humiliation. He died a drunk, bitter and broken, while Gene Stusick succumbed even more horribly, crushed in the famous collapse at Baker Twelve. Anyone would say their sons had good reason to avoid each other. Any conversation between a Devlin and a Stusick could only lead to ruin.

Dick poured the doctor a whiskey, himself a club soda. Mindful of his father's end, he went easy on the sauce. "We need to get a handle on this, pronto. Carnicella's a hothead. I'm afraid of what he'll do."

"Could be trouble," the doctor agreed. "None for you?"

"Next round, maybe."

They clinked glasses.

"The thing is, I have nothing against Sunny Baker, or any of them. Old Chessie wasn't a bad guy, my dad said. They did some drinking together. I guess you heard."

This was dangerous territory—his father's alleged chumminess with Baker. But Rege and Gene were long dead, their sons old men. Baker Brothers, the Mine Workers, and the whole mining industry were relics of another century, never to return.

The doctor grinned. "I've never seen Davis Eickmeier so worked up."

"I thought he was going to swallow his snuff." Dick splashed whiskey into his glass. "He's right, though. It's her property, and I don't like the idea of poking in her business. And yet—"

"The prison," the doctor said.

"Goddamn if we don't need those jobs."

They drank in silent agreement. Nudo Construction, though based in Harrisburg, would use local subcontractors: electricians, plumbers. The prison would hire sixty full-time corrections officers and nearly that many janitors, secretaries, and cooks.

"Not union. Not like our dads had," Dick admitted. "But no one in their right mind thinks those are coming back."

The doctor nodded. Even after a drink, he was a man of few words, a trait that made Dick talk too much.

"Hell, I wouldn't mind one of them for Richie," he continued. His oldest son—the only one who'd stayed in town—earned minimum wage driving a truck for Miners Medical, delivering oxygen tanks. It wasn't much of a job.

"I worry about his generation. We all want to keep our kids around, but . . ." He trailed off, remembering that Len had no children. "My point is, we need that prison. It seems crazy to lose it because one lady won't clean up her yard."

. . . .

LEO QUINN SHUT off the ball game. He had never been a Cleveland fan—the Pirates were his team—and loyalty, like drink, was essential to the spectator's enjoyment. Watching baseball without benefit of either, he found himself agreeing with what his wife had said for years. It was, essentially, a slow and tedious game.

He'd left the council meeting in a dark mood, not even bothering to needle Dick Devlin about the late hour. In truth, he hadn't had the heart to: the old windbag had seemed as dejected as everyone else. The discussion of Sunny Baker had cast a pall over the room. Andy Carnicella's outburst, the way he'd resorted to name-calling, was a shameful lapse of civility, beneath his dignity as an officer of the law. Leo forgave him, a little. Rash judgment was a young man's sin. He'd been guilty of it himself years ago—free with his opinions, worked up about Communists and so forth. It had taken him sixty years to understand that compassion was the only virtue. He'd been raised to count faith, hope, and charity, but the years had eroded his confidence in the first two: his Mary was the true believer, and hope seemed foolish at his age, when life was all over but the singing. That left only charity, to the suffering especially. And who had suffered more than Sunny Baker?

Not that Leo knew her personally. Nobody did. But he'd run a tavern for thirty years. If he were a different sort of person, he could have told tales on half the town.

After her hippie boyfriend vanished, Sunny had lived alone for many years. Men came and went from the farmhouse at odd hours, according to Davis Eickmeier's wife; but who they were or what became of them, no one could say. Then out of nowhere, a rumor blossomed: Sunny had taken up with a local, or a near-local. Her new man came from Erie, a few counties to the north. His pickup was seen parked on Deer Run, its bed loaded with lumber. Sunny had hired him to work on her house. The pickup, a battered Ford with Pennsylvania plates, won the town's warm approval—a workingman's truck, the exact same model a Bakerton guy might drive.

The new man's name was Judd Crombie. Unlike Sunny and her famous family, he seemed at home in the town. On Monday nights he brought her to Quinn's, where they could get comfortable at a dim corner table and close the place, running up a steep tab. They were night owls, and why not? Sunny's kids were gone by then—off with their hippie father, some said, or with some distant Baker relative. (Were there Baker relatives? Or had the whole clan died off as this local branch had, its final fruit, Sunny herself, plump and dangling from the vine?)

Her plumpness was a new development, unusual in a Baker. Her aunt Rosalie, the actress, had been famous for her tiny waist, and even in her old age, Virgie was thin as a whip. The whole clan seemed congenitally slender, the men included, and certainly any women they deigned to marry. Sunny's mother, the English war bride, had a lovely figure, though few could claim to have seen her in person. Old-timers remembered the wedding portrait reproduced in the *Herald:* Ty Baker dashing in uniform, the beautiful Nola extravagantly gowned.

Sunny herself had been a slip of a girl, until Judd Crombie roared into her life.

The town agreed later that Crombie had been her downfall. True, the hippie had impregnated her twice, *out of wedlock*—a phrase still used in Bakerton without irony—and left a decrepit bus on her front lawn. But Judd Crombie had done her a greater disservice. It was Judd Crombie who taught her to drink.

Leo Quinn had been present at her ruination—had even, it could be said, facilitated her downfall. That first night at his bar, Sunny had ordered a glass of wine. (Bakerton women snorted at this detail, but the men found it touching: it made Sunny seem somehow virginal, despite the births out of wedlock; too innocent to order a real drink.) Leo tore apart his stockroom looking for a bottle but came up empty. Miss Baker thanked him for his trouble and asked for a Pepsi until Crombie interrupted: *She'll have a whiskey and soda.* Later she drank a second, and in the end Crombie half-carried her to his pickup, shamelessly paying the tab from her purse.

From that night onward, they drank often at Quinn's. Crombie, the working man, seemed on permanent vacation: Sunny's farmhouse was still falling to pieces, though his truck was parked there seven days a week. Their weekly tabs grew steeper. Soon Sunny— once so hammered on two whiskeys that she could barely walk— matched Crombie drink for drink. As women did, she wore it badly: her face round as a pie plate, her potbelly high and hard as a man's.

At first their Monday nights were gay and flirtatious. Sunny's laugh was never loud or ugly, never a drunk's laugh. After paying the tab, she left arm in arm with Crombie, her hand in his back pocket a kind of sight gag, as though she knew and didn't care what everyone said, that his hand was always in hers. Later they stopped flirting and started arguing, softly at first. More than once, Leo Quinn brought a fresh round and saw Sunny crying, silent tears streaming down her cheeks.

One Friday night in the spring of 1984—a date remembered

for obvious reasons, the town drinking away its sorrows—Crombie came into Quinn's alone. He sat at the bar like anyone else, drinking Iron Cities instead of whiskey—a frugal choice, with no rich girl-friend to pick up the tab. He chatted briefly with Leo: the game on television, the rising cost of fishing licenses. Sunny's name was not mentioned, Crombie sensing, probably, that it would be a breach. That the Bakers, while not exactly beloved, belonged to the town in a way no one else did, just as the town had once belonged to them.

For an hour or two he sat alone at the bar, until Barb Vance sat down beside him.

She was a local girl, a tough, skinny blonde with full-body freckles and a tiny heart tattooed on one shoulder. At the time in Bakerton, tattooed women were a rarity, and naturally Crombie noticed. Barb was freshly divorced then—her second—with a knockout figure she didn't mind showing.

Sunny had turned forty that year, her birth enough of a local event that the town would never lose track of her age.

Crombie and Barb left separately that night, an hour apart, but the next Friday they met again at the bar. A local band, Reagan Cheese, had a standing Friday gig at Quinn's, but the two did not dance. Instead they rose periodically to shoot pool, Crombie standing close behind her to point out the sight lines, arms around her to steady her cue.

He had his defenders. They pointed out that Sunny was a drunk, a repeat customer at the state mental hospital, a woman so unstable or incompetent that someone else was raising her kids. Others blamed Crombie for her troubles. No one had *forced* him to quit his job and subsist on what was left of the Baker wealth,

charging groceries and liquor to Sunny's credit card. He was making a fool of her with Barb Vance, and somebody ought to tell her.
Of course, no one did. Sunny's phone number, if she had one, was
unlisted. Anyway, who would have the nerve?

She had always been a recluse. And recent events had isolated
her further, clipped the delicate filaments connecting her to the
town. That winter Baker Eleven had closed, the largest Baker mine
and the most productive. The official explanation, reported the *Herald,* was predictable: the Eleven was mined out, its coal depleted.
The official explanation was crap. According to men who worked
there—Mitch Stanek, Lou Berks—there was plenty of coal down
deep, if Baker would spend the money to get it. New equipment
was needed, an investment of capital. But Baker Brothers had never
recovered from the disaster at the Twelve. The company had lost a
fortune, and lost its nerve.

Suddenly nine hundred men were out of work, nine hundred
families living on food stamps. In the school cafeteria at Jefferson Elementary, the free lunches outnumbered the paid ones. On
Saturday mornings at the American Legion, the line extended
out the door and around the block. Men who'd recently earned a
union wage stood waiting for free food, the humiliating block of
government-surplus cheese.

What did any of this have to do with Sunny Baker? Nothing,
maybe: her legal relationship to Baker Brothers was not known.
Her aunt Virgie had, until her death, sat on Baker's board of direc-
tors, which met quarterly somewhere in Pittsburgh. The meetings, summed up in a single dry paragraph in the *Bakerton Herald,*
attracted little notice. (Though in those years, with the town glued

to the TV for *Dallas* and *Dynasty*, board meetings came to seem glamorous, full of conniving rich women in power suits, showing décolletage.) Now, with Baker in real trouble, its board meetings had ominous consequences. Was Sunny sitting at the table where the decision was made, nine hundred men put out of work? Was it guilt that accelerated her drinking, driving her further into seclusion? Or had she simply guessed the truth about Judd Crombie?

That summer Crombie's pickup roared out of town, leaving behind a crashed motorcycle, a busted table saw, an old Plymouth he'd been meaning to work on. A new generation of junk took root on Sunny's lawn.

IT WAS NEARLY midnight when Dr. Stusick pulled into his driveway. The house was dark, an oversight. Usually he remembered to leave a light on. He'd been widowed a year and had adjusted to his aloneness, yet somehow the dark windows returned him to a state of fresh bereavement. He'd rather spend the evening at home alone than drive up to an empty house.

Inside, he poured himself a second whiskey, though what he really wanted, really wanted, was a Halcion. Without it, sleep was unlikely. The conversation with Dick Devlin had set his mind churning. Even a third whiskey wouldn't make it stop.

His father and Dick's, the famous grudge that had outlived them.

The idiot police chief.

Miss Baker has had her troubles.

A police cruiser tearing down Deer Run, sirens blaring, to the ramshackle farmhouse where Sunny Baker lived.

It was a well-kept secret in a town that believed it had none: years ago, in the early seventies, a much younger Sunny Baker had been Len's patient. He'd been leaving the hospital one night when Virgie Baker approached him in the parking lot. Though they had never met, he recognized her immediately—a tall, lean woman with an equine face, her gray hair cut short as a nun's. Her niece was suffering a depressive episode, she explained. She needed medical attention but refused to leave her room.

Len followed her back to The Mansion, where Sunny was holed up in a dark bedroom—a slender blond girl, younger than Len, lovely despite her greasy hair and unwashed face. He found her stubbornly mute, unresponsive. When Len introduced himself, she turned her face to the wall.

Later, over coffee, Virgie Baker explained the particulars. Her niece had been volatile since childhood, prone to crying fits, tantrums, rages. In adulthood the problem had worsened. When Sunny was happy, her exhilaration was boundless. At other times, despair swallowed her like a sinkhole. To the Baker family, both extremes were alarming. In both states, calamities occurred.

Naturally she'd seen doctors. Medications had been prescribed. Unmedicated, Sunny swept through life like weather: arrests for shoplifting and vandalism, for public intoxication, a situation with fireworks in Atlantic City, Virgie never got the details. There were car accidents in New York and Philadelphia and Berkeley, California— years ago, when Sunny was still allowed to drive. Finally a doctor in San Francisco had prescribed lithium, and for several months Virgie received polite, coherent letters in Sunny's handwriting. Then, abruptly, the letters stopped. From long experience, Virgie awaited the telegram, the late-night phone call—this time from a hotel manager in New York City, where Sunny had been living. She'd been taken by ambulance to Lenox Hill Hospital, for reasons unclear.

The reasons, it turned out, were the usual ones. Sometimes drugs were involved, sometimes drink. Sunny had complained for years that a stranger was following her. Occasionally she heard voices. She had never recovered from the loss of her parents. In Virgie's estimation, she had always been a troubled girl.

Len saw her twice that spring and again a few years later. Each time the girl was nearly catatonic. Twice Virgie had her committed to hospitals in Pittsburgh. In between, Sunny fled like an exotic bird bound for milder climes. When, exactly, had she stopped flying? What made her retreat to the decrepit farmhouse at the far edge of town, her wrecked life piled up around her?

What he wanted, really wanted, was a Halcion.

DEER RUN WAS a piecrust road, crumbling in places. That morning—cloudless, the trees bare—Len could see for miles. From the high ridge he had a clear view of the old Baker Twelve, the mine where his father had died. After the accident, the investigation and hearings, the tipple had been cleared away. Forty years later the valley was filled with clover.

Nature was willful, patient. Over time it always had its way. In Africa this had seemed a curse. Irrigation, road building, the earnest industry of the missionaries: untold months of human busyness could be wiped out overnight in a storm. He had spent three years there on a church-sponsored mission to Madagascar, his wife's idea—except for nursing school in Pittsburgh, Lucy had lived her whole life in Bakerton; and was restless. Len had needed little convincing. They were young then, and the great world beckoned. They were young.

Their clinic was a small one, the only hospital for miles. Like the roads and bridges, the huts and primitive sewers, it was regularly swamped by nature: cholera and dysentery, malaria and giardiasis; the starving girls miraculously pregnant; the rampant infections unstoppable in the heat. To Len's eye, it was all the same, cells replicating stubbornly, mindlessly. The defiant persistence of life.

In every case but their own.

Lucy's desire for a child would never abate, but in Madagascar she made peace with it. Life sprang up where it could, illogically, without wisdom or prejudice. To take it personally was a kind of insanity, but Len knew better than to say so. In Madagascar Lucy came to the realization all on her own.

He rounded the bend past the Eickmeiers'. No car in the driveway, but he knew Marcia well enough to treat the kitchen window as a security camera. A strange vehicle on Deer Run would not escape her notice. He gave the house a wave and continued up the road.

Even at this distance, the squalor of the place astonished him. The farmhouse looked deserted, the windows dark, the curtains drawn. He parked and plodded through knee-high grass. It had rained overnight, and the ground felt spongy beneath his feet. Galoshes would have been a good idea, or maybe the fishing waders hanging in his garage. How did Sunny do it, for God's sake? Did the woman wear gum boots to get in and out of her own house?

When he reached the front porch, he saw that two of the steps had caved in completely. The remaining ones, moist with rot, would crumble under a man's weight.

Well, now what? he thought, eyeing the wreckage. He sensed some scuttling beneath the porch: a raccoon if he was lucky, a skunk if he was not. Off to his left, a movement startled him. The animal was bigger than a cat or squirrel: a groundhog poking its head through the weeds.

"Sunny?" he called.

A bird whistled in the distance, the sound low and airy, like blowing across a Coke bottle.

"It's Dr. Stusick. Anybody home?"

He circled around to the back of the house, the wet grass soaking his pant legs, and spotted a faint trail through the weeds, in the general direction of the back door. The back porch appeared rickety but intact. A new satellite dish, clean and modern, had been bolted to its roof.

Len knocked firmly—once, twice—and listened. Voices inside, a faint music. Somebody was watching television.

"Sunny, are you there?"

The doorknob turned easily in his hand.

MARCIA EICKMEIER WAS scrubbing out the percolator at her kitchen sink—white vinegar, her secret weapon against coffee stains—when Dr. Stusick drove past in his van. Later the sirens attracted her attention: first the ambulance, then the volunteer firemen. Finally the police cruiser screamed down Deer Run Road, sending gravel flying. Chief Carnicella had been listening to the scanner when the ambulance was dispatched, and was the last to arrive.

Marcia and Davis rode over together in the pickup. By then Deer Run was lined with parked cars. "I'd a loved to get a look inside that place," she said later to anyone who'd listen: her daughters-in-law, her sisters, the ladies at the church. But by the time she'd arrived, a yellow tape cordoned off the property. The paramedics had already left.

Sunny Baker, too, was gone.

Dr. Stusick had found her on the sofa in front of the television, dressed in her plaid hunting jacket. The TV, at high volume, was tuned to the Travel Channel. The smell was indescribable. Judging by decomposition, she had been dead over a week. Had already been dead—Len learned this later—when Dick Devlin led the prison officials on their site walk, past the junkyard on Deer Run Road.

Despite the court's best efforts, Miss Baker's children could not be located. Her estate would spend years in probate, but Dick Devlin wasn't about to wait. Within a week her property was cleared of the motorcycle and snowmobile and junk cars; the tractor and generator and swing set; the hippie's starburst van. The beautician's sink was refused by Ruth Rizzo, who had her own, thank you, she didn't need a piece of crap that had spent ten years on somebody's lawn. Everything else went straight into a Dumpster: the ruined furniture and rusting appliances, the warped piles of lumber, the high chair and bicycle, the busted table saw.

The haulers were paid by the Borough of Bakerton.

In the fall of 2000, Deer Run State Correctional Facility was built.

DESIDERATA

Albert Chura is an early riser. Joyce awakens to the buzzing of his lawn mower. The days are getting longer, and already her room is filled with sunlight. Outside, the pale spring leaves have matured into a deep summer green. Ed's white birches—he planted them along the front edge of the yard—are in full leaf. Once again Joyce has her privacy, after a long winter of feeling exposed.

She dresses and goes downstairs to make coffee. From the front porch, she gives Albert a wave. After he finishes, he'll come inside for a cup. He always compliments her coffee, though she knows it's nothing special. She simply follows the directions on the can. It seems a ridiculous thing to learn at her age, but widowhood is full of such lessons. Ed, who rose before dawn, always had his first cup alone in the dark. He'd put on a fresh pot when he heard Joyce on the stairs.

She sets out milk and sugar for Albert—she takes hers black—as he raps at the back door. "Morning," he grunts, wiping his work boots on the mat. Albert is seventy-two, the age Ed would have been, and his boots look nearly that old. He wears what he always wears, green Dickie work pants and a clean white T-shirt that seems

to have shrunk in the wash. It's not unlike the uniform he wore
as the high school janitor, a job Ed gave him out of sympathy or
misplaced patriotism and helped him keep for thirty years. Albert
was a decorated veteran; at Anzio he'd taken a bullet in the hip. Ed
was 4F and, in Joyce's opinion, unduly impressed by such things.

"Lot of stones this year," Albert says, hiking up his pant legs to
sit. Every spring when the snow melts, Joyce's front lawn is littered
with gravel. The pebbles are spread by the township crews for trac-
tion on icy roads, and the first hard rain washes them into her yard.
Some years Ed had spent half a day raking them up.

"I need to reseed out back," Albert adds. "Them kids tore it
up pretty good this year." Every winter Joyce's backyard is a mecca
for neighborhood children. At the first snowfall they show up in
droves with toboggans and sleds. Their voices fill the air like birdsong, delighted shrieks as they careen down the hill.

He glances over Joyce's shoulder into the living room, where
she's left a couple of large Hefty bags, old clothes she will take to
Goodwill. "Spring cleaning, eh?"

Albert is handsome for a man his age; at least he still has a lot of
hair. It is snow-white and worn in the style he's favored since high
school, an extravagant ducktail held in place with Brylcreem. Joyce
hadn't known him in school—he is several years older, her brother
Georgie's age. According to Georgie, Albert had been a hothead and
a troublemaker. He dropped out in his final year, worked in the coal
mines until the army drafted him. That he returned with a hitch in
his step earned him some sympathy. When you came back wounded,
people forgot for a time why they'd been glad to see you go.

It is the fact of growing old in a small town: you know everyone's whole story, and everyone, like it or not, knows yours. Except for a brief period in her youth, Joyce has lived her entire life in Bakerton. When she looks at someone her own age—her neighbor Betty Bursky, for example—she sees the towheaded child Betty once was, the teenage siren, the young wife with too many children; the whole journey that landed Betty where she is now, widowed, morbidly obese, living with a dozen cats in a manufactured home on Locust Street, as though feeding a crowd is a habit she can't break.

Albert stirs his coffee. There is a mermaid tattooed on his forearm, green and fuzzy like mold on bread. "I've been meaning to ask, Joyce. That bike of Ed's is just setting in your garage. If you don't have any use for it, I can take it off your hands."

It startles her somehow to hear him use her first name. What had he called her when Ed was alive? Nothing. They simply hadn't spoken. It was Ed who'd phoned Albert when something needed to be painted or trimmed or sanded or graded, the chores he could no longer manage. Presumably Albert had called Ed by his first name, too; when had that started? After they both retired, probably, and were no longer principal and janitor. When the school's stiff hierarchy, like so much else, was made irrelevant by age.

"It's a good bike. Shame for it to set there." Albert is a keen negotiator, a *wheeler-dealer*, Ed used to say. When something breaks down at the house, Albert is a phone call away, but it is a call Joyce dreads. She overpays him, probably, but this is preferable to haggling. Talking about money embarrasses her.

"Well, what do you say?"

. . . .

EVEN THE TEACHERS had called him Mr. Hauser. In the beginning Joyce herself had. He hired her as the school secretary, and later, after they began dating, she carefully avoided addressing him by name. It would have been absurd to call him Mr. Hauser when the whole faculty had seen them together at the Legion dances, the Rivoli Theater, Keener's Diner for a bite afterward.

As the school secretary, she was simply Joyce. Like the cafeteria ladies, the custodial staff, or somebody's pet, she was thought to need only one name. Later, after she'd put herself through school and stood at the front of her own classroom, she truly enjoyed being called Miss Novak, the small formality like an umbrella in the rain. It distresses her to learn that her daughter, a college professor, lets students call her Rebecca, but she is trying not to be critical. *How times have changed,* Joyce says.

Later, after Albert leaves, she sees that he forgot to trim the hedges. Her own fault: she gave him several chores when one task at a time is all he can remember. He is a good worker as long as you don't overload him. Ed used to joke about his forgetfulness, even gave him a nickname, Addlebert. It was a private joke, one of many between them; a complex web of shared silliness that, now that Ed is gone, means nothing to anybody.

It offends her slightly, the way the world has gone on without him. There was a television show he liked—something about military lawyers, she couldn't make any sense of it, but Ed never missed an episode. All last summer he grumbled about the reruns. Then, the week after he died, a new season started. She could have cried at the unfairness of it, and did. You cried over the small things.

Her own memory is sharp, painfully so. She wonders when

Albert's started to go. Ed had blamed it on the drinking. Over the years Albert had been on and off the wagon. There had been times, more than a few, when he missed work or showed up soused, and Ed sent him home after a talking-to. A couple of students had seen him staggering, and the others pretended they had. The crueler boys aped his limp. Anyone else would have fired the man ten times over, but Ed could never bring himself to do it. *He's got a family,* he pointed out. *Albert's all right once you get to know him. He's not a bad guy.*

Ed did all the hiring and firing at Bakerton High, though the truculent school board had the last word. As in many small towns, the system stank of nepotism, which got worse over the years as the mines failed and jobs became more and more scarce. There were twelve board members, most with several adult children. (Bakerton was a Catholic town.) Add in the nieces and nephews and cousins, and you had a school system with too many employees and fewer and fewer pupils as the young families moved away. It isn't her imagination: Bakerton is aging before her eyes, the whole town subsisting on Social Security or, like Joyce, widows' pensions. Her own daughter went away to college and stayed away; she comes back only at Christmas, and Joyce doesn't blame her a bit. Rebecca would be miserable in Bakerton, though she was a happy child here, sunny and sociable, involved in school activities, a leader of teams. It was in high school that she became a deliberate misfit, proud of all the ways she didn't belong. Ed blamed himself: it wasn't easy being the principal's daughter. It was true that teachers' children were noticed and commented upon, their slightest misstep dissected in the faculty lounge. *Poor kid,* Ed would tell Joyce, shaking his head. *At least she only has one parent in the system. Good thing you got out when you did.*

Was it a good thing? Looking back, Joyce isn't sure, though at the time the choice was nearly automatic. Ed made a good living; they didn't really need her paycheck. She had two small children, one sickly and furiously attached to his mother. Teddy had been a babysitter's nightmare. Each morning he'd wept bitterly, sometimes for hours, when Joyce left him with her sister. Dorothy kept track of his medications, his twice-daily breathing treatments, but she was a high-strung spinster undone by tantrums. After a few months with Teddy, she was a nervous wreck.

So when the school year ended, Joyce surrendered her classroom—the place where she'd been happiest, the job she'd worked so long and diligently to get. She was no longer Mrs. Hauser. Gone was the companionship of the faculty lounge, the cheery sound of the morning bell ringing the start of a new day. Gone were the shy, studious girls, her favorite pupils; the obstreperous boys who made her laugh; *The Great Gatsby* and *Lord Jim* and *The Scarlet Letter,* books she has always loved.

For many years her small family occupied her completely. She was cook and laundress, chauffeur and nurse. She has never admitted to anyone—why would she?—that books have brought her as much joy as her children have, and considerably less pain.

IN THE AFTERNOON her daughter calls. It is six hours later in France, nine P.M. on a Saturday night, and Rebecca is lonely. Joyce can hear it in her voice, or maybe it's just a bad connection, hollow-sounding, as though they're shouting across a frozen lake. Additionally, there is a delay on the line, a few seconds' pause after each of them speaks, so they're always interrupting each other. She listens as Rebecca complains about a difficult student, her officious landlady, a transit strike that makes her commute to the university nearly impossible. (The French, it seems, are always on strike.) Joyce worries, but doesn't ask, about Rebecca's phone bill.

It isn't until the very end of the conversation that Joyce mentions Albert Chura.

"The janitor? We used to call him Prince Albert. I don't remember why." Rebecca pauses. "Why would he want Dad's bike?"

Joyce starts to answer, but Rebecca interrupts. "Well, it's not like *you're* going to use it," she says breezily, as if she doesn't know (perhaps she doesn't) that the words will sting. That Joyce never learned to ride a bike remains, even at her age, a point of embarrassment. Her parents had been poor and hadn't owned such things, and by the time Joyce could afford to buy one herself, she had little desire to learn. Now, apparently, she is the only adult alive who's never mastered this skill. (Her sister Dorothy, dead now, doesn't count.) Ed loved bicycles and offered many times to teach her. *I'll walk behind you, keep you steady. Just like we did with the kids.* For a while he badgered her, which made her even more determined not to learn. They had fought about it more than once, quite vehemently. It all seems stupid now.

"Prince Albert," said Rebecca. "He and Dad were friends, right?"

Well, no: not friends, exactly. Albert had a way of lecturing Ed on mechanical things—once, the proper use of a pressure washer—that sounded slightly belligerent, as though he wanted it known, again and always, that he was the more competent man. Joyce didn't appreciate this, but Ed had tolerated it with his usual good humor. He had an easygoing disposition and was not easily riled. Though occasionally, after Albert left, he'd seemed irritated. *That guy will talk your ear off,* he'd say, shaking his head.

"They knew each other a long time," Joyce says.

"Well, maybe Dad would want him to have it. He loved that bike," Rebecca adds, as though Joyce might not know this.

"Yes, he did," Joyce says.

HE FOUND THE bike the year he retired, in the pages of a catalog. It was a replica of one he'd ridden as a boy, red, with coaster brakes. At the time he owned a ten-speed with hand brakes, which squeaked no matter how often he replaced the pads. For many years, a bike with coaster brakes had been impossible to find.

He rode the new bike to daily Mass, where he served as a lector. (In one of the many ironies of their married life, Ed, the convert, turned out to be the better Catholic.) From the kitchen window, Joyce watched him pedal down the street. He returned exhilarated but winded from the effort. "It's good for the old geezer," he joked, huffing mightily. "Give the lungs a workout."

He had quit smoking for the second time, and each morning he woke with a rousing cough. Listening, Joyce thought only of Teddy. It was almost more than she could bear to hear Ed straining for breath.

. . . .

THAT EVENING JOYCE sits through Mass—it's quicker than the Sunday service—and eats dinner with her friend Eleanor Rouse at a new restaurant with an old name, the Commercial Hotel. The original Commercial went under when Joyce was a girl, and the second was destroyed in a fire some years ago. This new Commercial occupies the old Sons of Italy building, and Joyce hopes Dick Devlin can make a go of it. Bakerton, at the moment, has only three other restaurants: a pizza joint, a diner with bad coffee, and a Chinese takeout with a few tables in the rear. Every so often an unemployed miner would scrape together the money to open a new one. Within a few months, a year at the outside, the place would close.

"How are you making out with your cleaning?" Eleanor asks. She's been after Joyce for months to go through Ed's closets, his camera equipment, the basement workshop where he kept his tools. *You need closure,* she likes to say. Her own husband died ten years ago, and she considers herself an authority.

"I dropped off three bags this morning," Joyce says. That the clothes were mostly hers and Rebecca's is not, strictly speaking, Eleanor's business. "Tomorrow I'll tackle those boxes in the basement. And Albert Chura is interested in Ed's bike."

"Oh, *Albert.*" Eleanor rolls her eyes. At one time she'd been the school nurse; she remembers a younger Albert, in his drinking days. "He's always been a hoarder. A cheapskate, too. Let me guess: he didn't offer you a dime."

Joyce blinked. Until that moment money hadn't crossed her mind.

"Rebecca called," she says, changing the subject. "She wants to come visit in July or August for a couple of weeks." It is apparently the time to get out of France, which every summer is overrun with tourists. *Americans,* Rebecca said with disdain. She has spoken this way since high school. It seemed absurd then—except for a class trip to Niagara Falls, she'd never taken a breath in another country—but to Joyce, who as a child collected cans for the war effort, whose brother marched in V-J parades, it was also perplexing and sad. Her own parents had come over from Italy and Poland, a fact she's never advertised. As a teenager she was ashamed of their accents, and as an adult is ashamed of her shame.

It's no mystery where Rebecca learned to disparage Americans. Her junior year at Bakerton High, Ed hired a new language teacher, a woman named Marianne Blinn. And more than either of her parents, it was Marianne Blinn who shaped the course of Rebecca's life.

SHE WAS A doctor's wife, and in a town with only two of them, that was enough to make her a celebrity. All of Bakerton knew the story of the Blinns' courtship. They had married in Germany, where David Blinn was stationed, and after his residency came back to his hometown to live. It was considered a romantic story, in part because Bakerton was not generally a town people came back to. You were born in Bakerton and either escaped, as Joyce's brothers had, or failed to. Ed Hauser was a rarity: he'd grown up halfway across the state and was hired for the principal's job, over some objections, when no local candidate could be found.

In the same way, Marianne Blinn was a controversial hire. The other candidate, a recent Penn State grad whose uncle sat on the school board, had significant support. Marianne's degree from a foreign university was viewed with suspicion. More than one board member argued that, as a doctor's wife, she didn't need the job.

But Ed lobbied hard on her behalf, and Marianne Blinn was hired to teach French and Latin. Later a new course was added, introductory German, her native tongue. Each morning she was seen driving to school in her little Audi. (Foreign cars, in those days, were rare in Bakerton. Even now you don't see them every day.) She was a tall, striking woman, dark-haired, with a single dramatic streak of gray she didn't bother to touch up. This was a subject of much discussion at Ruth Rizzo Beauty, where Joyce reported each Saturday morning for her wash and set. *I don't know why she doesn't do something with that hair,* said Ruth as she scrubbed Joyce's scalp. *Lord knows she can afford to.* Like every woman she knew, Joyce got a fresh perm every three months. (The frugal, the ambitious, and the hard up rolled each other's hair at home.) Marianne's hair was shoulder-length, twisted sometimes into a loose bun. She wore no lipstick, ever, just rings of black liner around her eyes.

By all accounts she was a marvelous teacher. Still, there were critics. When parents complained that she graded harshly, Ed refused to intervene. *The teachers are on the front lines,* he told Joyce, as if she might have forgotten. *The least I can do is back them up.* Rebecca, a bright but erratic student, studied French with fierce intensity. In the evenings she barricaded herself in her bedroom with vocabulary tapes—recordings of Madame Blinn's own sultry voice, duplicated in the school's new audio lab. *J'irai, tu iras, nous irons, vous irez.* Each followed by a brief pause in which the student was to pronounce the words herself.

Joyce never learned a foreign language. In high school she

declined Latin verbs, but this had never seemed more than an exercise, a language spoken only by priests. Lingering outside Rebecca's door, she'd felt a deep loneliness she remembered from childhood. After her father passed the citizenship exam, he'd insisted they speak only English at home, but late at night, after the children were in bed, he tuned the radio to a Polish station from Pittsburgh. One night—she was very small, five or six—she'd crept downstairs. Listening, she had felt forsaken. It had seemed in that moment that her father was a stranger, thinking and dreaming in a language she would never understand.

In June Madame Blinn hosted a dinner party in her home for the handful of students who'd earned A's each quarter. To Joyce, who'd kept her own pupils at a distance, it was a startling notion. The Blinns lived in a stately Victorian on Indian Hill, an enormous house for a childless couple. Dr. Blinn had bought it from the estate of Virgie Baker, whose father and grandfather had owned the mines. As a girl, Joyce had walked past the house on her way to school, peering through the thick hedge of lilacs hoping for a glimpse of a Baker. The fragrance of lilacs in springtime had followed her down the street.

Joyce had planned to drive Rebecca to the dinner, but Teddy was running a fever; as he breathed into his nebulizer, he wouldn't let go of her hand. Instead it was Ed who ferried Rebecca back and forth and was invited in for coffee and dessert. The next morning Rebecca raved about the Blinns' huge dining room, the table big enough for twelve. (The couple apparently entertained a great deal.) Madame Blinn had cooked the dinner herself: a creamy leek soup (where, Joyce wondered, did you buy leeks in Bakerton?), a leg of lamb, crepes dripping with butter for dessert. Rebecca described these dishes in elaborate detail, and Joyce remembers thinking that her daughter seemed a little in love with Marianne Blinn. The night of the dinner she'd changed her outfit several times, as though dressing for a date.

Joyce cooked with margarine, still does. They'd both grown up with it during the war, and Ed said often that he preferred the taste.

AFTER DINNER WITH Eleanor, on her way home from the Commercial, Joyce drives past Albert Chura's house. It is a small, tidy place, yellow brick, with an attached garage. The lawn is shorn and well fertilized, as dense and green as Astroturf. In the backyard is a huge aluminum shed, nearly the size of the Churas' house.

As she approaches, Albert comes out of the shed. Recognizing her car, he waves her down. Local custom demands that she lower her window and make small talk for a few minutes. When they have exhausted the topic of her lawn—he agrees to come back Monday to finish the trimming—Albert says, "Joyce, have you ever seen my barn?"

Oh, hell, she thinks, remembering what Ed used to say: *That guy will talk your ear off.*

She parks and follows him into the shed, which is full of tools and equipment—a snowblower and several mowers, intact and in pieces; a lawn tractor, a contraption she believes is called a rototiller. In contrast to the tidy yard, the shed is dirty and cluttered, crowded with junk.

"Very impressive," Joyce says.

"I like to have something to work on." Albert points to an old bicycle propped against one wall, inverted, its wheels removed. "That's my latest project. Not worth the effort, probably. It's a piece of crap."

She notices in one corner a portable radio, its antennas extended. Beside it are several mugs and glasses, a plastic Pepsi bottle, round canisters of snuff.

Albert follows her gaze. "I come out here when I need peace and quiet," he says, and Joyce thinks of his wife, known to be a persnickety housekeeper. Joyce once spotted her at the foot of the driveway, spritzing the mailbox with a bottle of Windex.

"About that bike of Ed's," he begins.

"Sure, Albert," says Joyce. "I don't see why not."

SUNDAY MORNING DAWNS quietly, no lawn mowers humming. The neighborhood is populated with Catholics of Joyce's generation, and out of piety or habit, they avoid doing chores on the Sabbath—at least any chores that the neighbors can see. Joyce can recall the stern text of her Baltimore Catechism: *By the Third Commandment all unnecessary servile work on Sunday is forbidden.* Young people, of course, have never heard of this injunction. From her kitchen window, she sees Andy Carnicella puttering in his backyard, dismantling a Weed Whacker. Andy is Rebecca's age, and by the time they came along, the Baltimore Catechism had fallen out of favor. They'd been spared the endless memorization, the faith distilled down to hundreds of questions and answers Joyce had learned by rote.

What is servile work?

Servile work is that which requires labor of body rather than of mind.

Her whole married life, Sunday had belonged to the cross-word. Ed, the early riser, would have two pencils sharpened; over breakfast and again after church, they sat at the kitchen table happily filling the boxes, rising sometimes to consulting the atlas or the dictionary or the encyclopedia shelved in the den. Joyce hasn't touched a crossword since September. Now she drinks coffee and scans the headlines and wonders how to fill the day.

In the afternoon she goes down to the basement, a windowless corner Ed used as his workshop. Compared to Albert Chura's cluttered shed, it is orderly as an operating room. Against one wall are a dozen cardboard boxes, neatly stacked. Another wall is covered with corkboard; there are hammers and handsaws and other items she can't identify, all hanging by hooks. Three low shelves hold paint and varnish, various solvents, old coffee cans filled with hardware. Joyce peers into each one and touches its contents, the nails and screws and bolts and hinges her husband sorted carefully by size.

She sits at the workbench Ed built, on an old kitchen chair he salvaged from a set they'd retired years ago. She has resolved to sort through one box per day. It is the opposite of servile work. It is labor of the heart.

The boxes, for the most part, are unlabeled; there's no telling what a particular one will hold: vinyl records, 78s and 33s; camera equipment, books that had overflowed the shelves in the den. In Friday's box she'd found Ariel and Will Durant's *The Story of Civilization*. Ed had read the series years ago, all ten volumes; she remembered him lingering over *Rousseau and Revolution,* slogging through *The Age of Faith*. Joyce had marked the carton DURANT.

She would donate the set to the public library. It was not the sort of thing she'd ever read herself.

Today she chooses a box at random. This one is too heavy to lift, so Joyce kneels beside it. Ed had suffered twinges of arthritis, but Joyce, knock wood, has no such troubles. *Must be all those years of kneeling,* Ed used to joke. His own knees protested; they had remained Protestant. Joyce had *good Catholic knees.*

The box is filled with high school yearbooks, a decade's worth of the *Bakerton Banner.* For most of his career, for no extra pay, Ed had advised the yearbook staff. A passionate amateur photographer, he made sure Bakerton had a fully equipped darkroom, something no other local school possessed. On schooldays it was used by the photography classes; on weekends, Ed went there to develop his own film. In summer he spent whole days in the darkroom. Often he rode there on his bicycle, his camera bag strapped to his back.

Joyce selects a yearbook at random: *BANNER '75.* She opens to the frontispiece, looking for the familiar verse: *Go placidly among the noise and haste.* Another private joke: each graduating class voted on a poem for the opening page, and for most of the sixties and seventies—to Ed's amusement and despair—"Desiderata" had won the poll.

She remembers enough Latin to know it's a fatuous title. The poem, it seems to her, has little to do with desire.

> *Neither be cynical about love; for in the face of all aridity and disenchantment, it is as perennial as the grass.*

Joyce marks the box BANNER: another donation for the public library. Gratefully she turns out the light.

ON MONDAY ALBERT Chura trims the hedges. After they finish their coffee, Joyce takes him down to the basement. She points to the boxes marked BANNER and DURANT. "They're pretty heavy. Do you suppose you can get them up to my car?"

"Sure." Albert eyes the stacks of boxes. "What's in all them?"

"I haven't gone through those yet. So far it's mostly books."

Albert's eyes flicker. "Are you sure that's a good idea? Going through Ed's private things?"

"Someone has to do it." Joyce has imagined Rebecca some years hence, flying back from France for her mother's funeral. It seems unfair to make her sort through two parents' possessions, forty years' worth of memories in that house.

After Albert leaves, she chooses a lightweight box, one she can manage on her own. She has never been comfortable asking for help. The other cartons had been closed carelessly, the cardboard flaps folded end over end. This one is sealed with packing tape, as though its contents might escape.

Cutting it open, she understands why it's so light. Nothing inside but photographs, piles of them. Ed's hobby had vexed her in the beginning, since more than anything, she hated to have her picture taken. Early in their courtship she had submitted to the camera, her grim smile speaking for her: *Get that thing away from me.* Later, pregnant with Rebecca, she refused to be photographed at all. The children, luckily, were unself-conscious models, so Ed at last left her alone. Every few months she'd filled another album, Rebecca and Teddy at various ages and stages. *The little orphans*, Rebecca now jokes: their father invisible behind the camera, their mother hiding in the next room.

But these aren't family photos. They're black-and-white shots taken in and around the high school. She recognizes certain classrooms, the library, the cafeteria, the gym. Yearbook discards, then: unknown teenagers with outdated haircuts. She is halfway through the pile when she spots a familiar face.

Marianne Blinn is laughing into the camera, Marianne in a dark coat and earmuffs, her hair flocked with snow. Joyce stares at the photo a long time. Marianne clearly doesn't mind being photographed. She beams as though the camera were a lover, or simply a very good friend.

Joyce puts the photo aside. Beneath are more shots of Marianne. In her classroom, erasing the blackboard. In the cafeteria, holding a lunch tray. Sitting at her desk before a bulletin board decorated with snowflakes; Joyce picks out the words *Joyeux Noel*.

Other shots were taken in summer: Marianne in a tank top and long skirt, astride a bicycle.

Ed's private things.

Breaking her own rule, she opens a second box. This one, too, is sealed with packing tape. Inside is an untouched package of Kodak paper, and Joyce feels a momentary pang: photographic paper was expensive, and they were both children of the Depression. Ed had abhorred waste of any kind.

Beneath the Kodak paper is a slippery stack of plastic envelopes, each filled with amber negatives. At the bottom is a pile of color prints—red-eyes, double exposures, decapitations, the sorts of mistakes that usually ended up in the trash. Why would Ed keep these? she wonders. Why on earth? As she sorts through the pile, she understands. The photos weren't Ed's but Teddy's, taken with his new Instamatic the summer he was thirteen. It was, without question, the happiest time of his life, his weeks at Camp Aspire.

They had driven him there in their old station wagon, a long drive on winding back roads since there wasn't—still isn't—a highway running north to south, an efficient route from Bakerton to western New York. Rebecca had stayed behind with her aunt Dorothy, so Teddy had the entire backseat to himself. He stretched out full-length, surrounded by his prized possessions—his Evel Knievel action figures, the toys he hated to leave behind but in a day would forget entirely, distracted utterly by sack races and scavenger hunts, his new friends, his counselor, Zachary, a young medical student he'd idolize the rest of his days.

The camp was just over the state line, a woodsy spot, the small cabins built around a lake. In June and July it was overrun by Girl Scouts, but for three weeks at the end of the summer, it hosted kids with cystic fibrosis. Joyce had learned of the camp from Teddy's doctor. It was, he said, a welcome break for parents: a brief holiday from medical appointments, the daily gauntlet of aerosols and nebulizers, the endless, hopeless work of clearing mucus from the lungs. The kids, too, got a break from overprotective mothers, a chance to make new friends. They were treated to a few weeks of vigorous, lung-clearing activity—swimming, hiking, canoeing—in the fresh mountain air.

Of course, they got more than that. No one realized then that CF kids passed infections between them, that the camp's equipment—

the shared aerosols and nebulizers—were a breeding ground for bacteria, resistant strains that flourished in cystic lungs. Teddy came home with pneumonia. He spent the autumn at Children's Hospital in Pittsburgh, breathing through a respirator, visited daily by his camp counselor Zachary, a second-year resident at Children's.

It rained heavily the morning of the funeral, a cold downpour that soaked her coat in the short walk from car to church. Joyce scarcely remembers the long Mass, the droning eulogy—those details, mercifully, have been wiped from her memory. She recalls only the procession out of the church, the priest and the altar boys and finally the family following Teddy's small casket. Outside the wind had kicked up, a dizzy spiral of snowflakes. The church steps were edged with white, the first snowfall of the year.

As they stood waiting for the hearse, a tall woman approached Ed and clasped him fiercely. Joyce waited for the usual platitudes—*He's at peace now. An angel in heaven.* But the woman said none of these things.

Instead, on the steps of the church, she swore bitterly: *Jesus Christ, Ed.* The epithet was oddly beautiful in the low, accented voice of Marianne Blinn.

Joyce stood there awkwardly, watching them. They were nearly the same height. Marianne's cheek was pressed to Ed's. Her eyes, like his, were closed.

That day was like truth itself—colder than you expected, and full of surprises. In a year the Blinns would divorce, shocking the town. Dr. Blinn would retire and move to Florida, and Marianne would go back to wherever she'd come from.

But that morning on the church steps, a fine snow swirling the sidewalk, Joyce wasn't thinking of the Blinns. She was remembering

Teddy at the window in his pajamas, looking out at the other children sledding, an armada of yellow toboggans shooting down the hill.

IT IS TOO late in life to open all these boxes.

Joyce reseals them carefully, understanding—too late—why Ed had taped them shut: a protective impulse, a kindness to them both. Upstairs the kitchen is filled with a golden light. In another hour, the sun will set.

Where did the time go?

Albert Chura's number is written in Ed's neat cursive on the inside cover of the phone book. Albert's wife answers the phone. "He isn't here right now, Mrs. Hauser. Want me to have him call you back?"

"Darlene," Joyce says, "would you do me a favor? Give Albert a message from me."

She is sitting on the front porch when he wheels up on Ed's bicycle. He dismounts carelessly and drops it roughly on the lawn.

Joyce rises. She has rehearsed what she is going to say. *I'm sorry, Albert. I'm not ready to part with it.* He doesn't give her a chance to speak.

"Indian giver," he says, and she smiles. It is a phrase she remembers from childhood, and for a moment she is grateful to him for easing the tension with a joke.

"What are you laughing at? You should be ashamed of yourself," he says, his boots loud on the porch steps. "A teacher! And here you are going back on your word."

He stands too close to her. His face is very red, his breath beery. He wears the alcohol like a subtle cologne, a fruity reek that seems to come from his pores.

"I'm sorry," she begins.

"A teacher!" he repeats, shaking his head in disgust.

"Ed was a good friend to you." The words come out more softly than she intends. She is dismayed to hear a tremor in her voice.

"Well, maybe so. But it was a two-way street. I was a good friend to him, too."

Joyce glances across the street. Betty Bursky's windows are open. She wishes he would lower his voice.

"I was *trustworthy*," he says. "That's hard to find these days. In them days, too. Hard to find, period, in this town."

Joyce stares at him.

"I'm not saying Ed owes me anything," says Albert.

Yes, you are, Joyce thinks. That's exactly what you're saying.

"The way I figure, we ended up even. So." He nods once, decisively. "Keep your goddamn bike."

He stomps off muttering and cursing, into the sunset like the hero in a Western. Calmly Joyce watches him go. Ed's bike lies in the grass like an abandoned toy. She lifts it carefully and rolls it toward the garage, one hand on the handlebar, the other on the seat.

I'll walk behind you, keep you steady. Just like we did with the kids.

More than anything in life, she wishes she'd let him. That she'd smiled for the camera. That she'd said yes. Life was gone before you knew it; how foolish she'd been to refuse any of it. In a couple of months Rebecca would arrive from Paris. They would rise before the neighbors and practice in the driveway, hidden by Ed's birches: fresh cool mornings, dew on the grass. Her daughter would get a kick out of that. It was just the sort of project she'd enjoy.

ABOUT THE AUTHOR

Jennifer Haigh is the author of four critically acclaimed novels: *Faith*, *The Condition*, *Baker Towers*, winner of the L.L. Winship/PEN New England Award for Fiction, and *Mrs. Kimble*, for which she won the PEN/Hemingway award. Her short stories have been published in many places, including *The Atlantic*, *Granta*, and *The Best Americna Short Stories 2012*. She lives in the Boston area.